J.J. MEYER

Hearts

Burning Desire

Other Books You Might Enjoy

The Cooper Family Series
Volume 1 – 7
(Shoshone Pass, Separate Trails, South Creek,
Double Edged, Legacy Trail, Courage Trail and Sherando)

Virginia Byway History (non-fiction) **2021**

All the above-mentioned books are available
www.Ingramspark.com
www.Amazon.com
www.Kindle.com
You can also follow me on Facebook –
Jim Meyer Western Author
Or
On my Author Page
https://www.amazon.com/Jim-Meyer/e/B0182S590W

Characters

Todd Morgan - Civil War Survivor; husband of Priscilla Parker, owner of Stony Creek Ranch, Wyoming Territory; Co-owner of Wind River Ranch and Mining Company, Wind River Township, Wyoming.

Priscilla Parker-Morgan – Owner of The Parker House Inn, Lander, Wyoming Territory; wife of Todd Morgan, Co-owner of Wind River Ranch and Mining Company.

Megan Parker Morgan- Priscilla Parker's daughter

Jonathan "Crusty" Harrison – Co-owner of Sweetwater Ranch, Wyoming Territory.

Elizabeth "Liz" Connolly Harrison – wife of Jonathan Harrison

August McDavitt – A West Point Graduate, lawyer. Legal Counsel for the Wind River Mining Company.

Farleigh McDavitt – brother of August, partner in McDavitt & McIntosh, Assayers.

Shoshone Joe – half-breed, a friend of Todd, who raises dogs and horses

Maud Bricker – New owner of trading post at Ft. Washakie

Walking Many Places – Sioux Chief, friend of Todd, brother of Feather In Air and Bright Star.

Ned Hogan – works for Todd.

Hiram Bender – wagon maker, horse trainer, owner of Bender's Farm, Lander, Wyoming Territory

Moon On Sky – shaman, friend of Todd's

Colonel Johnson – Commander, Ft. Washakie, Wyoming Territory

Tom Murphy – US Marshal, Lander to the Yellowstone, Wyoming Territory

Elizabeth "Beth" Sanderson-Murphy – helps Priscilla around the inn and soon to be wife of Tom Murphy.

Gus & Turk Langstrom, Pete Byrd – Owners of Langstrom Mining & Engineering Company.

Edith, Mabel and John – boarder's at Parker's Boarding House.

The Thompson's – Richard, Emma, George, Mary

Prologue

After having successfully discovered gold while out on his trap lines Todd Morgan made immediate plans to marry Priscilla Parker. He now faces the toughest challenge in his life, balancing family life and working to secure both his ranch and mining claims.

Priscilla Parker Morgan must see to it that Todd does not overwork himself so they can have the life they have planned.

Many factors will challenge both of them.

-1-

Priscilla Parker was sitting on the settee in her living room, while Todd Morgan was kneeling in front of her holding a small box, open. He was about to ask her an important question when her daughter, Megan, came in the kitchen door as she had done everyday and called out, "Mom, I'm home."

"Megan, I'm in the living room, I'll be out in a minute. Todd, you were going to ask me something?"

"Where was I? Oh, I remember now, will you marry me?"

"Now why would we want to go do something like that?"

"'Cause I love you and Megan. I don't want Johan what's-his-name to take advantage of you anymore."

"I don't know, I mean, I love you too, but it's so sudden."

"Sudden, what do you mean sudden? We just spent the last three days making love up at Stony Creek. I thought you wanted to get married. Was I wrong? There are times when you're so unpredictable. I could have asked Mable or Edith, but I want you to warm my bed, keep me happy and in turn, I'll keep you safe and our lovemaking will be wonderful."

"You promise you'll keep me safe?"

"I promise."

"You'll be intimate at my beck and call?"

1

"I promise."

"You'll treat Megan like she was your own?"

"I promise. Now are you going to answer me or not?"

"I'll give you my answer after supper."

"I'm not sure I can wait until after supper. You are skating on very thin ice."

"Just think if I fell through you could rescue me."

"Don't change the subject. I have been on my knees for the last half hour waiting for your answer." He replied, determined to get an answer.

The front door opened, Mabel and John, two of Pricilla's boarders, came in the hallway and saw him on his knees. John said, "I guess we're interrupting something important Mabel, perhaps we should come back later."

"It's nothing really, she won't give me an answer to my question anyway," Todd replied.

"What was your question, Mr. Morgan?" John asked getting interested as to why Todd was on his knees.

"I asked her if she'd marry me, but she is the biggest tease in Lander and she won't give me an answer one way or the other."

She winked at them and said, "I'm just not sure, he's… always in such a hurry and it's an important question. I don't want to rush into anything if you know what I mean?"

Mable replied, "It is an important question and I'd think that he should be asking your family first. After all it is the proper thing to do."

John interjected, "I don't know Mr. Morgan. She is constantly talking about you especially when you're not around; she is the happiest when you are. The last four days the two of you have been gone and we've missed her cooking, watching over us, making this our home. I think she'll give you an answer when she's good and ready. By the way Priscilla, what's for supper?"

"I was trying to get back to the kitchen to finish getting the food in the serving dishes and out to the table, I am torn between getting supper on the table and giving him my answer."

Before anyone else could answer, Edith, the third boarder walked in and said, "Were we supposed to have a meeting? Is anything wrong? Why is Mr. Morgan on his knees?"

He lowered his head and said, "I give up." As he started to get up Priscilla stood up and gently pushed him back down and said, "Go ahead ask me again?"

"Are you sure you'll give me an answer in front of everybody?"

"Of course I'll give you an answer. What was the question again?"

Exasperated, Todd blurts out, "Will you marry me!"

She looks at the three boarders, then back at him and replied, "Yes".

"Yes, what?"

"Yes, I'll marry you."

"What a relief, I thought this was going to take all night at the rate we were going." John came over and helped Todd get to his feet and shook his hand; Edith and Mabel hugged Priscilla. Megan came in the room and said, "Mom, why is everyone so happy? Why is Mr. Morgan rubbing his knees?"

"Mommy, will explain it to you later. Will you help me get the supper out to the table?"

-2-

Todd woke from a deep sleep and said, "Got to get back to Stony Creek."

He'd been staying at the boarding house for a month already and Priscilla had made it perfectly clear that she didn't want him to go, but knew that he would have to leave sooner or later. He had new responsibilities now that he was going to get married. He sat on the edge of the bed and rubbed the stubble on his face, breathed in the fresh morning air drifting in through the bedroom window and decided he'd leave the day after tomorrow.

They had an appointment at the lawyer's office this morning to sign the mining documents, wills and the trust they set up for Megan and any subsequent children. Once that was taken care of, Priscilla was going to pick up a few staples at Henderson's and they would walk home from there.

After lunch, Todd was going to Tom Murphy's office and the two of them were going to talk about finding someone to help him run his ranch near Bull Lake. Once that was accomplished, he would have to find someone to help him with what he planned to do here in Lander. While Todd was away, Tom was going to keep an eye out for anyone who might fit with Todd's personality.

He also needed to find the right people to operate the mine. As much as he wanted to hire at least five people, Tom suggested he concentrate on one thing at a time. He never had to hire people before, but things were changing all over the territory. Settlers were moving onto their homesteads that had been granted to them by the Territorial Governor.

He rode the Appaloosa mare to town, while Priscilla took a nap.

The US Marshal's office in Casper had assigned Marshal Tom Murphy to the new office in Lander. He was at his desk when Todd walked in and said, "You're looking well and contented."

"And you the same."

"I need to get done what we talked about last night."

"Do you know the type of person that you want to hire?"

"Well, in the past, I have been able to judge a man by looking him straight in the eye and see how he responds. Some men look away while others look right back at you without blinking. I actually prefer the person who looks away. At least you can tell they are honest enough to acknowledge how they feel."

"You and I are a lot alike. I look to see if their hands have calluses or if their hands are smooth. You know someone who says they have done this and that but their hands are smooth, they don't know what hard work really is. You don't need anyone like that."

"I need you to let me know if they are wanted by the law. I have to trust the people that I am going to hire and to make sure they are going to give me an honest day's work for an honest day's pay No one, including myself, is perfect or hasn't done some things they wished they hadn't. I just need a person to be honest with me, that's all."

"Well, let's see if we can't get that done, today." Tom replied. "Why don't we go down to the Cattlemen's Association office and see if anyone is looking for work, with all the new settlers coming into town there should be at least one, maybe two who could use a steady job, even if it is only for six months or so."

Two young men were sitting on the bench outside of the Cattlemen's and one said to the other, "I guess we should try South Pass City or maybe go back to Green River. It sure doesn't look like there are any jobs around here."

Overhearing the one-sided conversation, Todd said, "Are you looking for work?"

"Yes, yes sir," a tall, lanky young man replied. "We both worked for Timber Creek Ranch over near Green Springs until a month ago."

"You don't say. What a coincidence, I... I think I have heard of them, big operation, lots of work, I would think? Why did you leave?"

"We were getting' tired of doing all the work that the other ranch hands didn't want to do."

"Well, what type of work are you looking for?" Tom asked.

The tall, lanky one looked at his partner and said, "We figure with all the experience we've had, we should be able to handle a foreman's job or lead wrangler at least."

Enjoying the conversation so far Todd asked, "Either of you ever heard of a fellow named Todd Morgan?"

"Yeah, they thought he was God's gift to horse wrangling. One day he just up and quit. Seems he wanted to hunt and trap up in the Yellowstone wilderness."

Tom spoke up and said, "Either of you wanted by the law for

horse stealing, cattle rustling or bank robbery by any chance?"

"No Sir!"

Tom decided it was time to show them his badge and said, "Tom Murphy, US Marshal from Lander to the Yellowstone. I always ask on the off chance I'll catch someone in a lie."

Todd continued his line of questioning, which he thought was fun in an odd sort of way, "What type of wages are you looking for?"

"We were making $35 a month and found, a horse and we had one day off a month, the tall, lanky one said"

"You say $35, what do you think Tom?"

"I do believe the going rate around here is maybe $25 or $30 for a person starting out; $35 for some experience and maybe, just a possibility of course, as much as $40 for the right person." Tom replied knowing fair well that Todd would pay that amount for just such a person.

"Before I hire anyone," Todd remarked. "I like to check with their old boss to see what I should be paying them in a new position, especially someone who has experience such as yourselves that is. Would that be a problem?"

"None that I know of."

"Where are you fellows staying here in town?"

"We're over at the Mayfair Hotel."

"I'll have to think about it some. I might need one person to work on one ranch and the other to work on a separate ranch. Either of you have a problem with that?"

"No; No, Sir. We just need to find some work before the winter gets here, is all."

Todd said, "I'll let you know in the morning." As he is walking away, one of the cowboys said, "What's your name mister?"

"Todd Morgan."

All of a sudden, the one doing all the talking said to his partner "Our goose is cooked. If I'd known who he was up front, I would have kept my mouth shut. Our chances are nil around here now."

The other less talkative one, replied; "Now you understand why I let you do the talking. I know when to keep my mouth shut and I don't bad-mouth anyone either."

After Todd and Tom were out of earshot, Todd said, "I think the one who was smart enough to keep his mouth shut will do just fine for the ranch up near Bull Lake; the other one needs a lesson in humility. Do you think you could detain him for a while until I get back?"

"I'm sure I could. What have you got in mind?" Todd explained that he'd need someone here to do the tree cutting, land clearing and getting the section next to the boarding house property ready for a barn and fencing. "I'll send a telegram to Charlie Cooper to get some information about Mr. Big Mouth, and then I'll know what to do with him once I get back here. But like I said, a good dose of humility is what he needs right now."

$$-3-$$

Later that afternoon, Todd, Priscilla and Megan were sitting on the front porch, Megan asked, "Mr. Morgan when you came here about a month ago, you said you would tell me a story about the name I gave the doll you gave me, but you never have."

"I'll tell you the story tonight after you've said your prayers and before you go to sleep. Will that be okay with you?"

"Oh, yes!" Before she went down the stairs to go play with her dog, Jasper, Todd said to Priscilla, "Have you told her about us yet?"

"The night you proposed and gave me the ring, I told her that I loved you very much. She accepted that, but I've been waiting for the right time to explain everything to her. I don't want her to think that I'm going to be spending all my time with you and that I'll be ignoring her. I was thinking that tomorrow afternoon, you and I would take her out for supper at the Wind River Inn, and afterward we would explain everything."

"That's a good idea. Do you think you'll have any time for me before I go up-country?"

"Well, I'll have to think about that. Could you help me in the pantry for a few minutes?"

"Sure." he smiled. As they both rose from their chairs and

went inside on their way to the pantry, she was right behind him and slid the pantry door closed. She turned him around and kissed him, deep, long and wanting more.

"I need air," he said after a couple of minutes.

"Why aren't I giving you enough of it?"

"Well, I guess you are at that, but I was hoping for more than just some kisses."

"Later, after Megan goes to bed and you tell her your story, I'll take you into my bedroom and we can do more than just kiss. Just then, the back porch door slammed and Megan said, "Mom, where are you? Mr. Johansen from the bank wants to see you outside." They both hear her skipping through the kitchen and down the hall going out the front door.

"I've been dreading this, but it had to happen sooner or later."

"Do you want me there when you talk with him."

"No, I think I can handle him, but if he grabs my elbow as he does sometimes when he's trying to get his point across, you might have to step in."

She opened the pantry door, smoothing her dress before walking out to speak with Johan, who was pacing back and forth in the barnyard, "You wanted to see me?"

Todd on the other hand does what she suggested and goes up the front stairs to his room, grabs his holster, straps it on, and ties it down. He looks out his window to see Johan using his hands to make a point and talking to Priscilla, who puts her head down. Johan puts his hand under her chin and lifts it up and begins his tirade once again. Todd would like nothing better than to jump out of the window and confront him. Instead, he goes down the back stairs and sits at the kitchen table within earshot of the backyard.

Johan's voice continues to rise, "I've been hearing rumors that you and that, that no account trapper, Morgan, have been seen together. Who do you think you *are*, humiliating me like that?"

"He's a friend and he was going into town, so we were walking together. He said he'd be glad to help me when he was done with his business and I was done with my shopping. Besides, what business is that of yours?"

"We're a couple, and you can't take up with riff-raff like him. What will people say?"

"I have never led you to believe that we were a couple as you seem to think we are. You have asked me out to lunch and I have accepted out of courtesy. We are on the same committee at church, but a couple we are not." He moved closer to her and grabbed her arm and said, "I think that you and I should go in the barn, and I'll make you understand how important it will be that you do it my way or there'll be trouble for you."

"You're hurting my arm, please let go." Before he can say anything else, Todd walks up and says, "If you don't let go of her, you'll regret it the rest of your life which could be very short from where I'm standing."

Johan let's go immediately, "Are you threatening me?"

"No, not at all. But I won't let anyone hurt the lady I'm going to marry. *Comprende*?"

Sputtering, Johan replied, "Marry? You can't be serious Morgan. You're no man for her; she's too sophisticated for the likes of you. She'll see the light one of these days and come running back to me." With that, he turned, mounted his horse and galloped out of the barnyard.

There were tears on her cheeks. Todd held her head in his hands and wiped away the tears with his thumbs saying, "You won't have to worry about him anymore. I doubt he'll cause you any more trouble from now on."

"Oh, if I could only believe that, but with you away, he'll castigate me and Megan. What am I going to do?"

"Priscilla, you might think that, but like I said to you awhile back, no one is ever going to hurt you and what he says and how he acts toward you, whether it's on the streets of Lander, at the church, or at a restaurant with your friends, they're just words and they alone can't hurt you. Now if he touches you at all, I want you to do what you just did a few minutes ago, I want you to yell at him and say, "stop hurting me," so that anyone can hear you. Then I want you to go to the sheriff's office or see Tom Murphy and file a complaint against him. You are going to have to be brave like I know you can."

"Why don't we go in the barn where we can be alone and pick up where we left off in the pantry?"

"Lead on."

-4-

After supper, Megan went up to her room to get ready for bed and said her prayers with her mother kneeling next to her. When she finished, she said in a loud voice, "Mr. Morgan, I am ready for my story now."

He was in his room down the hall and heard her. He walked out of his room and down the hallway to where Priscilla and Megan had their private living quarters. He knocked on the door before letting himself in and went into Megan's bedroom. She was already under the covers holding the doll. Priscilla was sitting in a rocking chair in the corner by the window with her knitting on her lap.

"Well ladies! I have a story about 'Molly'." Megan blushed. No one had ever called her a lady before. He told them about growing up in the hills of Tennessee with his older brother Hank and his sister Molly. She was the one who always protected him from the bullies at school when he was little. She sang to him, and dried his tears when he was afraid and told him what he meant to her. He hasn't seen his sister Molly in years, but he knows that she is out there somewhere wondering what happened to him after he went off to the war and whether he was dead or alive. In his heart, he wished she lived just down the street and that she could be here with

Megan, 'Molly' and her mom.

Megan said, "My 'Molly' will try and find your sister. I don't want you to worry Mr. Morgan. My mom and I will be your friends when you need someone to talk to or when you need someone to protect you, too. Thank you for sharing your story with us. Goodnight, Mr. Morgan."

"Goodnight, Megan." He walked out of the room, shut the door and decided to go down the back stairs and out to the barn to check on the horses for the night. Priscilla tucked Megan in, kissed her forehead and went out to find Todd.

He was standing in front of the stall scratching Misty's forehead. Priscilla touched his arm and said "Thank you for telling Megan and me that story. I am sure you'll find your sister one of these days." As he turned towards her, his cheeks were moist, "I do miss her and hope she is okay." She took a handkerchief from her skirt pocket and wiped the tears on his face. "I love you more and more every day," she said before giving him a kiss on his cheek. They worked in unison for the next several minutes, making sure that all the horses had enough feed and water; closed the windows and finally the barn door. They walk arm in arm across the barnyard and into the house.

"Let's talk for a few minutes about what you have to get done before you leave the day after tomorrow. Would you like some coffee?" Priscilla asked.

"No, but a nice glass of buttermilk will help me sleep better tonight. Tomorrow, I have to see Hiram Bender; go to the bank and close out my account and put the money in my new account at McDavitt & McIntosh's Private Bank and get signature cards for you to sign; I have to hire that new young man that I told you about when I came back from town this afternoon; get the buckboard over to Henderson's so they can put the supplies on it for the trip back to the ranch and probably more little things than I care to count."

"Why don't I take the buckboard up to Henderson's and I'll walk back and stop in to see my friend Mary. I'll meet you here at 2 pm, and after Megan gets home from school, she can do her homework. When she finishes we'll go the Inn for supper, afterwards we'll drive over by the Wind River so that we can talk with her."

"You know we are going to have to set a date to get married. Have any ideas along those lines?"

"I thought we'd see how Megan takes our news first. I want her to be a part of all our decisions that will affect her one way or another."

"You know Priscilla, it's going to be hard for me to leave you, but I will come back and you will always be in my heart. Once things get settled up-country, I'll be here more than there. Do you think you'll be able to handle all the attention that I'm going to give you?"

"I'll have to think about that." She replied with a smile.

"By the way, have you had any luck in finding someone to do the cooking and some of the other chores around here?"

"Not yet, I am still looking for the right person. Enough said, we better go to bed like I promised you earlier this afternoon." She made sure the covers were on the cook stove, the back door was latched and all the gas lamps had been turned down or were out. He made sure the front door was locked before they went up the stairs to their respective rooms, he gave her a few minutes to get ready for bed before he walked back down to her room, carrying his boots and dressed only in his long johns.

-5-

Priscilla woke earlier than normal and left Todd sleeping soundly knowing that he needed to sleep given what he had to accomplish today. She had to get breakfast ready for everyone else and would get him up after everyone had left for work and Megan left for school.

When he woke, the house was silent. He padded back to his room, slipped on his jeans, put on a clean shirt and pulled his suspenders over his shoulders, combed his hair and slipped on his boots. He locked the door to his room and walked down the back stairs. He saw her standing at the sink washing dishes and humming. He walked up behind her and put his arms around her waist and kissed the back of her neck; she almost dropped the plate she was holding as she leaned back against his chest and said, "I could get used to that every morning."

"I hope you do. Why didn't you wake me, I could have helped you get breakfast ready?"

"Because you needed to sleep and I have been making breakfast all these years without anyone helping me."

"Once we become partners, so to speak, you can be the one who sleeps in and I'll get them all breakfast, or once you find someone to help you out, we can both sleep in or do other nice things to each other."

16

"We don't have time to continue where we left off last night, but tonight we will. What do you want for breakfast?"

"I'll get a cup of coffee, put some bread on to toast, and put two eggs and bacon in the skillet, while you finish up with the dishes."

"You'll find some sweet rolls and bacon already made. I have pancake mix sitting next to the stove. I thought perhaps you'd want a filling breakfast given all the things you have to get done today."

"Actually, I think a cup of coffee and you would fill me up a lot better," he suggested with a smile.

"I can see that you only have one thing on your mind, but you won't have any strength left if I let you make love to me again. You'll have to put off leaving another couple of days."

"I didn't hear you say 'no' to what I am suggesting."

"You know that I don't want you to leave, but you have to get things done up at Stony Creek and when you get that finished, you can come back here and we can make love every day."

"I'll concede to your wishes, my lady, but tonight you better be ready for me."

"You know I will be."

After he had breakfast, he said, "I should be back by 1 pm. Are you sure you want to drive the buckboard over to Henderson's for me?"

"Yes, I need to get a few things and I want to see my friend Mary. I'll be here when you get back."

* * *

"Mr. Bender, it's me Todd Morgan."

"'Todd, I didn't expect you back so soon is anything wrong

17

with the wagon?"

"Quite the contrary, it's just fine and it has been a workhorse. The way you built it has exceeded my needs completely. I need another bucket of axle grease, however."

"You couldn't possibly have gone through that whole bucket already, too much is just as bad as too little."

"I had to use most of it for another reason," explaining how he used it to alleviate his friend's pain from burns to his body.

"Well, that's a first, who knew that my grease would have medicinal properties. Maybe I should start going from town to town like a 'snake oil' salesman to make my fortune."

"Then who would make or repair all of our wagons?"

"You do have a point there."

"I also need to find out if you can make sleigh runners for the buckboard. Being where I am up-country, I'll need to change out the wheels for something that can get me through the snow. I am not in any hurry mind you. Can you look into it and if it's possible, make me a set and I'll get them on my next trip back here in November."

"I'll look into it and if it's possible I'll have them ready for you when you return."

"Any chance you are going into town later this afternoon?"

"I am."

"Could you drop off that bucket of grease at Henderson's and have them put it on the buckboard along with my other supplies? I have so much to do to get ready for my trip and I won't be able to lug it around with me all day."

"Sure, no problem at all."

Todd paid him for the grease and gave him an advance on the sleigh runners for the buckboard. He waved goodbye and headed to his next appointment. Arriving at the bank, he waited his turn to talk with a teller. The head teller opened another window and Todd went up to it and said, "I would like to close my account."

"Are you dissatisfied with the service here at the bank?"

"No, I just decided to consolidate my holdings."

"If you'll fill out this withdrawal slip, I'll process it for you right away. Do you want a bank check or cash?"

"I prefer cash, if you don't mind. I would like that all in double-eagles."

"I'm not sure we have that many. I may have to give you half and the rest in paper. It's the best we can do on such short notice." He finished writing out the withdrawal slip and slipped it under the grate. Surprised, the clerk said, "There must be some mistake. According to our records you only have $1230.00 in your account."

"I'm positive that I have $2600.00 in my account and now you tell me that my account is less than half that! Something isn't right here. May I see the bank president?"

"I'm sorry, but the president is in a meeting and can't be disturbed."

"You tell him when he gets out of his meeting that I would like all $2600.00 in double-eagles and I want it by 1 pm, today. Understand?" He left the bank slamming the door as the glass in the door rattled back and forth nearly breaking. He walked around the corner of the building and in through the side door, walked up the stairs to the law office of August McDavitt. His secretary, Lucy said, "Hello Mr. Morgan, did you want to see Mr. McDavitt?"

"Yes, if he's available for a few minutes?"

"I believe he is. Please have a seat and I'll check with him.." After a few minutes, she came out of Mr. McDavitt's office and said, "Please come in and take a seat." In his office there is a rather tall, thin gentleman that Todd had never seen before and August said, "Todd, this is Mr. Price from the Territorial Governors Office. He is here to investigate monies missing from several of the bank accounts of the Lander Bank & Trust Co. Unfortunately, yours happens to be one of them."

"What did you say? Did I hear you right?"

"Yes, during a recent audit of accounts, it was discovered that the original starting figure and subsequent deposits in most accounts were correct, but every time a draft was written or cash was taken out of some of the accounts, a duplicate transaction occurred the next day. We believe that the bank president, the bank manager, the head teller or all three of them were in cahoots in taking the money for their own use. Had it not been for the audit, no one would have caught on. We know where the manager and the head teller are, but when Mr. Price went downstairs to talk with the President, he was told by the head teller that the president was in a meeting and couldn't be disturbed."

"I just went to close out my account. I compared my balance to what they said I had and there was a discrepancy. I just thought that perhaps I wasn't writing down my withdrawals correctly. The teller also told me that the president was in a meeting and couldn't be disturbed. I think it's time we get the US Marshal over here and he can disturb the president."

"When you came in, I was just about to send Lucy over to his office and ask him to come over here. When he get's here, I'll have him deputize you and you can cover the back door; I'll cover the door that is down the stairs and Mr. Price and Marshal Murphy will go in through the front door of the bank and demand to see the president. If anyone tries to leave we'll arrest them."

"What will happen to the accounts in the bank?"

Mr. Price replied, "Until a judicial trial can be conducted, all accounts will be frozen."

"Well, I'm not worried about me so much, but most of the people in town depend on that money to pay their bills and get by from week to week. Couldn't you or the Territorial Office loan the people say $100 each until the trial is over and then give them the balance of their accounts, less the $100 so that they can survive?"

"That sounds fair to me and I'll clear it with the governor's office once I get back to Cheyenne." Tom Murphy arrived and the plan was laid out for him. He said to Todd, "Raise your right hand and repeat after me: I do solemnly swear to uphold the laws of the Territory of Wyoming and the United States of America, so help me God."

"I do. I mean so help me God, oh you know what I mean." He lowered his hand and Tom gave him a badge before they all left the office. August said to Lucy, "I want you to stay here. I don't want you hurt, no matter what you hear, including gun shots." After a few minutes there was a lot of shouting, a few gunshots and then quiet. Todd was standing behind the building where the back door of the bank was located. Suddenly, the door opened and Johan Johansen walked out of the building carrying a bulging satchel. "Going somewhere Mr. Johansen?"

"It's none of your business Morgan. Get out of my way."

"I'm afraid it is my business. You see, I have been deputized by the US Marshal and told not to let anyone leave the building. You're under arrest."

"What's the charge?"

"Bank robbery and evading capture by the authorities. We'll see when you get to court. I'm guessing you'll be found guilty and sent to the territorial prison for a long, long time. Guess I'm not so dumb after all now, am I?" Sputtering, Johansen is paraded around to the front of the building with Todd holding a gun on him and carrying the satchel. Sheriff Hughes, the US Marshal and Mr. Price are all standing out front with the bank president and the clerk in handcuffs. Many of the townspeople had gathered to see what all the commotion was about. Sheriff Hughes put another set of handcuffs on Johansen; he and two deputies take the three men to the jail. Todd gave the badge back to Tom, handed the satchel to Mr. Price and said to August, "I was going to ask you about something, but for the life of me, I can't remember what it was. Mustn't have been too important. See you gentlemen later." He touched the brim of his hat, mounted his horse and headed back to the boarding house. Upon his arrival he saw Priscilla picking flowers and said to her, "Do you mind if we go out to supper later? I need some time to be by myself."

"Are you okay?"

"I'll explain it to you later. I need to be in the right frame of mind to take out my two favorite girls."

"Why don't you sit on the chaise on the side porch where no one will bother you; I'll come get you in a couple of hours."

"I should be rested by then."

After Megan had gotten home, she asked her mother, "Why is Mr. Morgan sitting on the side porch?"

"He needed some time to be alone. I thought it would be a good place for him to rest where no one would bother him. After he get's up, he is taking us out to supper at the Wind River Inn. I'd like you to get your homework done and when you are finished, come upstairs. I'll need you to wash your hands and face and put on the pretty pink dress that I have laid out for you on your bed."

After Pricilla got ready, she went back downstairs and out to the side porch to wake Todd. As she walked up next to him, he was twisting from side to side. She hadn't seen him like this in a long time and wondered what he was dreaming about. She sat in a chair across from him and waited. After he settled down, she got up and walked over to him kissed his forehead before returning to her chair. When he woke, he looked at her sitting across from him and said, "How long have you been sitting there?"

"About twenty minutes. You were tossing and turning in your sleep. Please tell me what is bothering you?"

He took a deep breath before sitting up in the chaise and told her what happened at the bank.

"You must have been shocked when Johan came out the back door carrying a bulging satchel."

"He put on airs that he was an upstanding citizen and all that time he was stealing from his friends and neighbors. I don't understand why he would do that?"

"Well we won't have to worry about him any more. When did you want to leave for supper?"

"Give me about twenty-five minutes, I need to get the horses hitched to the surrey before I go wash up and change into some decent clothes. I'll meet you and Megan out in the barnyard."

After their arrival at the Inn, Todd left them off at the front door of the inn while he parked the surrey and walked back to where they were waiting for him and escorted them inside. They were shown a table near a window that overlooked a flower garden and the river. As they are viewing the menus, Megan says, "What is Gordon Blue?"

Todd replied, "Cordon bleu is French for "blue ribbon" but on the menu it means chicken with ham and cheese with a bread crumb topping and a white wine sauce. Are you interested in trying that?"

"I don't think so. I do like chicken and dumplings though, do you see that on the menu, mom?"

As Priscilla scanned the menu, she said, "Here it is. Why don't I order that for the both of us and I'll share part of mine with you"

"That's what I'd like for dinner. Mr. Morgan, what are you having?"

"Well, I have been eating everything your mother makes at the boarding house when I'm around, but when I am at my ranch in the mountains I eat a lot of rabbit and venison. I think I'll have a ham steak, with raisin sauce, boiled potatoes, and asparagus tips with coffee and when we get back to the boarding house, I'll join you for a glass of buttermilk and some cookies." After they placed the order Megan and her mother talked about school, while Todd just listened.

After a delightful dinner, Todd drove the surrey to the section where the Wind River crossed under the road that went right passed the Inn.

Priscilla said to Megan, "Mr. Morgan and I want to start a family."

"Well, I know you like Mr. Morgan a lot and when he's around, everything is fine, but sometimes he has to go away and that makes you sad. If 'We' become a family will he be my daddy?"

"In a manner of speaking, he will. Is that alright with you?"

"Yes, I like him a lot. He got Molly for me and he likes buttermilk and cookies. The only thing that I am worried about, will you be going away with him and live somewhere else, and leave me here at the boarding house, and have a nanny to watch over me?"

"The answer to your questions are no, I'm not going away from you, which is one reason we brought you to this spot by the river. Mr. Morgan and I are considering buying it together and if we do, we would like to build a house for all of us to live in together."

"Can I have my own room? Can Molly come live in the new house? Will Jasper be coming with us too?"

Todd touched Priscilla's arm to reassure her, looked at Megan and replied, "Yes, to all three questions. I love your mother very much and I want to marry her; I want you to be my daughter, too. So, can we be a family?"

"Yes."

He kissed her cheek; kissed Priscilla's lips and in return they both hugged him back. He said, "Ladies, I think it's time to get back 'home' and have some buttermilk and cookies."

After Priscilla helped Megan get ready for bed she came down the back stairs and noticed Todd sitting on the back porch, "Well that went better than I expected. You seemed distant what's wrong?"

"Just trying to sort things out about what happened today and what I have to get done tomorrow. I have to talk with that young man about the job and I have a few other necessities to take care of. I'll need to be here an extra day. Will that be okay with you?"

"You don't have to ask. I don't want you to go and as Megan said, I will be sad after you leave."

He pulled her down on his lap and began kissing her neck. She put her head on his shoulder and whispered, "Let's take this upstairs."

-6-

In the morning, Todd decided to walk rather than ride into town. As he turned the corner and walked up the stairs to the boardwalk everyone who walked past him was very cordial, shaking his hand or patting him on the back, saying, "Thank you." As he walked into Henderson's Mercantile, the storeowner, Joshua Henderson, came over and said, "I heard what you did for everyone yesterday. You're the talk of the town and we are all very grateful. Your wagon is all ready, but when you didn't come by, I had my son cover it and secure the sides; we put your horses in our barn out back. Do you want to pick them up now?"

"Actually, I wanted to pay you for the supplies and I'll be back in about an hour or so to get the wagon."

"You don't owe me a cent, your bill has already been paid for."

"By whom?"

"The town; they wanted to do something for you. You saved everyone from financial ruin by having the governor's office okay the $100 to cover each of us until the trial is over and we can get the rest of our money. It was the least the town could do for you."

"I'd protest, but I'll accept their generosity." He smiled as he left the store and went across the street to McDavitt & McIntosh.

"Mr. Morgan, we were expecting you yesterday," the security guard said, "but because of the incident at the Lander Bank & Trust we weren't surprised that you didn't show up. Unfortunately, Mr. LaDeux is not here today."

"I didn't want to see him specifically. I need a signature card so that my wife-to-be has access to my account when I am not here. Can you get that for me or do I have to see either Mr. McDavitt or Mr. McIntosh?"

"Well, neither of them is here either. If you wait a moment, I'll get one of their secretaries to bring a card down for you and you can bring it back tomorrow. If I'm not here, just give it to the guard that is here and he'll get it to Mr. LaDeux. Will that be okay with you?"

"Yes, that will be fine." Mr. McIntosh's secretary brought a card, explained where he and his wife had to sign and gave it to Todd. After she left, Todd said to the guard, "I'll bring this back early in the morning, say around 8 am. Will Mr. LaDeux be here then?"

"He should be; I'll make a notation that you would like to see him if he has a few minutes. Good day, Mr. Morgan."

After he left McDavitt & McIntosh, he walked the six blocks to The Mayfair Hotel and said to the hotel clerk, "I would like to speak to… you know I never did get their names. One is tall and lanky, and doesn't know when to shut up and the other one is quiet and reserved." Oh, that would be Ned Hogan, he's the quiet one; Curt Strom is the one with the big mouth. They both are in the restaurant next door, shall I get them for you?"

"No thanks, I'll go and see them in there myself. Thanks for your help."

"Sure thing, Mr. Morgan." He went through the door that connected the hotel to the restaurant and saw them sitting over in a corner. Curt was cradling a cup, while Ned was eating breakfast. Todd thought to himself, *he's going to need that breakfast. I'm going to have him start today with some chores around the boarding house that need to be done before we leave tomorrow.* He walked over to their table, "Mind if I join you?"

"No, sir," replied Ned.

"I told you, that I'd give you my answer yesterday morning, but due to circumstances, I had to wait until today. Ned, you never said anything while Curt did all the talking when you were sitting outside of the Cattlemen's, I take it that you don't speak unless spoken to directly."

"Generally, that's the way I am."

"I appreciate your directness and you're hired. After you finish eating, I want you to go and get your things and meet me in the hotel lobby in a half hour. Your hotel bill has been paid in full. Mr. Strom, I was informed by the US Marshal about a half hour ago that he was looking for you and if I happened to see you to tell you that if you didn't get over to his office by 11 am, today, he'd come looking for you. He had a wanted poster with a picture of someone who resembled a likeness of you. I suggest that you get your things, pay your part of the hotel bill and get over to his office before he comes looking for you."

Todd touched the brim of his hat as he rose from the chair and walked back into the hotel to pay one half of the hotel bill for Ned, telling the clerk, "Mr. Strom will be in shortly to pay the other half of the bill. He won't be back for any more nights."

After Todd left, Curt said to Ned, "Lucky you, at least the

old man hired one of us; I wonder what the marshal really wants to see me about?"

"Other than getting upset with **José** and telling the guys in the bunkhouse that they cheated you, I have no idea. I'll put in a good word for you if you want?"

"Naw, I can take care of myself. I'll be seeing you around. Don't let him work you to hard, ya hear?"

"I've always done an honest days work for an honest days pay and I don't expect anything more or less. You take care and I'm sure our paths will cross again one of these days."

Todd walked across the street to the Marshal's office, and upon entering said, "Mornin', Tom. I just wanted to let you know that Curt Strom will be over here shortly. He's the one with the big mouth who needs a dose of humility. I'd like you to put him in jail for a night or two under a charge of disorderly conduct, then let him out and tell him that to work off his fine of say $15.00; he has to clean up the office, the cells and whatever else you can think of for 15 days and that he can sleep in a cell during the night. I should be back by the third week of November and by then, I can hire him to work on my section's here doing some manual labor. He should be ready to work by then. Is that OK with you?"

"Sure. Say, do you think we can get lunch today down at Los Frijoles?"

"Yes, I like that cantina."

"Is one o'clock good for you?"

"See you there." Todd walked back over to the hotel as Curt was stumbling out of it, trying to get all his stuff together as he made his way to the Marshal's office. He found Ned waiting for him and said, "Are you ready to go to work?"

"Yes, sir." They made small talk as they walked over to

Henderson's. "Mr. Henderson, this is Ned Hogan, my new ranch hand for my place up near Bull Lake. I want to establish a credit line for him of fifty dollars, so that if he comes to town and needs anything, he won't have to worry about paying for it until after he get's paid for the month."

"Mr. Hogan, pleased, to make your acquaintance. Is there anything you need today before you go up-country?"

"I'll need two pairs of leather work gloves, two pairs of Levi's, size 30-30, two wool work shirts, two pair of long-johns, a heavy coat with sheepskin lining, a scarf, no make that two, a box of cartridges for my.45, and a bag of those root beer sticks."

"Just so you know that comes to $19.45 on your credit line and as Mr. Morgan said when you get paid, you can pay the bill at that time."

"Ned, if you'll go out the back door, you'll see a buckboard with a double team ready to go. Bring it around to the front of the store and I'll meet you there." He hustled out to do as he was told. At the last minute, Todd decided to buy a 12 gauge shotgun with a box each of slugs and shot, saying to Joshua, "good for keeping' varmints at bay. See you in about a month."

-7-

"I see you had some trouble getting the horses and buckboard around to the front of the store Ned." Todd remarked as he stood on the boardwalk watching.

"Well, I've driven a buckboard, but none as fancy as this rig and never one with a double team before. I had to get down and grab their harnesses and walk between them. After a little coaxing, they came along. I guess I'll need you to show me how to drive your buckboard with the double team."

"When I worked at Timber Creek, I had to learn how to drive a double team as well. One of my first jobs was to take a buckboard full of fence posts and barbed wire, and do fence repair from the timberline to the lane that ran up to the bunkhouse. I had never driven a two-horse team before. The secret is that you have to get the two horses to work together no matter what. I'll drive and show you how it's done; hold this new shotgun for me."

As they pulled into the barnyard behind the boarding house, he said, "Grab your things and I'll show you where you'll be bunking tonight." He took Ned to the tack room where a cot was set up and where he could put his satchel. "You won't need your gun so put it in your satchel. The lady that runs this place has a little girl by the name of Megan and I'll introduce

32

you to Mrs. Parker and her daughter later. Dinner is at 6 pm sharp. Come clean, be polite and no spurs. We'll also be having breakfast tomorrow morning. This afternoon, I have a list of chores that need to get done around here. You do know how to read and write, don't you?"

"Yes, sir. My Ma taught all of my siblings and me how to do both."

"Good. Around here call me Mr. Morgan; up-country, it's Todd."

"Yes, sir, I mean Mr. Morgan." Todd gave him the list: 1. Check all the fence boards and make sure they're tight; if not, re-nail them. 2. Clean out the stalls that need cleaning, put down new straw; make sure all the stalls have fresh water, new feed and a half bale of hay in each corner. 3. Put the straw with the manure in it out back on the pile that is already there. "If you get done with all that, take a nap, lay out in the sunshine, read a book, but don't go into town. If you do, you're fired!

Todd walked up the stairs to find Priscilla talking with a young lady in the kitchen about the job she needed to fill. Priscilla said, "Mr. Morgan, this is Miss Elizabeth Sanderson she is applying for the position."

He removed his hat, extended his hand and said, "Please to make your acquaintance ma'am."

"He is one of our out of town guests who stays here on a regular basis. He's also the man I'm going to marry."

He smiled and said, "Would you excuse us for a few moments while I tell Mrs. Parker something."

"Certainly," the young lady replied.

Todd and Priscilla walked down the hall toward the parlor. "There is a young man out back working on some of the chores we talked about this morning, his name is Ned Hogan; I have to meet Marshal Murphy in about 15 minutes or so."

"Miss Sanderson is just the right fit for the boarding house; I plan on offering her the position."

"You do what you think is best. I'll be back in a couple of hours and you can let me know what she said." He kissed her before he went out the front door and walked towards town. He greeted Tom at the cantina where they both ordered enchiladas, an extra large portion of refried beans and a small salad for each of them. Tom ordered coffee; Todd asked for lemonade. "So how is Mr. Strom liking jail life?"

"Well, he claims he didn't do it and I should be looking for his partner, Ned Hogan. He resembles the picture also."

"Really, you know I just hired Ned. I wonder if he's the one you should be looking at?"

"Naw, Curt's my man. I think I'll let him stay for a week, maybe longer as a guest of the territory and feed him bread, beans and water. He not only needs a good dose of humility, but he needs a good swift kick in his you-know-what and how not to pass the buck. Unfortunately, you won't be here to see how he turns out. I hope he's ready for you, when you need him." Their meal arrived and they eat heartily. As they finished, Todd said, "This meal is on me."

"I can pay for my own meals you know. I'm not that poor, but if you insist, I accept."

"Will I be seeing you up-country this fall?"

"Might be sooner than you think. Those hombre's that burned your friend and his property are still out there. I got a message from the mayor of a small hamlet northeast of here. He said one of their townsfolk was beaten up pretty badly and his horse was shot dead, just like what happened up near you.

I am asking the territorial governor to offer a bigger reward for their capture. We need to arrest those cowards before they do any more damage."

As they left the restaurant, they both noticed that it was starting to cloud up. "Might be a wet one come morning. As much as we need the rain, I am hoping that it blows over. It will make it a tougher go for me if it does rain," Todd remarked.

"You take care and I'll see you in a few weeks."

Todd arrived back at the boarding house to find Megan playing catch with Ned in the backyard. "I'm guessing that you got all the work done and this is how you spend your free time?"

"Yes, I did. This young lady was bouncing the ball off of the side of the barn. She reminded me of my little sister so I told her I would play catch with her if she wanted me to. Do you have anything else for me to do, Mr. Morgan?"

"No, just remember dinner is at 6 pm and tomorrow, we'll be leaving early for my ranch. He went in the house and found Priscilla washing potatoes in the kitchen sink. He grabbed her around her waist and pulled her against his chest and kissed the back of her neck. She sighed and said, "You give me goose bumps when you do that."

"I aim to please. I think I'll take a nap before supper."

"I'll get you up around 5:30."

"Do I get kisses with that?"

"We'll see." She replied, smiling.

After supper, Ned helped bring the dishes into the kitchen and put them in the sink. He excused himself and went out to the barn to take care of the horses before going to bed. Todd, Priscilla and Megan took a walk down towards the property near the Wind River; Jasper and Mike chased each other with the three of them watching. When they got to the section where a house could be built eventually, Megan asked her mother, "Can I go with the dogs?"

"Go ahead," she replied.

Todd yelled after her, "Please be careful!"

"I will," Megan replied. He held Priscilla and gazed into her eyes. They were a bit misty and he said, "Tears already? I haven't gone anywhere yet."

"I know, but I don't want you to go; you know how I worry that something will happen to you and I'll never see you again."

"I promise that I will be back in time for Thanksgiving and that's six weeks from tomorrow. I'll keep a calendar in my pocket and mark off every 7th day so that I know when I am getting close, alright?"

"Maybe, I could have Mary take care of Megan and I could go with you."

"We've had that discussion and you promised Megan that you'd be here for her."

"Yes, but…"

"There are no buts. I need to get my new ranch hand settled in; I'll either take Gus, Turk or Pete with me up to the mine, so that I can decide after one of them has seen it who I should hire to get the mine up and running. I can't do that if you came along, I would be too distracted to get anything done and besides you'd miss all the fun you're having here. I promise when I come back that we will spend lots of time together, either wrapping Christmas presents or making a family. Which one do you prefer?"

"I prefer both. I think I'll talk with Megan on when we should get married. You have any preferences on who you want to stand with you and who we should invite?"

"I'd like Crusty to stand with me. Also, I would like to invite Liz Connolly, Crusty's wife, Tom Murphy, the Henderson's, August McDavitt, Hiram, and Mrs. Bender and You!"

"Sometimes you are so silly."

He held her at arm's length, twirled her around and said, "You're the only one I want." They made sure that Megan wasn't looking as he caressed her and kissed her for a long time until Megan came back with a bunch of wild flowers for her mother. Jasper and Mike looked exhausted from their run. Todd said, "Time for us to go back home."

She got Megan to bed and came downstairs to find Todd washing the dishes and setting them on the drain board, she started to dry them; he brought the serving platters into the pantry, she followed and closed the door.

-8-

With breakfast finished, the rest of the boarders had left for work and Megan left for school. Todd told Ned to get the horses harnessed and hitched to the buckboard, put a saddle on Misty, put the double-pack frames on top of the supplies in the wagon and tie them down tight, turn the wagon around so that it was headed out, put a rope halter on the mule and the gray mare and tie them to the rear of the buckboard, find a couple of empty burlap sacks and fill both half way with oats and buckwheat and put them under the seat and wait for him in the yard. He watched for a few moments to make sure that Ned was in the barn, before he swept Priscilla off of her feet and carried her up the backstairs and said, "We have fifteen minutes, let's not waste a single second of it. They made love and when they finished, he got up and went into her private bathroom to take a quick bath. He walked into her bedroom drying off. She said, "I see what I like…"

"I'm sure you do. I've got five minutes before I have to get out to the barnyard. He sat next to her on the bed and pulled her up to his lips and kissed her passionately before saying, "I want you to stay in bed. I will lock the front door; close the back door when I leave. I don't want you to get up and watch me go down the road; most of all, don't cry. I love you Priscilla." He walked out of her bedroom door, down the front staircase, locked the front door, went down the hall to the kitchen and grabbed three biscuits off of the stove on his way out of the house, and closed the back door as he left. He gave Jasper a scratch behind his ears before he got up in the buckboard and said, "Mike, up" and to Ned, "Time to go up-country."

He stopped by the assayers and gave the guard an envelope and asked that it be given to Mr. LaDeux when he came in. He got back in the buckboard and drove down a side street to the main road and headed for Stony Creek Ranch. He showed Ned how to handle the team when driving the wagon and after having gone a couple of miles they switched places. Ned picked up the reins and did what Todd had told him to do. He handled the team like he had been doing it for years. Todd had him stop while he got down and mounted Misty and said, "Follow me!"

They took the trail that went toward Ft. Washakie and Todd said, "I want to stop and see an old friend; take the horses down by the river, let them graze a bit, then let them drink after they have cooled off. I'll be back within the hour." He rode to the fort and as he approached the gate, the corporal of the guard said, "Who goes there?"

"It's Todd Morgan, I'd like to see if my friend Pete Byrd is still in the hospital and I'd also like to see the commander if he's in."

"Mr. Byrd went back home about a week ago and the commander is out on maneuvers. I'll tell him you called. Good day, Mr. Morgan." He rode at a leisurely pace back to where Ned was and let the horses graze several more minutes. He and Ned led all the horses and the mule to the river to drink.

He decided they'd stop at Shoshone Joe's for the night. He had Ned rein left and up along the dry creek bed arriving late in the afternoon. Joe hadn't seen his friend in a long time and said to Todd, "You bring a tenderfoot this time, I prefer your princess."

"I prefer my princess too, but I have to get my new helper squared away at my ranch."

"I suppose you want to stay the night?"

"Only if you have room, my friend?"

"I always have room for friends; it's my enemies that I try to keep out." They both laughed. He introduced Ned to Joe and told Ned where to put the buckboard and the horses for the night. Todd asked, "Why are the gates closed at the fort again?"

"A rider came through about two weeks ago saying that a wagon train had been attacked by Indians. They shot several of their horses, burned their wagons, killed several of the men, took advantage of the women and beat up some of the older children. It didn't make any sense that the Indians would kill the horses, take advantage of the women and hurt the children. They stopped doing that when the military presence became so widespread. It has been peaceful for several years. Even if they were renegades, they'd still want the horses. The commander decided to take two companies with him and find the culprits and bring them to justice. He's been gone from the fort for almost two weeks."

"While I'm here I'd like to get another dog like Mike. They make excellent watchdogs, are friendly with children and are very protective. Do you have any?"

"My bitch had a small litter of four just five weeks ago,

they're not weaned yet. How about I bring one up to your ranch in about two weeks and you can show me around."

"Two weeks is fine, but I may not be there; Ned will be. Just bring the whole litter. I have three friends who have homesteads right next to my property and they could use good dogs, too. Is it a deal?"

"For you, it's a deal. Time to eat, then we will rest?"

Before they left in the morning Todd said to Ned, "Get the horses harnessed and I'll take care of the mule and my horse. Once we leave, Mike and I will be ahead of you, but you will always be able to see me." As they rounded a bend, Todd slowed after seeing smoke up ahead and thought to himself, *this can't be happening again.* He stopped and waited for Ned to catch up, and when he did, he said, "I'm tying my horse to the wagon; I want you to come along after I send Mike back to get you but do not under any circumstances come before that. You do know how to use a repeating rifle, don't you?"

"Yes," he said with some hesitation.

"Good, now get down from the buckboard and stay with the horses up front, I don't want them to get spooked when they smell the smoke." He carried his Sharps as he walked forward. It was as he had anticipated, Gus & Turk's cabins were fully engulfed. He saw a fleeting glance of someone running toward the woods to the right of the cabins, but since he didn't know how many of them there were, he didn't pursue him. He decided to backtrack and pick up the trail to the west and come around on the north side, hoping to flush out whomever it was that ran into the woods on the eastern side of the buildings. Again, he saw a glimpse of a man going for a horse; he estimated where he would come out, aimed his Sharps and fired. He followed the shot and about 100 yards northeast of the cabin, one of the men who invaded his property last spring, lay dead. He kept walking east, saw another person and fired. This time, however, he only wounded one of them and when he got to where the man was he looked down. It was the man who had stepped in one of his bear traps so many months ago and said to him, "Stay right where you are and don't move. Mike, guard!" The dog stood his ground and gave a throaty growl. The man dared not move; Todd went to get a rope to tie his hands before standing him up. When he came back he said, "How many more are there?" The man didn't answer. Todd repeated his question. Again, the man didn't answer. "So you're going to make this tougher than it has to be, answer me damn it!

"I ain't saying a thing, so stop asking me."

"That's not good enough. Todd whistled for Mike who trotted over to where the man was and Todd tapped his shoulder. Mike put his jaws on the wounded shoulder and started to bite down harder and harder until the man said, "Get this mangy mutt off me! There are two others besides me and the one you shot dead back a ways."

"Where were they headed when the job was done?"

"We were supposed to meet up at Bull Lake around sunset tonight."

"I'm going to get you up off the ground and I want you to walk the way I point you. Don't try anything. My dog would love to sink his teeth in your throat or I could give you a running start and see how far my Sharps will "talk" for me." The man did as he was told. Todd marched the man back to where the buckboard was and said to Ned, "Keep and eye on him until I get back with his horse; Mike will help you guard him." Todd went and got the horses that were left in the woods; he took them over to where the dead man was and wrapped him in a poncho that was tied to the back of his saddle and threw him over it and tied him down. He brought the two horses over to where the other man was, tied his hands tight and helped him get up in the saddle. He tied the horse with the dead man to the back of the buckboard and put a rope around the other horse's neck and led the horse, while Ned drove the buckboard. Once they arrived at the back gate to his ranch. He opened it and told Ned to follow the lane. Once Todd led his horse through, he ground tied it, walked back to the gate and closed it. He secured it with the piece of rope like he always did. He told Ned to drive down the path toward the barn and when he got there to take the horse with the dead man on it over next to his cabin before he started to unload the wagon. Todd led his prisoner over to a large oak tree, got him down off the horse. He had him sit on the ground and tied him to the tree; put a hat on his head to keep the sun off of it. He hoisted the dead man over his shoulder and took him to the shed where he skinned animals and laid the body on top of the boards off the ground.

He had Ned unload the wagon and put everything in the barn to the right of the door next to the covered pile of cut lumber and said, "Welcome to The Stony Creek Ranch. This is what I want you to do while I am gone. I need you to separate everything that you brought into the barn, put everything marked Langstrom in one pile, Byrd in another. Put your things over in the tack room and make yourself a place to sleep tonight. Put my things in the cabin, along with the bucket of axle grease. You'll find a fire pit over by the stream, build a fire and make supper. A frying pan is hanging from the end of the table, vegetables are in the barn and in the cache you'll find some venison that you can cook for yourself and our prisoner. You can either untie one of his hands or you can feed him. If you untie one of his hands don't take your eyes off of him, because if he gets loose, you're dead. He'll not think twice about killing you. I was going to take Mike with me, but I've decided to leave him here with you. I'll be back either later tonight or sometime tomorrow. Since our prisoner is injured, I want you to clean out his wound, you'll find a bottle of Kentucky bourbon under my bed, pour some over your bowie knife and put it in the fire, then rinse it with the whiskey; pour some of the whiskey directly on the wound and then using the knife get the bullet out, once you do, pour some more whiskey on the wound, then heat up the knife again and *cauterize* it. Take a clean sheet from the cabin and cut apiece about two feet long and about six inches wide and wrap it around the wound. If he passes out, just leave him be, he'll wake up sooner or later. I know you think I'm being cruel about all this, but there is more to it than meets the eye. I'll explain everything to you when I get back. Remember, do not take your eyes off of him and have Mike guard him while you eat."

He put his Winchester in the scabbard, grabbed a box of shells from inside the cabin. He also tied the 12-gauge on the side of the scabbard and took the box of slugs and shot and put them in his saddlebag, got a bedroll and tied it behind the saddle. Then he took some jerky and the three biscuits he took from Priscilla's stove and started toward Bull Lake.

It was important that he got there by sunset to take care of what should have been done months ago.

-9-

Priscilla didn't get up and look out the window as Todd drove down the road. Her tears were being absorbed into her feather pillow; she had an uneasy feeling that before he got to the ranch something terrible would happen. She finally got up around noon and washed her face, put on a camisole under her spring dress. The tears would be gone by the time Megan got home from school, but you could see the sadness in her eyes. She still had to get the breakfast dishes done and get the evening meal started. To make it easier, she decided to have baked ham with raisin sauce and after it was in the oven she'd peel potatoes to mash and string beans for a vegetable. She'd make a batch of sourdough biscuits to go with dinner and sugar cookies with cinnamon sprinkled on top for dessert. She decided to tell the boarders that from now on she would announce what the breakfast and dinner would be for the following day, so that if they wanted to eat at a restaurant in town, they could. She had planned on having pancakes for breakfast, and baked fish for supper tomorrow night.

Megan came bounding up the back stairs and said, "Mom, I'm home." She was surprised to see her in the kitchen washing the dishes and said, "Are you alright mom?"

She turned to face her daughter and Megan saw that her mother had been crying. "Are you worried about Mr. Morgan?"

"I was, but now you're home and you always make me happy when I see you."

After dinner, Priscilla wrapped a shawl around her shoulders and took Megan and Jasper for a walk down by the river. Jasper saw a squirrel and took off after it with Megan cheering him on, while Priscilla watched in amusement. She had started to feel better during supper and she was surprised that the boarders were happy to find out what breakfast and dinner were going to be for the following day; they weren't surprised to hear that she was only going to make Sunday dinner from now on also. Mabel remarked, "it's about time you started to take care of yourself, we've noticed how exhausted you look lately."

Now that Todd was up-country she could get back to doing the things that made her happy when he wasn't around. She told Megan that she would take her to school in the morning, and that she had an appointment to see the doctor after that. She arrived at his office around 9 am and after her examination, the doctor confirmed what she had suspected all along, or at least for the last couple of weeks. She was with child. This only seemed to complicate things, however. She wasn't married, yet. She didn't know how she was going to tell Megan, let alone Todd. She also didn't want anyone at her church or in the community to know lest she be ridiculed for being pregnant out of wedlock. She would have to start taking better care of herself for the baby's sake and now might be a good time to have Beth Sanderson take over some of the duties at the boarding house. She had decided that she would have her move into the room that Todd used when he came to stay. He could sleep in her room; it was no secret that she was smitten and had told several of her friends that they were going to be married, soon. Miss Sanderson's references had all given her glowing reports. Priscilla had decided that she could pay her $40 a month, plus her room and board and use of a horse or the surrey if she asked; she would have one day off every two weeks. The only restriction would be that she could not have any men friends on the second floor. After all, there were other people who lived on the 2nd floor and they rightly deserved their privacy as well. After her doctor's appointment, she drove the surrey to The Mayfair Hotel to tell Miss Sanderson that she was hired; could she start Monday?

"Yes, that would be perfect," Elizabeth, replied.

Priscilla went back to the inn and changed into her work clothes. She had to clean out the room that Todd had been using, re-paper the walls, and rearrange the room for Elizabeth to move into.

Todd rode hard for the first hour wanting to get to Bull Lake before anyone else showed up. Without the dog or other backup, he'd have to plan it just right. He wanted to be able to take whoever showed up back to Ft. Washakie to stand trial. With one dead already, he really didn't want to make it more than him.

While Todd sat his horse he had a commanding view of the lake and the trails on the far side of it. From what the man said, Todd anticipated two men, but to his surprise there were seven angry men who rode in and perhaps this large group could be responsible for the raid on the wagon train. He needed time to plan an effective assault. He thought about all possible scenarios and decided to stay where he was. He'd use the early morning sun shining in their faces to mask seeing how many men they were facing. He let the horse browse in the hollow behind him with a rushing waterfall to deaden any sound; he took the shotgun and put a slug in one chamber and buckshot in the other; next he loaded the Winchester carbine and his pistol. He figured he'd use all of these weapons, maybe even his bowie knife before it was all over. He took one lariat and cut several pieces of it into four-foot lengths to tie their hands and set the other lariat down on the ground. Guessing that there was at least seven hours to go before the night gave way to a steel gray dawn. He chose to have a cold camp and rest close to the stream that tumbled over the rocks at the end of the lake. He was using the same maneuver he had used during the war and the same one he used when he went elk hunting last winter. He had a greater advantage, he understood men, even the ones that were as ornery as this bunch was.

As dawn started to break, he took the Winchester and fired three shots in the air for effect, and another round of three directly at the camp. One man stood up and quickly went down with a shot in his knee. Todd laid the smoking rifle in the bushes. He shouted out, "This is Deputy US Marshal Todd Morgan, drop your weapons! Any attempts to make this a firefight will result in your deaths. You are surrounded on all four sides. What's it going to be?"

"Bring it on Marshal, we aren't giving up that easy." He knew they were stupid, but he didn't think they'd make a firefight out of it. From his vantage point, he picked up his rifle and continued to fire in rapid succession and reloaded as quickly as he could. He winged one in his left shoulder, another with a shot to the gut with the man screaming in agony as the blood flowed out of the wound as he lay dying. Another man next to him decided to make a break for the horses. Todd pulled the trigger of the left side of the shotgun where the slug was, killing the horse. He came at them running full speed through the brush and across a stream. He reloaded the shotgun and sprayed the camp area with enough buckshot to make them think that there were more than just four men shooting at them. He slung the rifle over his shoulder and kept firing his pistol, winging one and then another and again he asked, "What's it going to be, all dead or some alive or wounded, it's your choice?"

After a few seconds and no answers he fired another two rounds of the buckshot, reloaded and fired two more for effect, then a couple of rounds from the pistol through the brush blindly at the men. He saw a white piece of cloth tied to a stick go up amongst where they had hunkered down and a shout out, "Name's Shorty, we've had enough; we've put down our guns!"

"I want to see all of you in a tight circle to the right of your dead partner and make sure that all knives, pig stickers, pocket guns and the like are in front of you in one pile; if anyone of you gets any crazy ideas, you're dead." The count was one dead, four wounded and the other two had buckshot holes in their clothes. When he came near them, he said, "Which one of you is Shorty?" He stepped forward. "I want the rest of you to sit on the logs around the fire pit. Shorty, I want you to take these ropes," handing him the four-foot ropes, "and tie their hands behind their backs, nice and tight, then loop one end through their belts and back up through the knot once again." He did what he was told to do, when he was finished he said to Todd, "their all done mister."

"Come over here so I can tie yours in front of you and when

I'm finished you can sit right in front of me."

Todd said to all of them, "You twitch or try to run while I get your horses I'll blow you to kingdom come with my scatter gun."

One of the seven remarked, "We're tired, hungry and want no more trouble with you. We will stay where you've put us."

He went and got their horses, first he tied the dead man over the saddle of one of the horses; next he got the four wounded ones up in the saddles of the next four horses securely tying them to the saddle and each horse tied to the one in front of it; next he told 'Shorty' to mount the final horse and said to the last man, "guess your horse is dead, sorry I had to do that. You can walk or you can ride the horse with your dead partner, your choice."

"I'll walk."

"Suit yourself."

Using the other lariat, he looped it over the horse's neck with the dead man on it. He whistled and Misty came down out of the hollow, across the stream and reined up next to Todd. "Excuse me for a minute," as walked over to the bushes and relieved himself. He walked a few paces to retrieve the Winchester and the shotgun.

"Shorty, you're the lead rider. Go south and don't try any funny stuff. I'll be watching all of you; my trigger finger is a mite itchy on this new shotgun that I got. It might accidently go off and I would surely be sorry if any of you 'varmints' got hurt before you got to Ft. Washakie. Now move out!" He trailed behind the last horse with the dead man tied to the saddle. Sometimes he rode along side of them, sometimes the trail in front, but mostly from behind them. After five miles or so, they came to a stream and he said, "All horses in the water, let them drink first then ride to the opposite side of the stream; "Shorty get yourself down. I'm going to untie your hands, your going to help each one of your partners down and get them into the stream to drink, one at a time, then retie them in the saddles and take the ropes I give you to tie their feet under their horses' bellies; he had the man who had walked all this way get down on his knees and drink from the stream. When he was done, Todd led the horse that the dead man was tied too over to the opposite bank while the man followed the horse and sat on the riverbank. 'Shorty' when you're done, you can get the last drink, and then come over here and I'll retie your hands. I will put in a good word for you at your trial." One of the men said, "Where's the rest of your posse Marshal?"

"You're lookin' at him."

"You mean that's all there was, just you?"

"In a manner of speaking, I have my Greener, a Winchester, pistol and my Bowie knife, which, by the way, none of you have met yet, but it would slit your throats from ear to ear, clean as a whistle."

"Well if that don't beat all," the man said.

As he rode into view of the fort, a soldier looking through a pair of binoculars saw the single file of men riding towards the fort. He said to one of the others, "Go and get the colonel, we have a column of men coming this way." The colonel got on the top of the wall, a pair of binoculars was given him and he peered out at the men riding single file. He saw that Todd Morgan was trailing behind the line and said to a sergeant who was standing next to the gate, "Open the gate and get five or six troopers to help bring those men in here." He yelled out, "Is that you Morgan?"

"Yes, Sir."

"Why are all those men tied to their saddles?"

"These are the men you've been looking for. The ones who hurt my friend when they burned down his cabin with him in it and killed his horse and who attacked the wagon train. I am doing my civic duty to bring them here for justice." The colonel had the dead man taken to the morgue and the wounded ones to the hospital under armed guard. The two with buckshot wounds were first taken to the infirmary to have the buckshot removed and afterward, were taken to the guardhouse. Todd said to the colonel, "I've got two more back at my place, one is dead and the other might be if my dog got hungry while I was gone. Can you spare a couple of troopers to follow me back and get them?"

"You need sleep Todd. I'd like you to go to the barracks, get a bath, some hot food in you and a good night's sleep, tomorrow will be soon enough."

"Yes, Sir."

Word spread fast, that someone by the name of Morgan had rounded up a gang of killers that had been plaguing the surrounding area. In Lander, people cheered, Priscilla cried and prayed that Todd was all right.

-10-

As Todd slept, he was plagued by nightmares from his days in the prison camp. He tossed and turned, shouted out at times while he slept not realizing of course that he had been asleep for two days. The colonel was informed about his outbursts. He summoned the fort's doctor and said to him, "Should we wake him or just let him sleep?"

The doctor replied, "We all have demons and some of us allow them to take over, especially when we are asleep. Where the mind is involved, we have no control over what we are doing, eventually he will have to deal with those demons. The best we can do for him at the present is to just let him sleep. As he sleeps, he presents no harm to himself or others and usually, when he wakes, he'll have no recollection of what transpired, other than to say that he still feels tired."

When Todd woke on the morning of the third day, he was still tired. He got the sleepers out of the corner of his eyes, stood up, yawned and walked out to the barrack's front porch where he stretched, and yawned again before saying to no one in particular, "Guess I better go see the colonel after I wash up, change my clothes and have some breakfast." An hour later he walked into the colonel's office and asked the private if he could see the colonel.

53

"Have a seat Mr. Morgan and I'll see if he has a few minutes to see you." The private knocked on the colonel's door and when told to enter said, "Mr. Morgan would like to see you sir."

"Have him come in," the colonel replied.

"Sorry that I slept so long, colonel, I guess I was more tired than I thought. Can I still get a couple of troopers to go with me back to my place and get those two other varmints?"

"Corporal Haines and Private Miller will accompany you. They'll be ready to leave when you are."

"Thank you sir for your hospitality."

"You're welcome."

They arrived at Stony Creek Ranch at sunset. Todd said to the corporal, "The only place I have where you can sleep is the barn, but it's dry providing you don't mind sleeping with the horses."

"That's fine, Mr. Morgan, if we were on maneuvers we'd be sleeping on the hard ground."

Todd noticed that the prisoner had been moved. Ned had been sitting down by the campfire when Todd arrived, he got up and grabbed the bridle of Todd's horse as he dismounted and said, "Our prisoner complained that he had cramps in his legs and had to relieve himself. I sent Mike with him so that he knew that he wouldn't get far if he tried to run. After that I put him down near the creek so that he could get water by scooping it out with a tin cup that I gave him. He hasn't tried to escape. Your neighbors, the Langstrom's and Pete Byrd arrived yesterday and asked me who I was and whom the guy tied to the tree was. I explained that you hired me in Lander and the man tied to the tree was burning buildings just south of here about 4 or 5 miles. I told them where you were and that you've been gone for four days to find the man's partners and bring them all to Ft. Washakie for trial. Gus asked me if I needed any help. I asked if he could watch the prisoner for a couple of hours so I could get some things done in the barn and made sure that the horses were taken care of. Once the chores were done, I caught an hour of sleep and hope to get some more tonight now that you're back. Gus is down by the campfire making sure that our prisoner doesn't go anywhere."

As Todd approached, Gus said, "We met your new man and his prisoner. Did you get his partners?"

Corporal Haines was standing next to Todd and replied, "You could say that; he single-handedly brought in seven men wanted in killing, burning and maiming people across the area over the last several months. We are here to take the dead man and this hombre back to the fort to join his partners."

"Todd, is this the man who hurt Pete?" Gus asked.

"He's one of the gang. I am not sure if he did the burning or not, only Pete can tell us that. By the way where is he?"

"He and Turk went over to my homestead. While you were in Lander, I was able to put up a barn with six stalls and a tack room. Up in the hayloft, we made half of it into our sleeping quarters and the other half for hay storage."

"Sorry I wasn't here to help you. I'm sure I'll be around to help with Turk's building and whatever Pete decides to do. For the time being, I suggest we get supper going and after a good nights rest. We can decide what needs to be done on all the properties and in about a week I have to go to my claim."

"What claim?"

"I filed on two pieces of property that I found while I was out trapping. I'm going to need one of you to go with me for about a week, I need some advice."

During the night, the prisoner disappeared; no one heard a thing.

* * *

Todd was up at the crack of dawn having gotten a restful night's sleep. He walked out the door of the cabin, yawned, scratched his beard and stretched. He noticed that the prisoner was gone; nothing except a couple of shod hoof prints leading off into the woods could be seen. He grabbed his rifle, which he had been keeping by the door of late, closed the door and made his way through the woods. He saw the prisoner tied upside down, with flames from a fire nearly touching the man's head. Pete was sitting on a stump teasing the man and pushed him with a limb so that he would swing past the flames as they grew higher and higher. He of all people knew how angry Pete was, but still it wasn't right to seek revenge this way. If it meant stopping his friend to keep him from doing something he'd regret the rest of his life, he had to do it. The man would stand trial and pay for his crimes. Clearing his throat, Todd said, "Morning Pete, I see that you've got my prisoner in a rather compromising position. Why you'd almost think that you were going to roast him alive?"

"Look what he or one his friends did to me," stripping off his shirt. "How'd you feel if what you see happened to you?"

"It would make me as angry as hell, but I'd like to think that I was a just man and that he ought to be standing trial not only for what he and his 'friends' did to me, but for all the other people, especially the women and children they terrorized and the animals that were killed for the sport of it; the buildings that have been burned, and innocent people who have been maimed, like yourself. He'll either be hung or face a firing squad."

"I'm angry and I want to make him suffer like I have over the last two months."

The prisoner said, "Please mister, do something. I don't want to die this way; please help me?"

"I can't say that I blame you Pete, but if you go through with this and he dies, you'll be the one who ends up going back with the soldiers to the fort and standing trial. You might get off because a jury felt you were out of your head, but eventually you'd see the error of your ways and you might try to kill yourself so the demons would just go away. Turk, Gus and I don't want to lose a friend and we will help you any way we can. Cut him down and let me take him back to the soldiers' so that they can take him back to the fort."

Pete took out his bowie knife and cut the rope as the man was over the flames. He fell and his shirt caught on fire, he rolled over and over in the dirt just trying to get the flames out, yelling and screaming from the pain. Todd got him to his feet, his hair was singed, his shirt torn and burnt. Some of the skin on his right shoulder was burnt just enough, so that he knew what it felt like, but he was alive. Pete returned to the stump, sat down and began to cry.

Todd marched the prisoner back to his homestead thinking, *maybe he'll make a run for it and I'll have to shoot him* but dismissed that thought as they neared the corner of the barn. He explained everything to the corporal and asked, "Make sure we're notified when the trial is so that Pete and I can testify?"

"The way these things usually go, it should be within a

month from now at least. I would be at the fort the fourth week of November for the trial. If there were any change to that date, we'll send a soldier out to tell y'all.

-11-

Tom Murphy swung by the boarding house to see how Priscilla was doing and maybe she'd have a letter for Todd. He went up the front steps and used the doorknocker; a pretty young lady came to the door and said, "Can I help you?"

Taking off his hat, he said, "I was wondering if Mrs. Parker was here?"

"She is, won't you come in and have a seat in the parlor? If you'll give me your name, I'll tell her you're here."

"Tom Murphy is my name, ma'am." She left and he thought *maybe I should get a room here instead of sleeping down at the office.* His thoughts were interrupted when Priscilla came in the parlor, "Tom, how nice to see you. I'm so glad you came by."

"I was just on my way out of town headin' up-country and thought that maybe you might have a letter for Todd and I could take it with me. I should see him in a few days."

"You must have read my mind, why don't I get you some coffee and you can relax while I finish the letter."

"A cup of coffee sounds just right to me, one sugar and a touch of cream, please." She went down the hall and said to Beth, "Would you please bring a cup of coffee with one sugar

59

and a touch of cream to Marshal Murphy. I have to finish the letter I was writing to Todd and he can take it with him."

"I'd be glad too." She brought the coffee. He thanked her and said, "Care to sit and talk for a few minutes?"

"I'd be happy too."

They made small talk; he asked her, "Would you tell me your name and how long you have been in Lander?"

"My name is Elizabeth Sanderson, but everyone calls me Beth. I came here from Casper about a month ago after I was hired for the housekeeper's position that was advertised in the paper."

"What a coincidence, I moved from Casper just over three months ago to keep law and order from Lander to the Yellowstone. Do you have a brother named Peter by any chance?"

"He's my younger brother. How do you know him?"

"We're both members of the Grange. When I come back from this trip, perhaps I could take you out to dinner?"

"I certainly don't know you well enough for that. I suppose over time that I will and then we'll see about having lunch sometime."

"You're right of course. Please excuse my poor manners. I'll be back in about two weeks or so and under Mrs. Parker's watchful eyes maybe we could become friends? Tell your brother I said hi, the next time you write him."

"I'd like that," She replied with a bit of a blush in her cheeks. "I'll mention you in my next letter home." Tom was thinking about the possibilities for the future. As he sat in the chair, relaxed, a thousand things going through his mind as he sipped his coffee. Priscilla came back in the room carrying an envelope for him to give to Todd and said, "As everyone knows, he is a hero for ridding the countryside of those killers, but please tell him that as much as I applaud his efforts, I need to have him keep focused on getting back to me in one piece."

"I plan on having a long talk with him. The territorial governor applauds his efforts too, but it puts a harsh light on the sheriff's and Marshal's service across the entire territory. Sometime it's easier for one man to tackle a problem and get the results that a posse might overlook. We all agree that it is more important that Todd remain a rancher for the good of his future family and the territory of Wyoming; I will give him your message as well."

"Thank you. Will you also give him a package from Megan?"

"It smells delicious, but I don't think it will make it to his ranch in one piece."

"You can take a couple of cookies, we won't tell Megan."

"I have enjoyed this short visit with you and Miss Sanderson. I must get to that new township of Wind River by early this afternoon; the day after tomorrow I'll be at Ft. Washakie for a couple of days and by weeks end I should be at Todd's ranch." He placed the coffee cup on the saucer before rising. He grabbed his hat and gloves and walked out the front door, stood on the top step for a few seconds and as he was about to step off, Beth, who had been sitting on the front porch said, "Please tell Mr. Morgan that I am worried about Priscilla. She is always tired and hasn't been feeling well in the morning. I'll keep an eye on her and he shouldn't worry unnecessarily. I can handle anything that goes on here. The boarders have been helping with the horses and the other animals, as well. Please give him our best. Priscilla will be glad when he comes back toward the end of November."

"I'll relay your concerns. I hope you have a nice day." Once he got on the trail, his thoughts quickly turned to why he was making this trip. The sheriff in Lander received a telegram about a lone rider who was riding from village to village inquiring about Morgan, no first name, just Morgan. Tom is not sure if Todd should be worried or not. He hopes to catch up to the rider; he isn't wanted for anything that he knows of, he just wants to know why he is making all these inquiries.

* * *

Todd was worried about Pete and walked back through the forest to go talk with him. Smoke drifted up through the trees where a campfire had been burning just a little while ago. He saw Pete sitting on the stump with his hands on the side of his head looking down at the ground.

"Pete, I'd like to talk with you."

"Not now, Todd, I've got to get my head on straight before I do something else stupid."

"Come and see me when you're ready. Do you know where Gus and Turk are?"

"I'd go down the fence line towards where my line meets Gus's."

"Thanks."

He found the two of them walking along the fence line and overheard their conversation. "You know he can't do any more mining. Do you think he'd be interested in guarding the mine when we're not there?" Gus asked his brother Turk.

"Actually, I'm not sure what he can do in regards to the mine, you know how hard working he is. Maybe Todd will have some ideas. Speaking of the devil, here he comes."

"Hey you two, Pete told me I'd find you down here. You

both look like you lost your best friend and don't know what to do next."

"In a manner of speaking, we have. Neither of us have any idea what Pete can or cannot do. The doctor at the fort told him he'd have a hard time being a miner ever again. His physical strength would certainly not be what it was before the incident and the fire damaged his lungs as well. It's unfortunate because that's all he knows how to do. He knows how to keep a mine safe and how to place the timbers in the right places to shore up the roof and walls to keep them from caving in on us." Turk responded.

"Well, I was going to suggest that he could ride up with me to my claims, make suggestions on how to get the gold out of the ground, the type of men I'll need to hire and guard the mine, especially when I'm not there, and probably a thousand other questions."

"That's a great idea," Gus remarked. "Why don't we have dinner over at our place for a change? We can discuss what you need to have done and when you plan on leaving," Turk added.

Gus said, "and while you're there, we can figure out what we all need to get done around all of our places before winter get's here. We see you hired someone to help you out."

"I hired him in Lander. He knows enough to get things done around here while I'm out trapping. I was working from sunup to sundown every day and it's taken a toll on my health. Every time I took a break, I felt guilty because I wasn't working to get this or that done. I hope he works out. If he isn't doing things around my place, I was hoping that he could help each one of you too; you're going to have to figure a way to pay him for any work he does for you though. I stopped at Shoshone Joe's on my way up here and he is bringing four dogs with him in about a week or so. I told him that I had three friends who needed good dogs for their places, too. Y'all can pay me back after he brings the dogs. Mike has been a great watch dog and he's good company too."

Turk asked, "that other dog you had, did she ever come back?"

"Yes, but she turned part wolf and…" as Todd looked away, "I had to kill her."

"Sorry, to hear that you had to put her down, it probably was for the best though."

"It was. Ned and I will be over around six or so. I'll bring some lemonade with me."

As everyone was sitting down on the benches at the table that Turk had built in his spare time, Gus said, "I hope you like turkey, boiled potatoes, carrots, sourdough biscuits and coffee." In unison, both Todd and Ned said, "We can hardly wait to start eating." Gus and Pete had constructed a raised cooking hearth including a beehive oven and storage for pots, pans, dishes or utensils. Pete said grace before they began to pass around platters of food. They made small talk during dinner and when they were finished, the dishes were cleared and Ned said he'd be glad to clean them all.

The four men sat at the table each lost in thought when Todd said, "Before we all decide to fall asleep after that dinner, I suggest we talk about the four homesteads and what needs to get done before winter gets here in about a month or so."

Pete spoke first, "Well I only plan on putting up a one room cabin, part for sleeping, part for storing my mining equipment, tools as well as a small barn where I can stable my horse; Turk spoke next, "Well I'd like to at least get my footings dug and a foundation wall up before winter gets here; Gus spoke last, "I need to finish the barn, especially upstairs where we are all sleeping; finish putting in a tack room. I also need to finish my corral just north of where the barn is situated and all of us have to finish putting up the barbed wire fencing around our individual homesteads and the fire breaks, as well.

"I have a list of things for Ned to do, but the most important for me is adding a roof over the porch and to build a cooking fireplace on one end of the cabin. If he gets caught up on the list of chores that I am giving him, then he can help any of you but you'll have to pay him for his work." Todd replied.

Pete, who had been quiet during supper said, "Well that seems fair to all of us regarding Ned."

Todd said to Pete, "I would like you to go with me to my mining claims. I plan on leaving the middle of next week."

"I don't know what I can offer."

"Well since I am new to mining I need someone with experience to tell me who to hire to work and guard the mine; what type of timbers I should be using, safety concerns and probably lots of other questions that I can't think of right now. Can I count on you?"

"You know I am partners with Gus and Turk and they need my help with our mine."

"Gus said, "Turk and I thought you'd be the best person to go with him next week. We'll be working around here before we go back to our mine by the end of November or the beginning of December. So what do you say?"

Reluctantly Pete replied, "OK, I'll go, but I need to start cutting logs for my new cabin now and hopefully I can get some of it up before I leave with y'all the end of the month or so."

Ned came back with all the cleaned pots and dishes and set them on one of the sides of the fireplace. He and Todd left shortly thereafter.

-12-

Marshal Murphy got to Wind River around 2 pm and went directly to the Mayor's home. They had lunch and afterward the Mayor said, "Last week a tall thin man with white hair, white skin riding a roan mare came into our township and just started asking questions about 'Morgan'. Does he live nearby? What kind of horse does he ride? Does he seem like a reasonable man? Of course the whole territory has heard about 'Morgan', but it was the way he asked and it didn't seem to matter who he talked to. We just didn't know what to make of this fellow and as suddenly as he appeared, he was gone. Since we don't have a sheriff, the only thing I could think of was to send a telegram to the Lander Sheriff's Office. He didn't break any laws and he was polite, but it was just kind of eerie."

"I appreciate the fact that you let somebody know about this person and that he came this way. He has been in other towns and hamlets throughout the territory; I'd like to catch up to him to find out why he needs to find 'Morgan'. We don't even know which Morgan he is talking about; there are certainly other people with a last or a first name of Morgan. Thank you for lunch, now I need to get to Ft. Washakie before sundown. If you need any other assistance either from the sheriff's office or my office just send a telegram. Good day to you, sir."

* * *

Priscilla had gotten into a routine. Deal with the morning sickness, get up around ten or eleven, get dressed in her work shirt, jeans and boots if she was going to be working with the animals or playing with Jasper; or her long tan, gray or denim blue skirt and a white or almond color blouse with the crisp ironed sleeves, if she was going shopping for food for the boarding house or for fabric depending what she was doing on any particular day; then go downstairs for a light breakfast of toast with jam, pancakes, waffles, muffins and buttermilk to drink that Beth had made for breakfast. Sometimes she'd stop at Mary's house on the way back from town for some woman talk. Beth was doing a great job and Priscilla didn't have to worry about keeping any particular schedule because she knew that things were getting done and the rest of boarders were well fed and happy. She hoped that Todd had gotten her letter and that things had settled down up-country and that he was getting done what he had told her he would be doing for the next month.

She knew that Megan was curious as to why she was sick in the early morning and why she was taking naps in the afternoon. One of these days she would tell her why, just not yet. On Saturday, she and Beth would be canning some of the fruits and vegetables from the garden and fruit trees. She was looking forward to that. She'd let Beth do most of the boiling, while she put the fruit or vegetables into the mason jars before sealing them with paraffin and putting on the glass tops. They would put some in the cupboard, some in the cellar and she would give some to Parson Samuels' and his wife. But most of all, she'd save several for Todd to take back with him to his cabin up-country.

On Sunday, She and Megan were going to church and to the social afterward. She had promised herself that she'd say a prayer for him, the new baby growing inside of her and that everything would turn out all right for all of them.

*   *   *

Marshal Murphy made it to Ft. Washakie around suppertime and stopped by the commander's office to see if he could bunk in the barracks and put his horse in the stable for the night. He would be happy to pay for his brief stay. He needed to find out if the stranger had been to the fort and if so what had he been asking the folks here. Tomorrow he'd ride to Todd's ranch. The colonel didn't know of any stranger riding through asking questions about 'Morgan', but he should check with the trading post owner and the owner of the café just outside the walls of the fort. He would be able to sleep in the barracks and there was no charge to do so. The following morning he asked both the trading post owner and the café owner the very same questions, but got "No's" from both of them. He had breakfast at the café, three eggs, apple smoked slab bacon, and toast with plum jam and coffee. After he paid for his breakfast and walked outside, he stood next to his horse with a toothpick between his teeth and surveyed the land before he mounted and reined his horse northwest toward Stony Creek Ranch, thinking, *almost a fruitless search but I've got to keep going until I find this man and talk with him.*

-13-

During breakfast Todd asked Ned, "What experience do you have?"

"I grew up on a farm in Tennessee. but after awhile I decided that I wanted to move out west and see if I could make it on my own. I ended up in Green Springs and mentioned to someone that I was looking for work. He told me Timber Creek Ranch was hiring and how to get there. I got hired and did the usual jobs like cleaning out the stalls, mending fences and herding cattle. EJ was showing me how you and he used to break horses; I'd never done that before, but I'm a quick learner."

"After we're done here, I want you to arm yourself with a rifle and walk the property. I want you to study tracks in the soft soil, see where the corner posts and fence sections have defined the property lines. Also defined by a single or sometimes a double strand of barbed wire stretching form post to post; check where the corrals are; where the pond is; what fish you see in the streams that crisscross the property; where the hayfield and grain fields are; how the cabin, even the barn are situated on the property, so that when you start to work the property you'll be fully aware of how this ranch is laid out."

70

"Why do I need to carry a rifle with me?"

"We've had wolves."

"A good reason to carry a rifle."

"Can you work long hours being alone and with little time off?"

"Yes, sir, I mean, Todd. I actually prefer the solitude. I seem to get more work done."

"How did you get to be friends with Curt?"

"We came to work about the same time at Timber Creek and we were bunk mates. Mr. Cooper thought we'd be good workers together. Curt said he knew about cattle and mustangs; I was just a country boy learning new things every day. In the beginning, it seemed that we did work pretty well together, but it became apparent after a while that Curt was more bullshit than substance and I found myself carrying most of the load. One day he mouthed off to **José** and called him a *'beaner'*. I guess I was just too stupid to realize that was an insult and I backed Curt, a big mistake on my part. Mr. Cooper told us both to apologize to **José**, Curt refused and I didn't know what to say. He told us we were both fired, to pack our gear and meet him at his house to collect our final pay. After he paid us he said, "Don't ever come back." We'd been traveling together for several weeks, going from one town to the next looking for work when you found us sitting on the bench. I just decided to keep my mouth shut, seems for once I made the right decision."

"Well, that's quite a story. You told me you know how to write."

"I do."

"You'll find some paper on the table next to my bed and a pencil. I want you to write a letter of apology to **José**. He is a good man and a great teacher. If you had simply said, "I'm sorry, I meant no harm" you'd still be working on Timber Creek Ranch. Your friend Curt has some life lessons to learn and from what you told me, I am sure that I made the right decision about hiring you. After breakfast, I want you to write that letter first, walk the property and after you have come find me in the barn. I am going to show you what needs to get done around here. I made out a list last night before I went to bed so that you'd have something to go by while I am gone. I'll expect you to get a lot of it done, but not all of it. Some of the things on the list will have to wait until it snows. I'd also like you to stay in the cabin when I'm gone. After we go over the list today, you and I are going to start building a fireplace with a beehive oven and a chimney onto the cabin. Tomorrow and the following day we will finish that project, then I'll show you where you can hunt for food; you do know how to hunt don't you?"

"Yes, my pa took me hunting when we needed food."

The list that Todd had written out included: *1 - Cut all the hay, bundle it and put the bundles in the loft; if you run out of room in the loft stack the bundles next to the barn and cover them with a tarp. 2 - Put a roof over the porch on the front of the cabin, use the tin sheets that are in the barn; 3 - Chop all the stumps into useful firewood and anything left over, pile on the grain and vegetable fields and burn after the first snow; stack the firewood on the north side of the porch and put the rest in a pile on the south side of the cabin and cover it with a tarp; 4 - Pick all the remaining vegetables and wash and sort them before putting them away in the cubicles in the tack room. 5 - Nail any loose fence boards on the two corrals. 6 - Enlarge the chicken coop and yard. 7 - Keep the barn and stalls cleaned daily and spread the manure pile on the grain and hay fields every other week. 8 - Cut the timber on the thirty acres that I have marked for new hayfields or pastures, stack the logs after you trim them according to size and set them off to one side and pull the stumps. 9 - Reinforce gates on the rear of the property. 10 - Help Turk and Gus if you have time or want a break in what you're doing here on the ranch.*

11 - Keep all of us fed – hunting for deer, rabbit; squirrel even a wild turkey or two; skin the deer and rabbit and after you've scraped them really well, put the skinned side out, roll them and put them up in the cache; put the meat in the cache and finally, if you think it needs to be done, it does.

It was quite a list and he knew Ned wouldn't even get a third of it done while he was gone. He expected him to use some common sense and take the breaks he needed. He was sure the lad knew hard work, but if he was a bettin' man, he also knew that his pa probably took more breaks than most ranchers; most farmers did. He showed Ned where to find the rocks he needed for the chimney and had him take the buckboard, with Mike riding in the back, up one side of the creek bed and down the other looking for suitable-sized rocks. Meanwhile Todd started to dig out the footings for the chimney. He wanted to get it done today so the cement and rocks could firm up and tomorrow, they would start building the chimney, fireplace and beehive oven.

After they got the base done, Todd decided he'd take the time to show Ned where he could hunt and where they all preferred that he didn't, mainly their homesteads. He also showed him how set snares for rabbits, martens and squirrels and when to check them so that a wolf or fox didn't get it before he did.

He left Ned at a favorite area to hunt while Todd went back

to his homestead. An hour or so later, Ned proved he was an excellent hunter, bagging a six-point buck. Todd showed him how to skin and scrape the deer hide, as well as the rabbit and the marten, how he wanted them bundled and where to store them. He hadn't decided if he'd share the sale of the skins with him yet, but he probably would.

-14-

"Hello stranger, long time no see," Todd said to Tom Murphy as he rode in looking weary.

"And a good afternoon to you too. I need a place to sleep and some supper, I'm exhausted."

"I think we can fix you up on both counts. I'll have Ned take care of your horse, while you get settled in my cabin. You can sleep in my bed," Todd replied.

After a good night's sleep, Tom wanted to talk with Todd about his involvement in rounding up the nine killers and bringing seven of them to Ft. Washakie for trial. "Let's sit down at the table. I was about to make some breakfast. If you're interested, I'll throw in enough for you too." Todd remarked.

"I am!" After breakfast, Tom said, "The Territorial Governor appreciates what you did and you'll receive the reward for their capture. However, he wants you to know that you're not to do such a foolish thing again all by yourself."

"Foolish, is it? I rid the territory of scum like those murderers and the governor wants to make sure that it doesn't happen again. I assure you Tom, I had no intention of doing it in the first place, but I have a breaking point and their actions forced mine. First it was my property that I was defending; next they attacked my friend Pete who got so badly burned that he can't work again in what he loves to do; then they attacked a wagon train of settlers' who meant no harm to anyone. They burned, killed and took advantage of the women and hurt the children and the final straw was that they came back to the site where the cabins were and burned them to the ground. Just a total disregard for the law. I hope that a jury treats them the same way they treated others. The military couldn't find them; you were the only lawman covering 5000 square miles of rugged country and you couldn't find them either. I seized upon the moment and did what I had to do, since no one else was able to get it done."

"I am not going to argue with you over the specifics, I just want to make sure that you understand that we don't want you to take the law into your own hands again. You are right about the lack of judicial power out here in this wide-open country, but I do make it my business to follow up on any leads that I get about any real or potential problems. Like a lead I am following up on right now. There is a lone rider going from town to town in this part of the territory who is looking for 'Morgan'. We have no idea whether it's you, or someone else with a first or last name of Morgan. The only information that I have so far is that he's tall, lean, and polite. He has white hair, white skin, almost an albino. He rides a roan mare and asks a lot of questions. I have no hot or cold trail to follow; I'll just have to keep traveling this part of the territory until I catch up with him and find out his reason for wanting to find someone named 'Morgan'. It isn't going to be easy and it may take me weeks, even months before I get one solid lead that I can act on. That's why I get paid for the protection of all of the citizens, you included. I also made a promise to a very important person in your life right now who worries about you constantly, Priscilla Parker. I promised her that I would talk to you and let you know her concerns, as well."

"Let's not bring her into this Tom, she has nothing to do with it."

"But she does. She's heard the heroics of what you did and cringes. She told me herself that the day you left, she had a premonition that something bad would happen before you made it back here to the ranch and she was right, wasn't she?"

"Well, yes, but I had to do it, I had to defend the people who in essence couldn't defend themselves. What's the use? No one apparently is ever going to understand how I felt at that particular moment. I will try to keep my emotions in check and when you see her and the governor, tell them both that I'll let the law do their job and I won't act so irresponsible again."

Tom said, "On a personal note, I would probably have done the same thing; I don't think you were irresponsible either. I'll stay an extra day if you don't mind; I could use a break. I'll need to get back on the trail again by Wednesday."

"Say, why don't you trail along with Pete and me. We'll be leaving on Wednesday to travel up to my second mine. We'll cover about 30 miles to the west, staying a few days there before I go to the first mine which is a good 25 miles to the northeast nearer to Bull Lake. Then we'll ride back down here. You'll be able to cover close to 750 square miles of the territory. I often meet up with other trappers, miners, even some Indians. You might just get the information you are seeking if any of them have seen him and when; besides, we can always use the "law" where we are riding too."

"It's a deal; now what can I do to help you out around this

place? I need to earn my keep, you know. By the way, I have a gift for you from a young lady, her mother asked me to give it to you. It's missing a couple of cookies, I couldn't resist." Todd took the box and set it on the table, opening it he found about two dozen assorted cookies, a half dozen brownies and a half dozen each of apple and peach muffins. He decided to pour himself another cup of coffee and have a muffin; he offered Tom one also. Tom also gave him the letter that Priscilla had written; he would read it later. He put the rest of the gift in the cabin along with the letter, and then he started on finishing the fireplace and beehive oven while Tom and Ned finished with the chimney, making sure that it rose two feet above the cabin's roofline.

<h1 style="text-align:center">-15-</h1>

When the chimney was finished, they all stood back and admired their handiwork, *'not bad'* each one thought. Todd said, "Now we can be warm in the winter and have our meals cooked inside when the weather turns bad."

Tuesday, he took Ned, with Mike riding along on the back of the buckboard, to the hay field, "This is the first thing I need you to get started on. I put this in late and surprisingly it came in. Now comes the hard part. It has to be cut and bundled, and what can't be stored in the hayloft you'll have to spread a tarp next to barn and pile them there and cover it. Today, you are going to start the cutting; on the buckboard you'll find two canteens of water, a sharpening stone, two scythes and some biscuits, just in case you get hungry. I expect once you get in the rhythm of cutting the hay that you be all done by week's end. Try not to think that its forty acres and it will go by quicker than you think. You are going to get tired and sore, that will go away over time. If you need anything, Marshal Murphy and I will be in the hayloft most of the morning. This afternoon we'll be getting ready to leave tomorrow. Do you have any questions?"

"None that I can think of, I'll see you at suppertime. Is Mike staying with me, today?"

"Why not? He can keep you company while you work."
He looked down at the dog and said, "Stay!" Mike got back
under the wagon, put his head on his front paws and lay there
watching what was going on.

Todd walked back to the pond; sat down next to the tree
where he made love to Priscilla just a few weeks before, and
took out the letter she had sent him.

*"Dear Todd, I know you've only been gone a week, but it seems
like forever to me. I miss your warmth, your tender words of
encouragement when we are working and playing together, and
most of all, the love that you have shown me when I least expected
it. I have started to do the things that I enjoy like knitting, sewing
clothes for Megan, doll clothes for 'Molly' and a quilt that I am
making for a bed. I haven't been feeling well lately, but the doctor
assures me that it won't be long before I am better again. Megan and
I have been taking walks down to the river after dinner, while Jasper
has taken to chasing rabbits and squirrels on the property every
time that we go. Megan, with the help of Beth, made the cookies
and the brownies, while I had a hand in making the muffins for
you. We all hope that you will enjoy them after a meal or perhaps
with coffee for your breakfast some days. If my calculations are
right, by the time you receive this letter, you'll be back with us in
three weeks. You are either reading this at the picnic table next to
the fire pit or at the tree where we went in the pond for my first
of many swims that I can't wait to do with you again. I want you
to know that I am very proud of you for capturing those men but
for my sake and Megan's, please be more careful. I really don't
think that I could go on living if something dreadful happened to
you. I know that you are getting that young man that you hired*

squared away at the ranch and you probably are leaving soon for the mines." All my Love, Priscilla

* * *

He quickly read through the letter one more time and thought, *I'd rather be there with you Priscilla, but for the time being I have to get the ranch the way I want it and the mining too.* He got up, dusted the dried grass from his pants, folded the letter and stuck it in his back pocket; he'd read it again another time. He was almost at the barn when he saw a rider with white hair through the trees on the homestead next to his; the man was riding the roan mare that had been stolen from him nearly nine months ago. He didn't have a gun with him or he would have shot the 'horse thief'.

"Tom, where are you?"

"I'll be out in a minute," came an answer from the outhouse.

"There is a rider with white hair on the homestead next to mine. He's riding the roan mare that was stolen from me about nine months ago from the cabin that I first was in just south of here. I'll get our horses meet me out here as soon as you can." They rode out the front gate and turned east toward the next homestead, "We'll split up, you ride along the front of homestead and I'll try to flush him out to you." Todd said, after ten minutes or so, neither of them had caught sight of the man. Todd was perplexed, he thought, *He couldn't just disappear into thin air like a ghost or maybe I miscalculated on where he was in the woods. I'll go back to my place and ride the firebreak and see if I can see him., If I do, I can fire a shot in the air and hopefully Tom will figure out where I am and come that way or I could just shoot the son-of-a-bitch on the spot and not worry about it.* They backtracked and went down the firebreaks, but without any luck. Todd wasn't crazy, because they did find tracks leading west along the same trail that they would be taking tomorrow.

They rode back to the barn, unsaddled both horses and set them loose in the corral. He decided to move the old bales of hay out of the hayloft and stack them on the South side of the barn. Ned could put as many of the new bales up in the hayloft that he could fit. When Todd finished cleaning out where the new hay would go, he had Tom help him cut the lumber that he was using for storage bins for his skins so that he could separate them by animal. It would be easier to sort them come springtime to sell at the trading post and he'd still have time to lay out all the supplies and equipment that he was taking with him up to the mine. The room would have to wait until a rainy or snowy day; the cache could still hold a large amount of skins.

It was getting late in the day and Ned still had not yet returned from the hayfield. Todd decided not to wait and started the supper he had planned for tonight as everyone was coming to his place, to eat. He would have the rest of the smoked ham that Priscilla had given him before he left along with boiled potatoes and carrots, sourdough biscuits and coffee or water to drink. He'd also share the cookies and brownies with everyone. He made sure that he arranged everything in the barn for loading in the morning. If they got a good start by 8 am, they would get about half way or better to the mine, camp out that night and go the rest of the way the following day. He started to get worried when Ned hadn't shown up as the last rays of the sun were barely peaking over the mountains. He said to Tom, "I've got to go find out what happened to Ned, I'll be back shortly. If the others get here before we get back, don't wait for us; have supper."

"You sure you don't want me to go along with you."

"I'm sure; he's probably just lost track of time and is trying to get back here in the dark, which isn't easy if you don't exactly know the way." He walked maybe a quarter of a mile, when he saw the buckboard making its way along the path through the woods, very slowly. Ned was holding onto the reins, but it was apparent that he was asleep in the seat. It was only by instinct that the horses knew the way back. By the time they got him down, he was sore from head to foot; he didn't have enough common sense to know when to stop from time to time and rest his muscles. A hot meal, some horse liniment and a good night's sleep was what he needed. "I'm sorry, I let you down," he mumbled several times.

Todd said to him, "You'll be alright; you didn't let me down." He and Tom carried him to his bed after he ate something; Mike stayed by his side throughout the night.

Todd hated to leave before Ned woke up. Gus and Turk said they'd keep an eye on him.

"It will do him some good if he gets all the sleep he can. It won't always be that way," Todd said to Pete and Tom Murphy as they were riding along.

"I know what you mean," Pete replied, "When I was growing up in the hills of Pennsylvania, I wanted to show my pa that I could do a days work, even though I was only nine. By the end of the day I was sore all over. It took nearly a week for the aches and pains to stop."

"He'll learn," Tom, said, "y'all had it easy. In East Texas, my Pa expected all his children to do chores from the time we could walk. I remember one time when I was five or six that it was my turn to gather the eggs, feed the chickens and get their water trough filled before I left for school. I got everything done, but I forgot to latch the gate to the chicken coop. By the time I got back in the afternoon, my pa took me to the woodshed and wailed the tar out of me for not paying attention. It had taken him and my mother nearly 3 hours to catch all the chickens and get them back in the chicken coop. A lesson I'll never forget."

"You two got nothin' on me," Todd said. "Why, I can remember when I had to slop the hogs and I'm guessing that I was maybe nine or ten at the time. I put the mash and leftovers as my pa liked to call 'em in their feed trough, trouble was I'd used the mash from his still, instead of the mash that he had set aside for the hogs. He used the other mash for the still and everyone that bought the moonshine thought it had a peculiar taste, only when he found that I had switched the 'mashes' he took a switch[1] to me. I couldn't sit down for a week, but the most humiliating part of it was at school. Everyone teased me unmercifully for weeks on end about what slop to use on them-their hogs." As they rode along, they all had tales to tell and laughing through it all made the morning go by faster; they each said in their own way that the good ole days were over. Todd was hoping that his good ole days as a bachelor were indeed over and better days of being married to Priscilla Parker was just a few weeks away. He had hoped that by the time he got back to Lander that he could convince her that they should get married during Thanksgiving.

---

[1]   Switch – a branch usually taken from a willow tree.

-16-

In Lander, Priscilla had a particularly bad bout of morning sickness, and just wanted to stay in bed all day. She didn't want to see anyone, including Megan. Having not seen Priscilla all morning, Beth became concerned as she was dusting the rooms on the second floor. She knocked on Priscilla's bedroom door and a barely audible voice said, "Go away! I just want to be left alone." Not knowing what was going on with Priscilla, Beth said through the door, "I'll get you some toast and a cup of ginger tea; I'll put them on a tray and leave it by your door. Please try and eat something." Beth retreated to the kitchen and made the toast and tea, and by the time she got back upstairs she could hear Priscilla vomiting. Taking a chance, she opened the door to find her lying on the bathroom floor; she was white as a ghost and sweating. Beth got her cleaned up and back into bed and said, "You stay right here while I take the surrey to get the doctor."

"Nothing he can do. I'm with child and its just part of having a baby. I'll be okay if I can just get through the next two months. When I had Megan, I had an easy time of it, so I'm guessing it's a boy this time and he wants to make sure I know whose boss for at least the first three months of his life."

"Why didn't you say something? In Casper, I was a midwife

for a couple of years. I'll help you get through this. Does Mr. Morgan know that he is going to be a father?"

"No. I didn't really know until two weeks ago myself. I mean, I had my suspicions, but the doctor confirmed it when I went to see him last. I haven't even told Megan and she has been wondering why I am so tired all the time. I'll have to find the time to tell her soon, before she sees me like you found me this morning. I don't want to scare her." She managed to eat the plain toast and get most of the cup of ginger tea down; she felt a little better and decided to try and get some more sleep. "I'll be up before Megan gets home from school. I'll meet her on the front porch and have a nice little chat with her about her new baby brother or sister."

* * *

The three men had ridden several miles before they came to a bold rushing stream and decided to take a break, let the horses graze for a while and drink. Marshal Murphy said, "I don't know if you've noticed, but we are being followed; there's at least two, maybe more riders on the ridge just north of where we are. I can't make out whether they are white or Indian, but they are keeping pace with us. I'd check your rifles just to make sure you've got a full magazine in case it comes down to us versus them.

Todd replied, "If one of you will stand on the other side of your horse looking towards me, I'll get out my binoculars and have a look so at least we'll know who we are dealing with." He saw four Indians; he thought Cheyenne and they were coming down a trail off of the ridge. He put away the binoculars, checked his side arm. He said to the other two,

"Hunch down and hold the reins of your horses; Pete stay to the left of me in case they cause any trouble, Tom stay to my right. I've had some dealings with both the Sioux and Cheyenne while I was trapping this past winter; let's see what they want."

As the four Indians rode in they were not wearing any paint, one had a spear, one a bow and a quiver of arrows and two of them had the new Winchesters. "We come in peace white man. Speaking to Todd, they asked, "Are you the one they call 'Peacemaker'?"

"You can call me that if you wish. What they call you?"

"I am 'Little Wolf'[2] and these are my brothers; we are looking for a white man who rides a roan mare, he is tall, has white hair, skin, and asks too many questions about you Peacemaker."

"How do you know he is looking for me?"

"He has visited our village. My father told him that you were Peacemaker during the Great War between the men of the north and of the south. I know not what that means, but I know that you do not kill unless you have to. I think he is angry at your spirit and wishes you great harm. A shaman[3] has lived with us for several months called Moon On Sky. He told my father to be wary of this man and to find you and bring you back to our village if you are willing."

"If I go with you, will you provide protection for my friends?"

"Shaman say, 'No harm is to come to you; you are brave man' you help him when the same man came and hurt him long ago; he says that because you are friend it would be a

---

2   Little Wolf - http://www.indigenouspeople.net/littwolf.htm.

3   Shaman – a holy man.

good omen for my people to keep you safe and the people who are your friends and your family. We have been in the forests and in the sky watching over you for many moons. Will you come?"

"Let me talk with my friends and I will let you know my answer shortly." The Indians went back to the other side of the stream, dismounted, and let their horses graze while they drank from the stream and waited for an answer.

"Well, at least we've found out who the man is that you seem to have been trailing Tom. We don't have a name, but their description matches many of the descriptions that you have received. I am curious to find out what Moon has to say about all this. It will delay our plans to get to the mine, but going with them may actually keep us alive for the time being and possibly the future. If he is the man that beat up Moon then he should be brought to justice. You'd be the person to do that since it happened at Moon's cabin about six miles from where my homestead is and not at an Indian village. Otherwise, they would have administered their law since he hurt Moon."

Pete replied, "I never experienced anything like this in all the time I've been in the mountains. You lead such an interesting life, Todd." Tom was a bit skeptical, "I don't know, if we go with them and it's a trap, we're dead and no one would ever know what happened to us. Gus, Turk and even Ned could only say we left for the mine and haven't been heard from since. It is a dilemma that we will have to ponder. I suggest that we go to your mine without the Indians, and once we are all there, you could meet them three days from now near there; Pete could at least decide what course of action would be best for your mine while you are gone and I could help him. That way we could 'kill two birds with one stone.'"

Todd replied, "I like what you are proposing. I'll go see Little Wolf and tell him our decision. I will meet him three days from now where the moon sets on the valley." Todd walked over to the other side of the stream to talk with Little Wolf. They sign in peace and the four Indians rode away, while he motions for Pete and Tom to join him; they have several miles to go before they make camp for the night.

* * *

Priscilla put on a comfortable spring dress and went out on the side porch and sat on the chaise while she waited for Megan to come home from school. As Megan was dropped off by one of the parents, she saw her mother on the porch and said, "Mom, why are you are smiling?"

"I'm smiling because I have something wonderful to tell you, come and sit next to me. You know that I have not been feeling well and that I am always taking a nap in the afternoon, particularly when you're getting home from school. 'Molly' told me that you are worried about me. You don't have to worry about me because I… I am going to have a baby. Do you know what that means?"

"You mean like a new baby sister or brother."

"Yes, that's exactly what I mean. But for the time being, you, Beth and mommy are the only ones that know about it and we have to keep it a secret. Do you think you can keep it a secret, Megan?"

"Yes, I can. Does Mister Morgan know that you are going to have a baby?"

"He doesn't know about this yet. We will tell him soon though."

89

"OK, mom, I can keep it a secret, but when the baby's daddy knows can I tell Molly and Jasper, they'll want to know too."

"Yes; we can tell everyone."

"Yippee!"

-17-

When Ned woke, his whole body reminded him why he shouldn't have pushed himself so much. He was sore and achy from his neck to the bottom of his feet. As he shuffled along to the outhouse, he barely made it there. When he came out, he felt relieved and laughed at his faux pas and said to Mike, who looked up at him quizzically, "I can't do that again because it hurts too much when I laugh." He went over to the fire pit, stoked the ashes, added kindling and got the fire going; he took the coffee pot over to the stream, had a hard time bending down to rinse it out and filled it with clean water. He set it on the grate above the fire; he went to the table and took the top off the can where the ground coffee was kept, took a coffee cup and scooped out a cup of grounds and poured them in the coffee pot, put the top back on and waited for it to boil. He decided to stay close to the cabin and do some of the other things on the list that he knew he could get accomplished until the aches and pains subsided. While the coffee was brewing, he went in the barn and opened the side door to let the horses out into the corral and found a new horse in one of the stalls he had never seen before. He looked around cautiously, but didn't see anyone sleeping in the barn, but heard dogs yelping over near a corner. Looking down he saw four small dogs that looked like Mike. Now he was more curious than ever to find out what was going on; he checked up in the hayloft, no one; he heard someone in the outhouse and had no choice but to wait until that person came out, he retrieved the shotgun from the cabin and rested it over his arm. When the person came out he said, "Who are you?"

"You have a short memory, I'm Joe. You and Todd stopped by my place on the way up here about two weeks ago; you stayed the night. I said I would be here in two weeks with the dogs; Todd said you'd be here and he'd be gone. Remember?"

"Oh yes. How are you?"

"Can you put the shotgun down, please?"

"Sure, I'm sorry about that. I didn't remember that you were coming and was surprised to see you. Would you like a cup of coffee, I just made a fresh pot?"

"Yes, I would."

"Todd told me to pick out the runt of the litter, just like he picked Mike to be his dog. I should go find the neighbors who'll be buying the other three dogs. If you'll just wait here, I'll be back in about a half hour."

* * *

Todd, Pete and Marshal Murphy arrived at the mine around mid-afternoon of the following day to overcast skies, a northwest wind and a chill in the air. Todd checked to see what prints, if any, were on the ground and only found small animal prints. He showed Tom and Pete where to put the horses and mule; "I only built the lean-to for one, so the best we can do for the time being is to use it to store our saddles and saddlebags and we'll have to rig the tarp for sleeping, unless of

92

course you prefer the stars." He had previously stacked some firewood next to the lean-to; there was a family of chipmunks living in the logs. "We're lucky we didn't bring Mike with us, he'd have a field day chasing them little critters all day long around the campsite. Make yourselves at home. If the two of you will set the camp, I'll show you where the mine is once I get back after I set some snares near here so that we can eat tonight and for the next few days."

Tom and Pete set the saddles, saddlebags in the lean-to and the bedrolls in a half-circle around the fire pit, then took the tarp and using pieces of rope tied the back part behind the lean-to to two spruce trees and brought it over the top of the lean-to. Using long limbs, Tom sharpened the ends to points and jammed them into the ground at an angle as the two of them looped ropes around the front end of the tarp and tied them to the limbs to make a temporary shelter, covering everything and to keep them somewhat dry should it rain or snow. Tom made sure that the horses and the mule got fed, while Pete looked over the area. Todd had taken two traps with him; he might as well do some trapping while he was here. He set one just off the trail down the hill, the other in the field of wild flowers a bit further beyond. He set several snares along the way between the campsite and the last trap. He was anxious to show Pete just where he had found the gold, but apprehensive at the same time. No one knew that nearly every stream that he had crossed or camped at yielded some gold. He would keep that information to himself. It certainly would have been a god-send if he found gold on his homestead then he wouldn't have to travel so far away, thirty miles plus to this mine; an additional twenty-five miles or so to the next one. If he had to count on living in Lander it would be close to 100 miles round-trip for this one. He would have to see if the one north of Bull Lake yielded as much gold as the one they were at now. Maybe he could sell this one, though he had no idea what it would actually yield despite what the metallurgist guessed. Pete could do some preliminary work on how to extract the gold over the next several days and again at the other mine. After he had set the last trap in the field of flowers, he thought of Megan bringing back a handful of flowers from down by the Wind River to her mother.

* * *

Ned, Gus and Turk arrived back at the ranch just as Joe was coming out of the barn with four frisky, black and white puppies that looked like Mike. Mike had just come back from chasing squirrels and didn't know what to make of all of them as he rounded a corner. Ned introduced them to each other and picked the smallest one, while Gus and Turk took the other three. Joe told the three of them that these dogs were the same as Mike. Simple one-word commands like "Sit", "Stay", "Guard", "Protect" were all they should have to use when training their dogs, the shorter the command, the better. He had been training them for a week, but it was up to its owner to finish the training. He gave a demonstration on the dog that Ned had chosen. He took the dog from his arms and set it on the ground by his right side and said "Seek" and the dog trotted forward; as he walked past him until he came to the bridge over the creek, he said "Come" and the dog trotted back to where he was and Joe said "Sit" and the dog did as he was told. Next he took a rag doll from his pocket and threw it about 20 feet ahead of the dog and said "Protect". The dog trotted over to where it was and lay down on the ground. Joe said to Ned, "Try and take the doll." Ned did what he was told and immediately the dog grabbed his arm and pulled it down toward the ground. Even though he was only two months old and still just a puppy, he knew the commands that he needed to know. Gus and Turk were thoroughly impressed and knew why Todd had chosen this type of dog for them. "Thanks for bringing the dogs, as well."

"It was my pleasure; I hope you enjoy them."

-18-

Before their evening meal, Todd took Tom and Pete to the back of the arroyo and showed Pete where the gold seam was on the rocks. He had each of them bring a pick or shovel. He was going to start digging where the rocks met the ground, but Pete stopped him, saying "We need to determine if there is a shaft underneath the rocks that you found or if this actually runs horizontal farther into the hill behind it. Could one of you get a bucket or something to carry water?" Tom went and got the coffee pot, went to the stream and filled it. Pete said, "watch where the water goes," as he poured it on the cliff face.

The water pooled near the base of the rock and made a gurgling sound before it disappeared beneath the rock outcropping. He said to both of them, "I'm guessing that there is an opening below the rock face and until we do a little digging next to the boulders, we won't exactly know what is below the rocks. I'm thinking that we may have to dig a vertical well; similar to a well you'd have for water, until we see exactly where the seam is. We can hope that we won't have to go to far; the longer the seam, the better off you'll be. You're going to need a load of timbers from the forest that surrounds us. We shouldn't have a problem getting enough sturdy trees to use to shore up a mineshaft. The further you go, the more timber you'll need. Todd, why don't you and I continue to dig, and Tom can get supper ready?"

Todd replied, "Let me see if any of my snares and traps yielded anything yet. If they have, I can bring back something for supper and I'll make supper; you and Tom can do some digging." He went down the trap line to see if he was successful in any of this snares and traps; he only found one fat rabbit, while the rest of the snares had nothing and neither did the steel traps. He didn't really expect anything in the traps yet. Back at the campsite he skinned the rabbit, set the edible parts in a fry pan and put the remains aside for use on the traps. He turned the skin inside out and put it in the lean-to on top of his saddle; he got a fire going, put the fry pan over the fire, called the others and reminded them to bring the coffee pot back with them.

* * *

Beth and Priscilla worked together during the day, airing out the house, changing the bed linens and dusting. Beth had told the boarders at breakfast that there wouldn't be a meal tonight because of all the work they planned on doing today. Around two in the afternoon, they stopped for a lunch and Beth said, "I think you have good color and you don't look so tired now. I'm guessing that you haven't had the 'morning sickness' as bad since you started drinking the ginger tea in the morning and evening."

"The first time I was with child, I had no one to tell me what I should or shouldn't be eating or drinking, what I could do, etcetera. Now I feel like a whole new person since you got me

97

started eating differently and doing some things around the house. I have more energy and have been feeling much better. I think Megan hasn't been worrying about me as much since I told her why I wasn't feeling so well."

"Megan told me the other day that she was happy to be having a new baby in the house, so that she would have someone to play with."

"It has been hard on her for the last few years, being an only child has its challenges. She has friends at school and most of them have brothers and sisters, but she doesn't have the same experiences that they have had while growing up; it'll be like having two families, she'll be eleven in the spring and by the time the baby comes in late June or early July, she'll be out of school for the summer. I am hoping that I can give her little things to do to help me with the baby."

"Do you think Mr. Morgan will be as ready?"

"I don't know what to think. He doesn't even know that he is going to be a father, let alone know what to do when the baby finally gets here. The baby will arrive when we should be going up-country with the horses that we will be getting in the spring for summer grazing. Our plans will change and we'll have to deal with them as they occur. I can't wait to tell him and yet I'm scared about his reaction at the same time. I don't think he ever thought that I'd end up having a child when we were intimate and I guess I was a bit naïve to think that nothing would happen either. I can only hope for the best."

Tom and Pete got back to the campsite, sat indian-style[1] and enjoyed the rabbit, biscuits and coffee, speaking of which had not been made yet. They were both exhausted. Pete said, "damn hard ground around here, couldn't you have picked softer ground, Todd?"

"The Almighty chose the ground for me. If it was softer, I wouldn't need to have you come up here with me."

Tom suggested, "Maybe you should just stick to finding some of this gold in the creek bed and not worry so much about what 'might be available' under the surface. You'll be spending all your time trying to get it out and you won't have any time to do anything else. I'm bushed."

"Oh, your not that tired, you have a soft job, just riding in the saddle all day or sitting around your office just hoping something will happen so you'll have to get out of your chair." Todd said with a little laugh.

"Is that right? Well, I don't see where you've been doing anything strenuous. You bring us up here under the pretense that we'll have an easy time of it, then you go off looking for helpless animals, while your two friends bust their ass; you are sitting in camp, roasting supper over an open fire and resting on your laurels."

"Hey you two, who'd think that the two of you never worked a day in your life with nothing more too do except moan and groan about this and that? A real man knows what work is," Pete responded.

In unison they replied, "and who might that be?"

"You're looking at him."

"Don't say?" said Tom.

"You know all this bullshit is making me hungry again, let's eat what's left," Pete replied. They all have a good laugh. Todd took the coffee pot with him and went down to the stream, filling it nearly to the brim. Once back he put in some coffee grounds and set the pot to boil. After supper and before sunset, Pete wanted to show Todd what they had found so far;

Tom said he'd clean everything and meet them when he was finished.

-19-

While they were eating, Gus said to Ned, "You've got to learn to pace yourself. You're not going to do Todd any good if you go whole hog, and then take two days off to rest up. That's not how it works, regardless of what you're doing."

"Now, I have to decide what I should get done so he'll be pleased with me." Ned responded with a determined voice.

"It's also not a question of whether he'll be pleased or not, it's more of what should you do and do well. What are you going to tackle first and finish? If you can't, you need to tell him. If you can, then just get the work done and not complain. This is just a suggestion. Lay out all the materials you'll need to get the roof done, first frame it up; next day, do another part of the hayfield. I'm guessing that you got at least a third of it done the other day and that's what made you so sore and achy; the third day, finish the roof; next day do more of the hayfield; day after that pull the vegetables, clean the dirt off, wash them and put them away. Start to bundle the hay; reinforce the rear gate, he's always wanted that as secure as possible ever since we had trouble awhile back; bring the bundles of hay to the barn and store them in the hayloft and if its early in the afternoon, go back for a second load of bundled hay and

101

bring the wagon back, cover it with a tarp, and unload it the following day. Take the remainder of the afternoon off, go for a swim, go fishing, take a walk with the dogs, do something other than work and most of all, have a good meal, then get some sleep. Keep alternating like we're suggesting and you'll do just fine." Turk replied."

* * *

Todd, Tom and Pete had all come to the same conclusion, the water from underneath the ground was forcing the gold to rub off of the rock face and filtered some out into the stream. They decided to dig down next to where the water was coming out to see if there was an underground spring. The water pressure must have been very high to force the gold from underground up to the stream. In either case, they were going to have to work at it to find out. They alternated using the pick and shoveling the dirt and rock; they'd look at the rock later in the afternoon. They decided to take a break mid-afternoon; each of them had coffee, jerky and a biscuit. When they finished they took a short rest before starting up again going until sunset or later with the lanterns they had brought with them. Later that evening, they had roasted rabbit, potatoes, sliced tomatoes and some of the cookies that Todd had brought with him and coffee. Tomorrow he'd have to go with the Cheyenne to see Moon, while Tom and Pete continued to find the source of the gold.

* * *

Priscilla and Megan walked to Henderson's on Saturday

afternoon to buy some fabric, a new dress for Megan and some personal items for Priscilla. Joshua's wife was behind the counter when Priscilla walked in and just happened to say, "Mrs. Parker, your man friend hasn't been around lately. What do you do with your time while he is away?"

"I keep pretty busy with the boarding house. Why do you ask?"

"I heard from some of the ladies that you, well you know, were, were intimate with him; is that true?"

"It's none of your business."

"As head of the Lander Women's Association, it is our responsibility to make sure that our children are not exposed to morals unbecoming of our citizenry; it is our duty to uphold those morals for the community. Now are you going to give me an answer or not?"

"As I said before Mrs. Henderson, none of your business, now if you'll excuse me I have to finish my shopping. You can assume whatever you have a mind to.."

"Well, I never. You have a lot of nerve talking to me that way."

"Actually, with the way you are talking at me, I would think that with your upbringing that you would have been taught better manners and that you never ask personal questions of a lady. I don't have to qualify anything about what I do or say to you or anyone else, for that matter." She went, to the counter and paid Mr. Henderson what she owed, who looked apologetic for the way his wife was talking to her. She took her packages and Megan's hand and walked out of the store thinking *maybe we should just sell everything here and move up-country, then Todd, the children and I will have a peaceful life and we wouldn't have to worry about busybodies like Mrs. Henderson.*

Megan looking up to her mother while they were walking along said, "was Mrs. Henderson rude to you?"

"She was, but I think I put her in her place or at least I hope I did. Would you like to get an ice cream before we go home?"

"Oh, yes, that would be fun." They walked down the street to the apothecary and both of them sat on the stools and Megan had a dish of vanilla ice cream, while Priscilla had root beer[4]. She said to her daughter, "I have had a fun day with you; won't it be fun when you, me, the baby and Mr. Morgan can all come here for ice cream and root beer on a Saturday afternoon."

"Yes, it will be fun. I can hardly wait."

---

[4] Charles Hires' version of a root beer beverage was first introduced to the public at the 1876 Philadelphia Centennial exhibition.

-20-

Todd left mid-morning for the rendezvous with the Cheyenne in the Valley of the Moon. After he arrived where he thought they would meet, he hobbled Misty, took off her saddle and blanket and tied the reins together and let them rest on her withers, while he rested against his saddle waiting for them. He thought about what Priscilla might be doing on this Saturday afternoon; he also wondered what Moon had been doing for the last six months, not knowing if he was alive or dead only to finally find out that he had been living with a band of Cheyenne. He had done so much since leaving Lander that it seemed like years, not weeks.

Depending on what his two friends found while he was away, hopefully only for a couple of days, he might have to change his plans. If they found that it was a cave, would he need dynamite to blast rock or would he just have to use a pick and shovel to get the gold out of the ground? How far did the seam go? There were too many questions to think about. He brought Pete along to give him answers and it was good of Tom to stay and help, especially since he had important business he needed to take care of himself. Then, there was the ranch. He hoped that Ned was over his aches and pains and that he got into finishing the job he started on the hayfield and some of the other chores on the list. And finally, when he did get back to Lander, how he would ask Priscilla to get married before he had to come back to the ranch and the mining claim.

Todd drifted off to sleep waiting. When he woke, the moon was already rising in the east in a darkening cloudless dark blue sky while the sun was going down along the ridgeline of the mountains to the northwest. The Indian's still had not arrived. If he had known they would be this late, he would have made their meeting for tomorrow morning. He got up, stretched and went to the nearby stream so that he could wash his face, take a drink from the clear running water and make camp as nightfall was fast approaching. He took off Misty's hobbles and led her to the stream; When he stood up, he could see them coming. He counted at least eight braves, Little Wolf, and was surprised to see that Moon was riding next to him. He thought he was going to their village, but apparently someone had a change of plans.

Putting the hobbles back on Misty, he crossed the stream as they rode in; they reined up and in broken English said, "You only come by yourself? We expected all of you; Where are your friends?"

"My friends are back at my camp; I came because the man, 'white hair, white skin' wants me, not them." Little Wolf got down off of his horse and another brave helped Moon get down from his. He was quite feeble; more so since the last time Todd had seen him. The other braves took their horses and went off a ways, letting their horses graze, while they went to the stream to drink. Todd hugged his friend before the three of them sat on the lush green grass and wild flowers. Moon said, "It is good to see you again my friend. When you did not return right away, I thought perhaps you were dead. Men who treated me badly forced me from your cabin many months ago; they beat your dog and wouldn't feed her; I was tied up and put in your barn like an animal. Finally I managed to get my bindings off and while they were sleeping, I left. I felt badly for your dog. She was tied to the post on the porch, but I was afraid that if I tried to untie her and take her with me they would wake up. I am so sorry that I left her; she was a good friend to both of us. You remember when you found me in my cabin? I told you that a man beat me. What I didn't tell you was that he was looking for 'Morgan'; he kept repeating it over and over, until finally he beat me because I wouldn't answer him. I did not know you well enough to tell him where you were or how he could find you. I know that you could have handled yourself against this bad man. When I fled your cabin, I wandered for days that turned into weeks. The spirits guided me and despite many hardships I never gave up that someone would help me. One day, Man-bear, was eating berries. I cried out to him, "Man-bear come save me". He fed me, clothed me and brought me through the wilderness to the Indian village where Little Wolf lives with his father and many mighty warriors. I swept my anger and fears away from my heart and accepted my brother Cheyenne as part of my life. Little Wolf's father knew of my people and had heard through the spirits that a shaman would come to him one day and help his village. It has come to pass."

"I wish I knew where you were as I too thought you were dead." Todd replied looking relieved that Moon was not.

One day, 'white hair, white skin,' came to the village to seek answers to his question, "Did they know Morgan and where could he find him?" I spoke with Little Wolf's father that the man who sought answers to those questions had hurt me badly many, many moons ago and that you and the spirits were looking for him to make him pay for what he had done to me and to our friend's cabins. You must be careful riding alone, if he finds you without your friends close by, I fear he will kill you.

The spirits have told me that you are to be a father and that your squaw and her daughter live in Lander. He may be on his way there to find you and hurt them. The spirits can try and protect them but only you will be able to stop him. I asked Little Wolf to bring me with him when he came to meet you here where the Moon sets on the Valley. The spirits have told me that after I meet with you that I will die and go with them to the great beyond, to see my wife and children; my friends who have all gone there before me and to protect you your squaw and your children the rest of your life, especially your man-child who has yet to come into our world, but waits in the belly of his mother for his turn to come join all of you."

Todd didn't know what to make of all that Moon had told him, especially about a man-child yet to be born. Priscilla had not mentioned anything in her most recent letter to him and he had no inclination that she was with child when he left her.

The day had turned to night and while they still talked, the other Indians had built a fire and had hobbled their horses along with his; he would have to stay the night. In the morning, he would ask Little Wolf to send a couple of braves to where his friends were and tell them that he had to return to Lander and he would meet them back at his ranch. He would ride to Lander to protect Priscilla and Megan from 'white hair, white skin' and to ask her about the man-child.

In the morning, Todd woke early only to find that Moon

had died during the night as he had predicted, but before he died, he asked that his horse be given to Todd to make his journey to Lander.

He said a prayer over his friend and asked the spirits to protect him on his journey. He had already gone to the great beyond to be with his wife and children and to see his friends where they could all be together again. After Moon's burial, he thanked Little Wolf, mounted his horse and rode in the direction of his ranch. He would need several horses to reach his destination. He decided to ride Moon's horse first, change to Misty and back again to the other horse until he reached the ranch. There he would take the gray mare to Joe's and from there he'd borrow two horses for the final leg of his journey.

He rode at a steady gallop only stopping for water or grass for the horses. His intent was to make it to Stony Creek by mid-afternoon. Upon his arrival, he dismounted and walked to the gate, swung it open as well as the next gate. Once inside, he went back and closed and latched both gates. He led the horses to the corral where he unsaddled Misty, took the rope halter off of Moon's horse and let them loose. He whistled for the bay and she came up to the fence. He brought her over to the gate and slipped the rope halter over her mouth, put on the blanket, then his saddle and tied her to the fence. He took a few minutes to use the outhouse and grabbed some carrots from the bins in the barn. The coffee pot had vapors coming out of the spout and he poured a cup, sat down and took a few precious minutes to drink it. Just as he was finishing, Mike came bounding up the lane towards him and was so excited to see him he practically knocked him over, Todd got up and walked to the stream where he knelt down and splashed water on his face, refilled his canteen and mounted the mare. Looking down at the dog, he said, "Come." He rode toward the back gate and soared over it with Mike not far behind as he made his way towards Joe's, arriving late in the afternoon. He asked Joe, "Can you loan me two horses, and I'll get them back to you as soon as I can. I must get to Lander today, tomorrow may be too late."

"Take your pick." He left 20 minutes after he got there.

-21-

As the surrey pulled into the yard, they noticed two horses lathered, exhausted, their reins extending from their bridles dropped on the ground. John said, "I'll check the barn, why don't the three of you go inside."

Priscilla went inside with Beth and Megan, and said to her daughter, "You have to get right to bed."

She heard John yelling, "Mrs. Parker come quick." The three of them went back outside and into the barn where they saw Todd lying in an empty stall, drained of color, barely speaking, "Protect," while Mike's head was laying on his left leg, panting.

"Megan, go inside for mommy and get a clean face cloth, wet it and bring it to me as fast as you can; She said to John, "Go find the doctor and bring him back here."

Beth asked, "Is there anything that I can do?"

"Would you go upstairs to my room and turn down the covers on my bed, while we're waiting for the doctor to get here we need to get him up to my bedroom. Once you've done that please get the dog a bowl of water."

Todd was delirious and repeated the same phrase over and over, "Tired, need sleep. Can you help me get to Lander?" The doctor said to Priscilla, "I'll be back later this morning. Mr. Morgan is very sick, worse case of exhaustion that I have seen

111

since the war. Just keep him as calm as you can, make sure he gets plenty of water. I'll leave this bottle of quinine with you. Give him a teaspoon every other hour if you can. His fever should break soon. We'll get him through this."

"Will Mr. Morgan be alright?" Megan asked her mother, as she was getting ready for bed.

"He is very sick and we will do everything we can to help him. In the morning, I'll need you to get yourself ready for school; Beth will have your bowl of oatmeal on the table for you."

"Can 'Molly' stay with him while I'm at school? He needs to have a friend."

"If that will make you happy, bring 'Molly' to me and we will put her on the pillow next to him."

Priscilla continued to monitor Todd throughout the night, she kept changing the cloth on his forehead but his high fever did not break and both of them fell asleep around 3 am.

In the morning, Megan said to the doll, "You stay here with Mr. Morgan while I go to school and when I come home you can tell me how he was during the day." She gave the doll to her mother.

John, one of the boarders, knocked on the door to her private suite and said, "Priscilla, I hope that Mr. Morgan gets better. Is there anything you want me to do or get for you while I'm in town? I would be happy to get it and bring it back on my lunch hour."

"I can't think of anything at the moment, thank you for helping us last night."

"It was the least I could do under the circumstances."

Todd went in and out of delirium most of the morning, sweating profusely. The quinine was working slowly and when he was lucid, he only wanted water, lots and lots of water.

Priscilla needed sleep herself, but didn't want to leave his side. Beth brought a tray with ginger tea, two pancakes and said, "You have to eat to keep up your strength. When you've finished eating you can take a nap on Megan's bed and I'll stay with him. If there is any change, I'll come get you."

"I can't leave him."

"You won't do him any good if you get sick, too. Now, I'm ordering you to eat your breakfast, then go and get some sleep." As much as she wanted to protest, she knew Beth was right.

"Wake me if anything happens."

"I will."

Priscilla crawled into Megan's bed and immediately fell asleep.

Pete discovered a cave about six feet below the surface where a man could stand up in. He said to Marshal Murphy who was sitting under a pine tree drinking from his canteen, "I think we've found a way to get to the source of the gold. It looks like the seam is actually running along the bottom of the cave, which is just beyond this rock wall. Come take a look with the lantern that I put on the other side of the hole that I made. Todd was just lucky to be at this spot when he found the gold dust and flakes in the creek bed, otherwise he would have missed it. Now, all we have to do is find a way to get the rest of the gold out of there more efficiently than letting Mother Nature do all the work."

"Just how do you propose we to do that? We don't have the time or the manpower to get the cave shored up to make it safe before we can enter it? Todd isn't here to tell you what he would like to do."

"Well under the circumstances, I think that you should ride back to his ranch and have Gus and Turk get up here with a wagon full of tools, boards, beams and food. I know you will have to get back on the trail of that hombre which is the main reason why you came along with us in the first place. I'll stay here and do some planning."

"From what the Indians told us, Todd should be in Lander by now, but he, like you, has no idea where this 'white hair, white skin' man actually is. I am guessing that he is somewhere close by and means to do harm to him, Priscilla and her daughter. Why don't we climb out of here and I'll work getting my stuff together while you get some much needed sleep. I know how you think. You'll be constantly working all the time until Gus and Turk get back up here."

"You're probably right, I should eat something to keep my strength up. I also think the two of us should check the traps and the snares Todd put out and bring them back to camp; He would be relieved that we did that for him."

"We better get started, we have a lot to do before I leave in the morning."

'White hair, white skin' had been close by watching their movements just in case 'Morgan' came back from his rendezvous with the Indians. *If he doesn't come back by morning, I'll leave and go back by his ranch where he had been before he left for here. Time is getting short and I must avenge my family's passing one, last time.*

When he was just a young boy, it was that murderous bastard 'Morgan' who was among the gray bellies who killed his father at Sailors' Creek[1] near the Appomattox He could only hide in the hayloft overlooking the barnyard as the undisciplined hooligans invaded their property on that spring morning. They only wanted his mother and sisters. His father tried to protect his family but he was no match against them. The killing, raping and torture they inflicted upon his family would finally be avenged. He made a vow way back then to bring them all to justice, one by one. His way. Now only 'Morgan' remained.

* * *

Tom left early and promised Pete he would get to the ranch and relay the information to Gus and Turk and give them directions on how to get back up here. "If I don't see you soon, you take care. When I see Todd, I'll tell him everything from the time he left right up to last night. He'll be pleased with the take on the traps and really excited about you finding the actual source of the gold." With a wave and a smile, he was off for the ranch. Pete decided to have a couple of biscuits and a cup of coffee. He had to make a plan and now was as good a time as any to get it down on paper.

'White man, white skin' rode west along the ridge just out of sight of the lawman; though 'Morgan' did not come back last night or early this morning, *this friend of his must know where 'Morgan' is,* he thought to himself. *I will follow him until he takes me directly to Morgan and then I will make him suffer like my father and my beautiful mother and sisters did. I will cut his skin in strips, peeling it off one by one and feed it to the crows as he watches; I will disembowel him like they did with my father and feed it to him in his mouth so that he can taste the death of my brave father, who spit in their faces as they were destroying him and for my mothers and sisters, I will rape his woman and enjoy it.*

115

Then they can kill me after I have avenged my family's honor.

Tom had many thoughts, but 'white man, white skin' was not one of them. He had to concentrate on where it would be easiest for the Langstrom's to get a heavily loaded wagon up to the mine campsite. He felt the trail he was riding was the easiest, but crossing several streams would be their challenge and it would take them at least a week or more to make the actual trip. *If I can get back to the ranch by tomorrow, they should be able to get back to Pete by next Thursday, Saturday at the latest. I'll rest when I get to Todd's and from there I'll go to Ft. Washakie. I should make Lander in three days.*

-22-

Two days and nights Todd sweated, going in and out of delirium. Finally the fever broke and he slept soundly. During a dream, he screamed Priscilla's name and yelled, "Hide, so that he won't hurt you or Megan."

She gently woke him and said, "I'm right here Todd, and you're having a bad dream." He found her sitting by his side and putting a cold washcloth on his forehead.

"You're alright?"

"Yes, why wouldn't I be alright?"

"Moon had a vision that a 'white hair, white skin' man was going to hurt you, Megan and our baby. I rode day and night to get back to you; to protect you from him."

"How did Moon know that I was carrying a baby?"

"He was a shaman. The spirits guided him all his life and he had told me that you were with a man-child. Is that true?"

"Yes."

"Why didn't you tell me before I left or in your letters?"

"I didn't know when you left that I was with child, but I had my suspicions; it wasn't something that I wanted to write to you in a letter "guess what I'm having a baby" and leave it that. I felt that when you came back for Thanksgiving that would be soon enough. You have enough to worry about and

117

that would have been an extra burden that you didn't need. I guess I'm glad you found out, but I did want it to be a lovely surprise."

"Does anyone else know that you are with child?"

"Megan and Beth are the only other people who know. The three of us have been keeping it a secret, until now and since you know, it won't be a secret for long. Megan has been really excited since she found out that she was having a baby brother or sister. Beth has been helping me get through the morning sickness that I was having really bad, but over the last several days it has subsided quite a bit, which, by itself, is a relief. You have no idea what we go through with having a baby."

"Well, I'm glad that you're alright. I guess that means no more sex until after the baby is born."

"Why not, the baby is protected in my belly and he or she doesn't really care what its mommy and daddy do in bed, at the pond or even up in the hayloft. Come to think of it, Megan is in school and Beth went to town to do some shopping, so we are alone for at least a part of the morning. I don't want to exhaust you again for at least a week."

"Oh, I think I'm strong enough for a little intimacy, especially if you can be gentle with me for a change. What do you say?"

"You make it sound so inviting. I don't know, after all, I don't want to get tired out, and then both of us would have to stay in bed for a week. I have longed to be held by you ever since you left."

"Well, let's not delay…"

"I suppose that you'll have to leave soon and I'll be back to worrying and crying all over again."

"I won't be leaving until this issue with the 'white hair, white skin' man is settled. Moon felt that he was coming here to Lander to find you and Megan, but what he doesn't know is I'm going to be here waiting for him to show up. Do you think you can get a message to the sheriff to come see me, since Tom is up-country with Pete at the mine?"

"I'll have to wait until Beth comes back, then either she can go and get him or I'll take the surrey and find him. Why?"

"Better you don't know what I might have to do. I need to send two telegrams, one to Jonathan and one to Charlie Cooper at Timber Creek Ranch. Unfortunately, I need some help to get this settled once and for all. Since our physical activity for the week is now over, I have to tell you a story and in the end if you never want to see me again, I'll understand. He told her everything he did during the war, some he was proud of and some that he wasn't. I actually think the 'Morgan' he is looking for is Morgan Cooper, a cousin of Charlie's. He bragged about what he did during the war that no man would have thought honorable under any circumstances. Morgan is the most despicable person I have ever met, but with a name like Morgan no one would think he was bad. I am who I am, but my past is just that. Ever since I came here to Wyoming, I am a different person and ever since I fell in love with you, I am a better person for knowing and caring for someone I love. Just like with Johan, I don't take kindly to folks who want to hurt people I love and this 'white hair, white skin' man has his reasons for wanting to settle a score with 'Morgan', just not the one he thinks he is following."

"Todd, I am in love with you, not your past, not what you did in the war, just you. I'll do what it takes to make you happy all of the rest of our lives. Don't even think about ever leaving me; you're stuck with me no matter what." She reached over and pulled him into her, kissing him passionately.

* * *

Tom made it to Stony Creek just as the last rays of the sun were setting behind the mountains. He dismounted, held the reins and opened each gate. Once he went past the second gate, he ground-tied the horse retraced his steps and closed each gate. As he approached the barn, Ned was coming from the opposite direction on the buckboard loaded down with bales of hay and said, "Hi, Marshal Murphy, I thought you were with Todd and Pete. What brings you back here all by yourself? Is anything wrong?"

"Nothing that can't be fixed over time. Did Todd come through here the day before yesterday?"

"Not that I know of was he supposed to?"

"I just thought he would on his way to Lander. So you didn't see him at all?"

"No, I've been camping out in the hayfield with the dogs. I just thought it would make it easier, since I've been doing a lot of work out there. Come to think of it, I haven't seen Mike in a couple of days, either. Make yourself at home while I park this wagon over next to the barn. I'll hoist the bales up to the hayloft first thing in the morning. Are you going to spend the night?"

"I was, I don't think Todd will mind if I do."

"Oh, he won't mind and I could use a little company, as well. If you'll just tie your horse to the post, I'll take it and these two horses to the barn. I'll get some vegetables while I'm in there and a couple of venison steaks from the cache for dinner. I think the fire might have gone cold by now, but with a little kindling I'll have it going in no time." Ned positioned the buckboard under the hayloft doors; unharnessed the team and led all three horses to the stalls in the barn. Once they were all fed and watered, he opened the side door expecting the bay mare to come through the door, but Misty and Moon's gelding come through it instead with Ned saying to himself, *I guess Todd was here* and proceeded to get them in their stalls also. He closed the windows, doors and latched them so that they couldn't be opened. He climbed the ladder to the cache and took out two thick venison steaks. Once down on the ground, he went over to the table by the fire pit, setting them in one of the pans on the table along with the vegetables. He took kindling and within a few minutes he had a hot fire just right for boiling the vegetables and roasting the steaks. He set the coffee pot off to one side so that it got hot enough to drink in a few minutes. He said to Marshal Murphy, "I guess Todd may have been here after all. When I opened the side door to let in the bay, Misty and another horse were there instead."

-23-

'White hair, white skin' heard all he needed to know, Morgan was in Lander. Now it was time to get there and carry out his final revenge. He bypassed the usual places where people might be, settling into the draws and arroyos that dotted the countryside. He'd have plenty of time to figure out how to get Morgan out in the open. He'd make sure the little girl watched as he did to Morgan what Morgan did to his family.

* * *

Todd had been getting stronger every day. Between Priscilla pampering him and Beth's cooking he was looking forward to getting up. He had made sure that everyone knew what had to be done by sending the two telegrams. Everyone had arrived after they heard what had happened to him and what this other man was capable of. They would make sure he was stopped before he could do anything to Todd, Priscilla or Megan. If 'white hair, white skin' was everything that they had been finding out about him, the sheriff was no match for the likes of him. Having his friends close by and ready for anything gave him solace. He made sure that Megan was

122

guarded to and from school; Beth was watched over if she went out on any errands and he took extra precautions with Priscilla, especially now that she was carrying his child. He was going to make himself an easy target for 'white hair, white skin'. He hoped the results wouldn't be fatal.

Tom had ridden to Ft. Washakie and had little new information about his quarry; while he was there, he caught up with other news that could be of importance to him after he got to Lander.

Priscilla had set a footstool on the back porch before she went upstairs to see where Todd was. She found him coming out of the bath in her living quarters drying off. He set the towel on a chair next to a bureau, opened a drawer and took out a shirt and new pair of blue jeans. She leaned against the doorway watching him; he saw her reflection in the mirror and said, "just how long have you been staring at me?"

"Long enough to see that you are not only handsome with your clothes on, but definitely cute in your birthday suit, as well."

"Is that so, I wonder what you'd look like in your birthday suit? I can only see that little tummy of yours pushing against your dress. I suppose he'll be chubby when he comes out of that tight space. Why in a few weeks, you'll need help in tying the laces on your shoes because you won't be able to see them or reach them either."

"I'll have to tell your son or daughter that you thought he or she was going to be fat."

"Now hold on there, you'll do no such thing. If anyone is going to talk to him it's going to be me and you can just listen. Matter of fact come over here and I'll start talking to him right now. He might need to know that his mama is smart, funny, a good worker and most of all, loving. It's the loving part that I like the best. Do you think you could give me a little loving?"

"No, you insinuated that I was fat." They both looked at each other and Todd burst out laughing; she joined him. He came to her and put his arms around her and gave her a little squeeze, kissed her tenderly and patted her stomach.

"I came up here to tell you that I put a footstool out on the back porch so that you can put your feet up like the doctor told you to do until you were feeling better, but I got distracted."

"If I was feeling stronger, I'd pick you up and take you to bed, but I'm guessing Beth is downstairs and she'd get the wrong idea as to why you didn't come back down. You wouldn't want me to get you in a compromising position and have Megan walk in on us after she gets home from school either."

"No I wouldn't. We'll have plenty of time later in the week."

"We will? I thought I'd be going back to Stony Creek just as soon as my 'situation' was settled. I have to work harder now that there's going to be four Morgan's."

"I'll make time before we all go back to Stony Creek."

"I thought we've already discussed and decided about you going up-country."

"We did but I'm changing the rules. Are there any objections?"

"What's the use in arguing my point?"

"I knew I could change your mind if I tried really hard."

"We'll see; let's get everything settled before we make any rash decisions, alright?"

"The decision has already been made," as she gently squeezed his groin and lightly kissed his cheek. I have to go back downstairs, care to join me?"

"Yes, ma'am. I'm right behind you enjoying the view."

"Always the same thing on your mind, that's what got me into this condition in the first place."

"I didn't hear any objections?"

"No objections just make sure you don't stumble down the stairs because you're not watching where you're going." They both walked into the kitchen as Megan came in from outside and said, "Hi mom, hi dad, I mean Mr. Morgan. I got all my papers back from school today. Do you want to see them?"

"Yes, we do, put them on the kitchen table and you can show them to us, okay."

"Mr. Morgan there is a man in the barnyard who wants to see you; he says you'll know who he is."

Immediately, Todd's demeanor changed and he said, "Priscilla, take Megan up to your room and lock the door; under the bed is my saddlebag and in it is my pistol. If you need to use it, don't hesitate. I love all of you." He brushed past her and went out the door; 'White hair, White skin' was sitting on a roan mare that he stole from Todd several months before and said, "Finally we meet. It has been over eighteen years since the last time I saw you at my father's farm at Sailors' Creek. I have waited for this day since I killed the last bastard of your murderous bunch in Omaha about a year ago, Smithson I think it was. You lose track after having tracked down every last one of your band of hooligans[1]. I wanted your little girl to see who was going to kill her daddy and when I'm done with you, I'll find that wife of yours and rape her just like your murderous bunch did to my mother and my two sisters. I'll make that little girl watch so that she can hurt just as much as I did when I was a child. Got any last words, Morgan?"

"Well, I must say you seem thorough, but I don't suppose

that maybe you have the wrong Morgan, do you?"

"I remember your long arms, that birthmark on your backside as you were raping and torturing my sisters; I should have disemboweled you first, but since you were in charge of those bastards, I wanted to save you for last, but you can be rest assured that I disemboweled them in front of their children so that they'd remember who I was. I am surprised that word hadn't gotten to you that I was coming for you."

Priscilla took Megan up to their room and said to her, "I want you to take Molly and go hide in your closet. Mommy is going to lock the door; I have to get some help. Do not come out until I or Mr. Morgan comes and gets you, do you understand?"

"Yes, mommy," she replied, clutching her doll and looking frightened.

Priscilla locked the door and quietly went down the front stairs to find Beth, but Beth was nowhere to be found. She went out through the front door, down the steps and through the gate as quickly as she could watching where she walked so that she didn't stumble and fall, hurting the baby. US Marshal Tom Murphy, Charlie Cooper and his son HJ along with Morgan Cooper, Charlie's cousin was coming down the road. Tom reined up and said, "Priscilla, what's wrong? Why are you crying?"

"It's Todd, that 'white hair, white skinned' man has him cornered in the barnyard and from the little I heard he plans to kill him and then come find me and Megan to torture us."

"He isn't going to kill Todd, harm you, or Megan. Mr. Cooper, would you have your son accompany Mrs. Parker to the sheriff's office."

"Certainly. HJ, I would like you to accompany this lady into town. Ma'am, are you strong enough to walk or would you prefer to ride a horse?"

"I prefer walking, but thank you for asking."

Marshal Murphy took his pistol out to make sure the cylinder was fully loaded and said to Priscilla, "Tell the sheriff what you told me and have him come to the boarding house as quickly as he can. You can do that for me can't you?"

"I can, but please hurry."

-24-

Priscilla made it to the sheriff's office and nearly collapsed in his arms saying, "Todd needs your help; Marshal Murphy said to come to the boarding house, quickly. I, I...," before she passed out in his arms. Sheriff Hughes picked her up and laid her on the couch in his office. He said to HJ, "Who are you?"

"HJ Cooper, my father is Charlie and he asked me to accompany Mrs. Parker. I can verify everything the lady just told you. May I suggest you hurry."

The sheriff went out the front door and yelled, "Help!" Several people heard him and came running. "Get the doctor to come over here and tend to Mrs. Parker; then I need at least two of you to mount up and follow me. Marshal Murphy needs our help at the Parker House."

* * *

Todd said to 'white hair, white skin', "I was never at Sailor's Creek. I was in the First Battle of Fredericksburg[1], and then I was in a Northern Prison Camp[2] for two years. You have me mixed up with another Confederate soldier named Morgan Cooper, I'm sure of it."

128

"Lies, you'd do anything to save your sorry ass, blaming someone else is your style. I'm gonna' strip your skin piece by piece and feed it to the crows and buzzards."

"You say that I have a birthmark on my backside," turning Todd dropped his Levi's, unbuttoned his long johns to reveal his backside, but there was no distinguishing birthmark. "If you're so sure it's me, why would you travel hundreds of miles on the word of someone who knew someone named Morgan. I grant you it's not all that common a name and you might be right about me, I did some things during the war of which I am not proud of, but I also did some that I am proud of. Most of all, I would never just kill a man because he was defending his family, nor would I rape a woman or a little girl just for the sport of it. The man you are actually looking for is on the horse almost directly behind you, the one cradling the carbine in his arms. I asked him to come here because I knew some of the deeds he did in the war. The men to his left are Charlie Cooper and US Marshal Tom Murphy. They needed to hear what you said to me. Now are you going to lower that pistol you have pointed at me or are you going to be shot for the coward that you really are?"

'White man, white skin' replied, "I've heard enough. Once you're dead, I don't care what happens to me. I figured that sooner or later the law would catch up with me and hang me for all the men I've killed along the way. I planned it that way."

"But you won't ever know if you killed the right person who did those terrible things to your mother and your sisters."

"If I put my weapon down, how do I know that they just won't shoot me anyway?"

"Despite what you might think, I'd take a bullet for you just to prove that I'm right and you are dead wrong, that's why."

"Prove it! If you're right and I am wrong, I will drop my weapon and let the Marshal take me in, but if your wrong…"

Todd walked up to where Morgan Cooper was and said, "I've known you about ten or so years and I think you're the most despicable person that I know from the war. You came out here to get away from your transgressions; you had the audacity to brag about what you did and that's why none of us at Timber Creek wanted anything to do with you for your cowardly acts. I'm going to ask you once, are you the man he is looking for?"

"You're crazy Todd. I'd never do anything like what he said was done to his Pa and his Ma or his sisters. Like you said, there are probably only a few people with a first or last name of Morgan."

"That's true, I did, but I'm a bettin' man and I say you're him. One way to prove it is for you to get down off that horse and drop your blue jeans, unbutton your long-johns and we'll see if you have a distinguishing birthmark on your backside."

"I won't. Charlie, you know that I was in the war, but I would never do anything like what he said."

"Well Morgan, you were at Sailor's Creek, Emmett saw you there and there were times when you were supposed to report to him, but he could never find you. You always said that you got lost or you were with a whore in town, but I always wondered where you got that little locket with the picture of the two girls in it. What did you do with that?"

"None of your business. I'm tellin' y'all for the last time, I'm not him."

Todd walked back to where 'white hair, white skin was and said, "Well I tried, if you want to kill me, get 'er done, Reb," he lowered his head in prayer and when he was done he said to the man, "Shoot me!"

'White hair, white skin' sat the horse and looked at everyone, but he couldn't do it. There were too many witnesses, still too many unanswered questions. He started to ride past Morgan Cooper who said under his breath, "I knew someone else had to be at that farm. I so enjoyed your youngest sister most of all."

'White hair, white man' took out a boot knife and plunged it into his heart, then swiftly took his bowie knife and slit his throat before anyone knew what happened. He pulled a derringer, put it up to his head and fired, dropping to the ground right next to Morgan Cooper.

Later that afternoon at the undertakers, Charlie Cooper turned his cousin's body over, took his bowie knife and cut off his long johns. On his backside was the distinguishing birthmark.

-25-

On Sunday morning, Todd said to Priscilla, If we're going to get married at the end of church services this morning, don't you think we ought to at least get to the church before everyone leaves."

"I'm coming, I'm coming! Our baby simply won't stop making me nauseous or maybe it's a case of the nerves. Just wait for me on the front porch; I'll be right along." Tom Murphy had taken the surrey around to the front of the house and helped Beth up into the front seat; then he helped Megan get in the next seat, he left the last seat for Priscilla and Todd. He looked at Todd who was standing on the top step of the porch waiting for Priscilla and said, "She'll be along in a couple of minutes."

At the end of the service, Pastor Samuels' said to the congregation, "Before you all leave today, we're going to have a wedding. Priscilla Parker and Todd Morgan, will you please come forward? They both got up from their pew and walked hand-in-hand to the opening in the railing and faced each other. He took her hands in his and mouths to her "I love you" and she replied, "we love you" with a twinkle in her eye. The pastor said, "Who is standing for this man?"

"I am," his friend "Crusty" replied.

132

"Who is standing for this lady?"

"I am," Megan replied with a big smile on her face.

The pastor began, "Dearly beloved, we are gathered here today to join this man and this woman in holy matrimony. Is there anyone, who can show just cause as to why these two beautiful people shouldn't be joined in marriage? You couldn't hear a pin drop. He continued, "Todd do you take Priscilla to be your lawfully wedded wife, to have and to hold, for richer or poorer, in sickness and in health, until death do you part?"

"Well, I'm not sure. What do you think Megan?"

"I think you should say yes. Mommy really loves you."

"Okay, if you say so, Yes," with a big smile on his face.

Priscilla looks at him and if looks could kill he'd be dead before he got to the church door. The pastor repeated the vows to Priscilla and she says, "I'm beginning to have my doubts. He had to ask my daughter what she thought, so I'm asking everyone else, what do you think?"

A parishioner in the back of the church says, "If you don't want him ma'am, I'm available." Uproarious laughter broke out in the church and everyone in unison "Say Yes!"

"Yes."

The pastor said, "With the power vested in me and by the hand of God Almighty and apparently everyone else in this congregation, I now pronounce you husband and wife, so help us all." Todd kissed her, and shook Crusty's hand, "Thanks for being here, amigo."

Crusty replied, "I wouldn't have missed this for anything." By the way, Liz and I are going to have a baby; Todd whispers to him, *we're having one too.*

Todd, Priscilla and Megan walk down the aisle and out the front door to swirls of confetti and birdseed as they get up in the now decorated surrey for their ride back to The Parker House Inn.

Later that evening Todd put Megan to bed and said, "Well young lady you've had quite a day. Do you think it's time to tell 'Molly' and Jasper that you're going to have a new baby brother or sister?"

"Well, mommy told me that it was a secret, do you think she'll get upset with me if I tell them?"

"She won't get upset, but for the time being, why don't we keep it a secret from everyone else."

"Okay, Goodnight, Mr. Morgan, I mean daddy."

"Goodnight, Megan." He gave her a kiss on her forehead. As he was closing her door, he heard her whispering to 'Molly', *mommy and daddy are going to have a baby and I can't wait.*

Priscilla was sitting in a porch swing on the side porch rubbing her stomach, saying, "sleep tonight little one, your mommy and daddy are going to be intimate and I don't want you to disturb us." Todd overheard her as he walked around in front of her and got down on his knees and whispered to her stomach, "listen little one; if you don't like what mommy is doing to daddy, you just let her know, OK?"

"So that's the way it's going to be is it? You'd think that newlyweds could have some alone time to make love with each other without any interference from the children, but I guess we'll just have to find out, won't we Mr. Morgan?"

"You know, I'd take you out into the barn for a good talking to, but I think that Tom and Beth are out there discussing some possibilities and Crusty and Liz are upstairs exploring each others thoughts; I just put Megan to bed. We can't go to our room, so I guess the only place for us to find out what is going to happen is too move over to the chaise next to this swing."

He sweeps her up in his arms, kisses her tenderly and carries her to the double-chaise lying her down gently, "Give me a minute while I get us a comforter turn down the lights in the parlor and the dining room. We don't want to wake anyone, now do we?"

Quietly she replies, "No!"

Priscilla decides to sleep in, but as usual the baby has other plans for her; she is not alone, Liz is just as nauseous. As Priscilla is coming in from the porch and Liz is coming down the front stairs they look at each other and begin to laugh. They both go arm-in-arm toward the dining room. "Did you sleep well?" Priscilla asked.

"We did, actually, that's the best sleep I've had in months and Crusty was out like a rock. I don't think I've seen him sleep that peacefully since our wedding night, if you know what I mean."

"Oh, I know exactly what you mean and with all that's happened around here over the last few weeks, it was a pleasant surprise to see everyone happy for a change. Now, if I can just get Todd into a routine, I won't have to worry about him so much. He works too hard as far as I am concerned. Maybe we could get Crusty to have a talk with him."

"Good luck with that, Crusty is the same way, they are both cut from the same cloth. I think the only difference is that we have an established ranch and ranch hands who help us out all the time, where the two of you or should I say the four of you are just deciding what y'all want to do."

* * *

The following morning after breakfast, Todd and Crusty walked down the road with Jasper and Mike running ahead of them toward the Wind River. The dogs chased each other along the riverbank; the two men sat on huge boulders above the river. Crusty said, "If I didn't know you better you're wondering how I do everything and still look younger than you?"

"Reading my mind again, are you?"

"You know it's okay to do more than one thing at a time, but there comes a time when you'll have to start making some choices. I came to that conclusion when I was cutting down the trees in the east pasture. I stopped, looked up to the sky and said, "Lord, if I died today, what would Liz do with all this?" She was perfectly content with the cabin, the small barn, two cows, two horses, the dog and a few chickens. She had all the money she needed and wasn't worried about a thing. Then I came along. So I made a vow that once I fulfilled the lumber contract, that we would just do ranching on a managed scale and not go overboard. It's you, amigo that I am worried about. You have two mines, a ranch, you go trapping and hunting, take care of your neighbors, hunt down murderers, etcetera, but what does Todd do for himself, his family and I don't mean work, either."

"You know up until this weekend, I might have had an answer for you, but now everything has changed. I don't mean now that I'm married and have a new daughter, a baby on the way and a wife I adore, but I've changed. I stumbled, literally on the gold. It wasn't what I had intended to do. I got caught up with how you were managing your property. I thought the trapping was going to be enough to support Priscilla, Megan and we'd be happy and content. We were down here one day and I got the bright idea of homesteading the very land that we are sitting on, in addition to the land that she owns and the ranch that I built north of here. I made a lot of promises to her that I can't keep. I am so exhausted; I don't know how much longer I can keep going at this pace. I don't want her to be a widow with two children and a lot of responsibilities. I do know one thing, I have to make some changes in my life very soon."

"Well, I'm here for you and I'm sure whatever you decide, she'll be happy with your decision."

"Let's stop talking about work on this beautiful day. You know the two of us would jump in that river and think nothing of it, splash each other, get out and jump in again for the fun of it. Something I haven't done in a long time, but I've got to start having fun again for my own sanity."

"You want to go out to dinner tonight just the four of us or should I say seven?"

"I'll ask Beth if she can watch Megan for a couple of hours. You're leaving tomorrow on the 2 pm stage, right?"

"Yes, we have to get back to the ranch and by the way both of your horses are going to foal by late spring, we think by the palomino stallion."

"That's great news, I almost forgot about them. That will give us a total of thirteen horses. I have a plan to get more, but I'm going to need help during the middle of the summer, before fall gets here. I found a wild horse herd up near one of the mines, lead by a palomino stallion that's as feisty as the black was in Lost Canyon. Even if I have to share, I could end up with 40 or 50 mixed bred horses of all sizes, colors and temperaments."

"Just let me know when."

"I will!"

-26-

After goodbyes were said to Crusty and Liz, Todd and Priscilla decide to take the buckboard to the general store and get some supplies. Mrs. Henderson was waiting on another customer and when she finished came over and said to Priscilla, "You had a lovely wedding on Sunday. I was wondering if you thought about starting a family right away or were you going to wait a while?"

"Why are you asking me some very personal questions?"

"Just had an idea that perhaps you were with child. It seems that Miss Sanderson buys a lot of ginger tea; she isn't pregnant, is she?"

"You know Mrs. Henderson, if you paid as much attention to your husband and your child as you do about my family, they'd smile more; the rest of the town folks would be happier, too. I think it's time that the people of this town start to trade elsewhere, even if it means driving across the river to the new general store. That's just my opinion of course." Priscilla put everything down that she had picked up and said to Todd, "I think we'll start doing business with that country store on the other side of the Wind River, the people are more pleasant and they mind their own business." He didn't know what had transpired, but said to her, "Okay by me."

Later that afternoon… Todd said to Priscilla, "I've finally come to the realization that I can't do everything that I promised you. I work all the time and don't take any time off. I know you're going to be disappointed in me and I am sorry."

"Sorry for what? It isn't just you, you know, I've wanted you to slow down ever since we decided to be a couple. I want you to enjoy what you do best, but I don't want you to get so exhausted that you get sick again. We need you! But most of all, we love you no matter what. Come sit with me on the back porch and tell me what you're thinking."

"I can't be doing all these different things, the trapping, mining, ranching, etcetera. It's more than three or four people could do. As much as you and I love the property next to yours on the Wind River, I don't have the time to develop it. You have about 150 acres right here at the Inn that will work very nicely for our horse breeding. As soon as I go back to Stony Creek the day after tomorrow I need to make a decision about the two mines. I need to find a way to either keep one mine or sell both of them. It's going to take a lot of money that I don't have right now to develop them and as much as it would make us rich beyond our wildest dreams, it isn't worth it especially if I have to be away from you for months on end. Keeping the Stony Creek Ranch and with your help, developing the remaining acreage around here is all I want to do. I had talked with Tom and he was worried about me before I went up-country. Then I talked with Crusty before he left and he was worried about me going in so many different directions, as well. He told me that he and Liz have a plan and so far it is working for them. I want us to have a plan, too.

I think that raising quality quarter horse stock with a few thoroughbreds mixed in we can have a right fine operation.

We'll use the ranch upcountry from late spring to early fall so that the horses can free graze; the rest of the year we'll be here in Lander. We can expand this house to accommodate our family and still leave part of it as an inn, which by the way is what you do best, besides being a great mom and wife. The children will have their friends and be able to go to school here and we'll have a good life. I need to write all this down, have you look it over and then we need to go back and see August."

"I think everything you've said makes sense; now what's all this talk about you going back up-country in two days?"

"I have to find out what is happening with the mine. Tom told me that Pete asked him tell to the Langstrom brothers to bring a wagon full of supplies up to the mine. I have to make sure that Ned is doing what I hope he was supposed to do. I can't just stop being a boss and saying, "you keep busting your ass while I get married and have a good life in Lander, that isn't fair to him or us. I'll be gone until just before Thanksgiving. Once I get everything settled, I'll be here in Lander with you and the children. I should only have to go up-country once a month after that. In early spring, I have to go to the Sweetwater Ranch and get our horses and bring them back here. We'll all be going to Stony Creek for part of the summer with the children."

"I'm starting to worry already and the baby apparently doesn't like it either; excuse me." A few minutes later she came back, drained of color and held a cold washcloth to her head and sat down next to him. "I thought the morning sickness had passed, I guess I'll just have to keep drinking ginger tea until our son or daughter is born. I want you to promise me that you'll be safe up there and you won't get overly tired, either. What do we have to do to get you ready to leave?"

"We'll make a list and when we're done I need to go see Tom; he has been looking for someone to work for me here in Lander. I was thinking that maybe John would trade room and board for taking care of the horses and making sure that the barn is cleaned at least every other day. I know he works in town, but maybe he would be interested in helping us out for a while."

"We could ask him after dinner tonight."

"I'm getting tired just thinking about all this and if you don't mind, I think I'll grab a comforter and go out on the front porch chaise and take a nap."

"May I join you?"

"Its just to sleep you know."

"Just sleep; the mommy and baby are tired, too."

That evening after dinner, Todd said to John, "Could Priscilla and I talk with you after you've had a chance to get comfortable for the evening?"

"Sure, give me about a half an hour and I will meet you in the parlor."

-27-

After supper, Todd asked Megan, "How was your day at school?"

"Well the teacher had us draw a picture of our family, so I put mommy, you, Molly, Jasper and the baby down and colored them all."

"How could you draw the baby, he or she hasn't come yet?"

"I'll show you. She took her picture out of her school bag and said, "See, there's the baby," pointing to the picture of mommy with a big belly.

He laughed; "I think we should hang this family picture in the parlor. It's perfect."

Hearing his laughter, Priscilla joined them to see what was going on; he let Megan tell her mom what it was all about. She gave Megan a kiss on her forehead and said, "I guess it would be a perfect family picture to put on the parlor wall. Now, you have to get ready for bed. Do you want me or daddy to take you upstairs?"

"I choose," looking back and forth, "both of you." They all went up the front stairs to her bedroom. Priscilla helped get her changed out of her school clothes into her nightgown; Megan knelt on the side of her bed and said her prayers. She selected a book from the bookshelf next to her bed and asked her mother to read it. As she cuddled up next to her mother, soon she was fast asleep. Priscilla tucked the blanket around her and quietly left the room.

Todd and Priscilla meet John in the parlor where Todd asked him, "Would you be interested in doing some extra work around here in trade for room and board?"

"As you both know I work all week and every other Saturday, but for free room and board and a chance to do something other than paperwork, I will gladly help you out. When do I start?"

"We were thinking that tomorrow night right after dinner, Todd will show you what he has in mind and you could start the next evening." Priscilla replied.

"That's perfect. See you after dinner tomorrow night, Todd." John took his leave and went out to the front porch. He stretched before taking a walk as he has been doing every night after dinner and before he retired for the evening.

Todd said, "Well that's one thing I won't have to worry about. Why don't you and I take a walk back to the barn? I have to get the horses settled in for the night and you can watch me work."

"You're always trying to get me in the barn, you think that I don't know what you have in mind?"

"Why don't you come with me and find out." After a few minutes, she said, "Stop that, what will the boarders think?"

"Let them think whatever they want."

* * *

Todd got out of bed as quietly as he could so that he didn't wake Priscilla. He lightly kissed her forehead, she sighed and hugged her pillow. He grabbed his boots, saddlebags and walked in his stocking feet out of the bedroom and down the hall to the back stairs. In the kitchen, he finished dressing, and went out to the barn. He had put off leaving an extra day already, She would be upset that he didn't wake her, but he had to get back to Stony Creek. He saddled up one of Joe's horses and put a rope halter on the other one. He bent down and scratched behind Mike's ears and said, "No barking, when I open the door you follow the horses. You understand don't you?"

Mike turned his head to one side and looked at him quizzically, yawned, then gave his paw to him.

He brought the horses outside, closed the barn door and on the side of the house where the only open window was in her bathroom, he mounted and rode quietly down the road. He stopped by the café and bought breakfast and two-dozen fresh baked biscuits, figuring that his next meal wouldn't be until he got to Joe's. With Mike by his side, he walked the horses over to Henderson's. Joshua was outside sweeping the boardwalk and said, "Good morning, what brings you out so early?"

"I have to get back up-country. I don't suppose you have any barbed wire do you?"

"I have five rolls left until my next shipment comes in the end of next week. How many do you need?"

"If you can loan me a blanket and a pack frame, I'll take two rolls. I'm paying cash."

"Sure, let me get them out here and you can put them on the frame yourself, need anything else?"

"I guess I could use some of those sweet sticks that Ned likes, four pairs of leather work gloves, 4 wool blankets, 7 pounds of coffee, 2 pounds of sugar, a dozen cans of beans, a cured ham and a slab of smoked bacon. That should do it."

"That comes to $29.50."

Todd gave him $40.00 and said, "If the Misses or Beth comes in have her get some candy for Megan and whatever she wants. I'll bring the saddle blanket and pack frame back the next time I'm in town and if I owe you anything, I'll pay you then." He mounted and led the other horse, with Mike walking by his side, back down the street and headed north.

Megan came in her mother's room and said, "Mom, where's daddy?"

Priscilla had just woken, "Well he was here just a minute ago. I guess he went downstairs for some coffee. He likes to sit on the swing and watch the sunrise. We'll leave him alone; he has a lot on his mind. Why don't you go in the bathroom and wash your face to get the sleepers out of your eyes and I'll lie out your outfit for school. When you're ready, you and I can go downstairs and get your breakfast."

"Can I have pancakes this morning?"

"We'll see what Beth has made for everyone today and you can have that."

* * *

Up-country, Ned was up at the crack of dawn. As he sat on the edge of the bed he said to the dog, who had taken to sleeping under it, "We'll Mister, what shall I do today?"

The dog, now standing in front of him, moved his head back and forth as if to say, "I don't know." Ned heated some water, poured it in the washbasin, took the bar of soap and washed his face; the back of his neck and under his arms and grabbed

146

a towel to dry off. He took one of the newer shirts that he bought at the general store out of his satchel and put it on before grabbing his hat and gloves as he stepped out on the porch. The dog followed and stood next to him until he saw a squirrel at the bottom of a pine tree and whined. "What are you waiting for, "Seek." The dog padded over to the opposite side of the tree where the squirrel was and came around the corner just in time to see it scurry up the tree and jump from one tree to another.

Ned walked over to the fire pit, stoked it and added a couple of split cedar logs; the aroma filled the air. He took the coffee pot over to the stream, filled it, added two fistfuls of ground coffee and set it on the grill to boil. While it was boiling, he walked over to the barn, slid both front doors open and went inside. He opened the side door before leading out the horses one by one. When the last horse went through the side door, he closed the bottom half thinking, *I'll put some of the new hay in the corral for them and I'll put the remainder of the hay on the pile and cover it; Next on my agenda is to enlarge where the chicken's stay during the day and cover the top with chicken wire to keep the hawks and eagles away. I'll go fishing later and catch dinner; I've got a hankerin' for some fish tonight. I should check on the other three homesteads to make sure everything is okay. I'll do that right after I have some breakfast.*

* * *

Todd took the usual route back north toward the ranch, but instead of stopping at Ft. Washakie, he stopped by the river to let the horses graze and drink; Mike was his usual self, sniffing the ground, digging in the soft soil before he went down to the

147

river for a drink; lying in the tall grass and fell asleep. Todd stretched and sat under a nearby tree to let the sun warm him, and shut his eyes for a brief nap, waking to a wet nose next to his cheek. He looked up to see it begin to cloud up and said to Mike, "I guess we'd best get to Joe's before it starts to rain, otherwise it will be a tough go." Mike trotted over to where the horses were and waited for him. Todd stood under the tree for a few seconds, stretched and walked over to the horses, mounted and began his trek up a very dry creek bed, which by morning will turn into a raging current. He won't be able to leave Joe's for at least two, maybe three days until the rain stops and the snow begins. The creeks and streams will all have to settle down enough to allow him to cross over.

＊

Ned left the rifle at the cabin, and started off to check the neighboring homesteads. Todd had warned him several times, never go anywhere without some firepower, either the rifle or the shotgun in case he needed to use it to protect himself. He'd been gone about an hour, going from one homestead to the next one; nothing was out of the ordinary that he could see. Both Pete and Turk had barely started building anything on their property. Gus on the other hand, had sense enough to build a barn and to fence off a corral. He remembered that he had gone through the properties just a few days ago and he was positive that he had made sure the windows were all shut and the side door was closed and secured, but that wasn't what he saw after coming down the fire trail this morning. Suddenly, he remembered that he didn't have any weapon with him, but his bowie knife, and he wasn't as skilled with it

as Todd or the others were. He decided to go back through
the forest to the cabin and get the shotgun and do what Todd
had told him, "put a slug in one side and shot in the other and
don't be afraid to pull the trigger, it might mean the difference
between life and death; take extra shells with you in your pants
pockets; always be prepared in case something unexpected
happens." He decided to ride Misty bareback back over to
Gus' place. Whoever was in the barn wasn't going anywhere.

-28-

Priscilla thought it strange that Todd hadn't come in yet for his usual late breakfast after he watched the sunrise. He had said that he would need to leave tomorrow at the latest, especially after having put it off an extra day already. After showing John what needed to be done after he had gotten home from work and then securing everything in the barn, he came to bed, tired. She was sure that he meant tomorrow and not today; he would have at least woken her, wouldn't he? She decided to just check the barn and see if the horses were still there; they weren't. He would have at least kissed her, but she didn't remember that he had kissed her forehead before he left, quietly. Maybe it was getting harder for him to leave, she thought wistfully. He had said that he needed to make changes so that getting what he needed to get done would be easier, so that he wouldn't be working non-stop to near exhaustion every time he came back to her.

* * *

These next two weeks were going to be longer than anyone would have guessed, but she'd have to put on a good front for

150

Megan, Beth, and the boarders. Beth was finally taking a day off, actually two. She was going with Tom Murphy back to Casper, he to attend a meeting and she to see her family. Beth had confided with Priscilla that she asked Tom to meet her parents and to come for dinner the day after they got there. They would be back on Sunday, late.

At least it was the weekend, and Priscilla would only be making the morning breakfast on Saturday and dinner on Sunday. She would have the whole weekend to spend with Megan. She thought about taking her for an ice cream on Saturday afternoon. She didn't anticipate the weather turning bad, actually no one thought of that prospect. It hadn't rained in over a month and even though it was getting close to winter, this part of the territory hadn't had an early winter in more than a decade. This year, it would start as rain late Friday night.

* * *

"I don't like the way the sky looks, Pete said to the Langstrom's as they sat around the campfire eating breakfast. If I didn't know better I'd say we're in for a bad storm."

"You might be right about that," Gus replied as the wind had picked up. "We better pull in as much deadfall as we can; then make sure we have enough protection from whatever Mother Nature has in store for us. Being this high up in the foothills I think we'll get snow, and lots of it."

Turk replied, "I'll check the snares; Gus why don't you put hobbles on the horses and the mule just in case, and make sure they have enough of the hay that we brought with us; Pete, get the tools out of the shaft that was dug to get to the area

151

where the gold seam is, and if we all have time, I suggest we move the lean-to back into the draw as far as we can, restring the canvas cover, and cover everything in the wagon; we can get the dogs in with us and be as ready as we can for whatever comes our way."

* * *

Todd met with torrential rain every step of the way toward Joe's. Joe wasn't expecting anyone and was surprised to see him ride up, especially as the wind and lightning intensified. Todd remarked, "I need to get my supplies and especially the barbed wire inside and get your horses in someplace where they can ride out this coming storm."

"Follow me." He took Todd to a cave where he kept his supplies and stabled his horses. "Put the two of them in the last two stalls and put your supplies on the floor near the entrance. I know how heavy those rolls can be. I'll get some extra food just in case this get's really bad and we have to stay inside for a few days."

* * *

Ned was about to ride back over to Gus's when he heard the first rumble of thunder, *I think I better take care of the animals and get everything tied down before this storm gets here. Whoever is in Gus's barn can wait and they'll need the shelter just as much as I'll need to be here at the ranch."* He closed all but two windows in the barn, one on each side of the barn for cross ventilation, ran up the stairs to make sure the hayloft doors on each end were closed and secured before bringing in the horses and got them settled in their stalls just as the rain started. He slid the barn doors shut and went over to the picnic table and gathered up the coffee pot, pans and coffee tin and put them inside the cabin. Next, he went to the chicken coop and herded the chickens inside and locked the door they used to get into the yard and took the six eggs they had laid. He made a quick check on everything outside, and said to the dog "Inside." Before he went inside the cabin, he went up the ladder to the cache to get a couple of roasts. He made it to the porch before the rain started coming down heavy, more than he's seen in a long, long time.

* * *

"Mommy, I thought I heard thunder, do you think it's going to rain?" Megan asked.

"It's been cloudy all afternoon, and we haven't had rain in such a long time. If you thought you heard it, there must be a storm somewhere close by. Do us a favor and get Jasper in the house while I get the horses into the barn."

"Please be careful, mommy, we don't want anything to happen to the baby."

"I will; make sure all the windows are closed on the first floor and when I come in, you and I will make sure they are all closed in the upstairs rooms.

* * *

Todd said to Joe, "I never expected this, one minute it is thunder and lightening, then hail and then the rain comes back. Mother nature sure is fickle at times."

"Mother Nature knows when it's time to change the seasons, but like you said she is fickle. I remember when I was a small boy growing up in our village close to the Yellowstone, my father and my older brother were out elk hunting, I think, or maybe it was deer, I forget its been ages. The sky turned a bright orange in the morning and by the afternoon one hell of a storm came up. You couldn't see in front of you more than a few feet. I was the only one in the lodge besides our dog and my baby sister. We were so scared that the lightening gods were going to strike the lodge and we would all be killed. When my mother came in the door, her deerskin dress was soaked. Despite the lightening and pounding rain she picked up my sister and led the way to the far side of the lodge and covered all of us over with a buffalo hide; we huddled together for what seemed like hours until the storm passed. Because my mother made sure we were protected, we faired better than some of the other people in the village. My father and brother had ridden out the storm in a cave, where the smell of dead animals emanated. Apparently the cave had been used by a bear and he left what he didn't want, to rot; the horses were anxious, but my father knew that they would be safe there rather than trying to wait it out in a draw with hardly any cover; they were dry and since they were up high enough it just snowed. They could watch the storm clouds race to the south and he said it seemed like hours before it stopped in the valley below and moved away.

It kept snowing for the remainder of the day and just before nightfall came, the clouds looked like puffs of cotton with gold fringes as the sun's rays glowed in the western sky. Between twilight and moonlight they were able to make it back to the village. Upon returning, they found the village in total disarray. Our lodge was one of the few left standing. They told us how scary it was and they could see herds of elk and deer just racing down the mountainsides to get away from the heavy snows. It was a lean winter for our family that year, they had to go great distances to hunt."

Todd replied, "When I was around eight or nine, there was a bad storm up on the mountain that we lived on. One minute it was rain, the next snow, and then back to rain. It was like the storm couldn't make up its mind what it wanted to do. We couldn't do anything until it finally stopped. We all went outside after the sun came out, but by that time the storm had ended, it had stripped every tree of its leaves and the stark landscape was eerie. It looked like a firestorm had come through and when everything dried out, you could see into the forest, but all the animals were gone and my pa said we'd have to go far to hunt because no living thing could be found in the hollows or even down in the valley. It made for a hungry winter that year. I hope this storm isn't one of those. By any chance do you know a trapper by the name of Jake Johnson?"

"Yes, he comes down here about once a year to sell his furs at the fort and buy his supplies; then he goes back to trapping. Why?"

"He told me a while back that the mountain people and the Indians that live in the Teton's told him it was going to be a bad winter. I wonder if this is the start of it."

"I guess only time will tell, but I can see this as a bad winter if this storm is any indication of what lies ahead for all of us."

"We'll have supper and afterwards we can play cards, there is nothing either of us can do until the storm passes." The two of them and Joe's wife just sat around the table and played a card game that Joe knew, drank coffee until they decided to go to bed.

-29-

Ned was more worried about the horses than he was about himself and decided about halfway through the storm to take the dog and run from the cabin to the barn and stay there the rest of the night. The horses were agitated because of all the lightening and thunder, he managed to 'talk' to them and get them settled down. He knew he'd do well with them from then on. It was going to be a long night but it was warm and somewhat comfortable in its own way in the barn. The animals certainly gave off enough heat to fend off the chill in the air. The rain turned to snow shortly after midnight and blanketed everything with a mantle of white.

* * *

Megan was so scared that she didn't want to leave her mother's side during the storm, and every time there was a bolt of lightening followed by a thunder clap she curled up even closer to her on the couch. Her mother fretted about where Todd was and hoped he had taken shelter from the storm where he'd be safe and dry. Jasper was hiding under a table nearby with his paws over his face and nearly jumped out of his skin every time there was a rumble of thunder close

157

by. The animals were more aware of a pending change of the weather than their human friends, but he acted like he was just as scared as Megan. She said to her mother, "does the baby feel anything when it storms like this?"

"The baby is in a protected sack inside mommy's tummy and knows when I'm not feeling well, when I cry, or when I'm worried like I am right now about your daddy, but it doesn't get hurt from those things. The baby will be fine." Megan sang a little song to make sure the little baby knew its big sister was there to protect him. Two of the three boarders' had gotten home just before the storm and went to their rooms. No one expected Priscilla to make supper. While Megan had finally fallen asleep lying on the floor next to Jasper, Priscilla went up and knocked on their doors to let them know she'd be making a supper that evening, much to their surprise, but they were happy that she thought enough of them to do that. Since there were only two of them now, they decided to come help her just to keep busy during the storm and said they'd be down shortly. Each one took a different part of the supper preparation, vegetable, dessert, while she baked the fish and put the biscuits in the beehive oven. By the time they had everything prepared, the storm was beginning to move away from Lander. There would be lingering showers throughout most of the weekend, finally exiting the area early on Sunday morning.

* * *

Nearly a week passed before anyone, could make their way through the snow in the mountains and the surrounding countryside, while down in the valley near Lander, the Wind

River overflowed its' banks making travel nearly impossible. Until the water receded, it was difficult to get around to inspect what damage had been done to the roads, bridges, and some of the buildings.

The Langstrom brothers and Pete huddled in their makeshift home until the snow stopped. You could only see a drift of smoke coming up through the wall of snow in front of where the lean-to was.

"Well, we weathered this one pretty good," Gus, said.

"Yeah, we did at that, but I wish we could predict when it was going to snow. I'd rather be someplace else where it's warmer than where we are right now," Turk replied.

Pete replied, "It's too bad we didn't tunnel our way to the shaft, we could have been doing some mining while it was snowing".

"What would you have done if you decided to come back to the lean-to and you couldn't find it? Freeze your ass off or what?" Gus asked.

Turk added his thoughts, "We were where we were supposed to be when this storm came. Next time we may not be so lucky. I guess we should try to dig ourselves out and see how the horses and mule faired."

"We can worry about the mine another time; sooner or later we're going to run out of the basic necessities and what are we going do them?" Pete asked the two of them.

"We'll worry about that after we dig out and take care of the horses. We can make a bigger fire for warmth and cook one of the two rabbits that I brought back here just before the storm came." Gus replied, "We'll discuss what we need to do during supper."

They took turns cutting a snow tunnel through the mounds

of snow that had drifted right where they were. Once they were out they finally were able to stand up and see what it all looked like. The sky was azure blue, the air crisp and clean, and as far as they could see, the landscape was like a furry white rabbit. Although snow had accumulated on top of the blankets the horses and mule looked okay. Each was either pawing the ground for grass, or for the bundles of hay that had been covered with snow. The stream was still running so at least they had water to drink.

They had pulled the lean-to within a few yards of the shaft that Pete and Gus had built. They lined it with boards and put a ladder down to the where the cave started, some snow was on the floor of the shaft. Their only concern right now was to get another couple of rabbits or a wild turkey, maybe an elk or deer to keep them fed for a few more days, weeks even. Turk said, "Why don't we try to move the wagon closer to the lean-to so that we can have more space to spread out. This sleeping together is good for warmth, but the closeness is beginning to smell like a hog pen; no offense."

"No offense taken, but I think we should have thought of that before all this snow got here. It'll take us twice as long to move it now and besides, looking over to where it is, it just looks like a big mound of white," Pete remarked.

"Since it's your idea Turk, why don't you shovel a path to it and make it your new home. Pete and I will stay right where we are until we can figure what we're going to do next." Talking among themselves, they decided that Pete should go back to their homesteads and over to Stony Creek to get some supplies and let Todd know what they found so far. He would also bring back the skins that they had already collected. The three of them put together a proposal that

Pete was going to ask Todd once he got back down to where he was. The three of them were going to stay and work the mine throughout the winter months; they might as well since moving the wagon wasn't going to be an option, at least until spring. They found that the gold seam ran along the floor of the cave but using dynamite was not an option. It would have to be hand-chiseled out of the bedrock and it would take time to retrieve it.

-30-

Todd borrowed one horse from Joe and he would use his mare as a packhorse to get the supplies he had purchased in Lander for the ranch. He said goodbye and gave them a half-dozen of the biscuits he had purchased at the café as a gift for letting him stay with them and said, "Next time you come to Lander, stay with us." He led the horse with Mike following behind across the creek on his way toward the ranch. He figured with the slow going, that he'd be back there by late afternoon, at best.

Ned couldn't push the door open, guessing that the rain had turned to snow and had drifted against it. He went to the Dutch door on the opposite side of the barn and opened the top part of it, looked out to see bare ground just outside the door and about twenty feet in front of it. Most of the fence was snow covered and the corral, which looked like it was about a foot deep depending on which way the wind had whipped the snow during the storm. Some drifts here and there were over six feet high, but it was open enough for the four horses to run and play in the corral for a few hours. They had been in their stalls the whole time the storm raged and they needed the release! He made sure that the horses were taken care of while they were in the barn; he took them out one-at-a -time, rubbing them down with straw, before brushing their winter coats and finally scratched them behind their ears and along their necks. He cleaned out the individual stalls, putting down fresh straw, new feed and a half-a-hay bale in each corner, and for a treat, gave each one a couple of carrots. He opened the bottom half of the door and led each one out into the corral. Once they were all out, he closed the bottom part of the door latching it so that it didn't accidently blow open. It was comical to watch them run and chase each other in the powdery snow and as much as he enjoyed their antics, he had work to do. He had to get the straw with the manure in it thrown out the back door into the growing pile that, for the most part, was covered in snow, but melting here and there because of the warm manure being put on it. He opened all the windows in the barn to air it out; let the dog run out the back door while it was open to stretch his legs.

* * *

Priscilla could hardly wait for Beth to finally make it back from Casper. The roads Beth was travelling on weren't in any better shape than they were in the area around Lander. She hoped that Tom was with her; it would make for a more enjoyable trip if he was, rather than traveling alone with strangers. Megan hadn't gone to school in over a week. The storm damaged the school and the town council asked the pastor if he would let the children use the church during the week, until the repairs could be made. "By all means, but could you wait until Monday after church services this week? It would make it easier to move some of the bibles and song books out of the pews, rather than having to put them all back before church services only to have to take them all out again." That wasn't going to be a problem. On Friday after school got out, the older children would help to put the bibles and songbooks back in the pews. They expected the repairs to the school would take about three weeks.

She became concerned about what Todd might be going through from the reports that were coming in from up-country. The two supply wagons that went to Ft. Washakie every other week couldn't get through because of the deep snow and had to turn back. They'd have to find another way to get to the fort as the people in it depended on those supplies. Thanksgiving was in eight days and she knew Todd wasn't going to make it back by then; she could only hope and pray that he'd be back by Christmas. The worst that could happen was he wouldn't be back until the end of winter, four to five months from now. She cried herself to sleep nearly every night, just wondering if he was alright or not.

* * *

Ned woke after a short nap with the dog lying at his feet. He decided that sleeping in the barn for a fourth night was not an option. He went to the tack room, grabbed his gloves, scarf and hat and got the wide bladed shovel he used to shovel the manure and went out the side door nearest the corral, closing it. He began to shovel a path to the gate and around the front of the barn so the huge doors could slide open. Once he finished that he went around to see how high the drift was on the north side of the barn - the drift was over eight feet high! *I'll do that one tomorrow, perhaps it will have melted down by then.* He shoveled a path to the cabin, cleaned off the porch and finally a path to both the chicken coop and the outhouse. Afterward, he went back to the cabin and opened the door, turned and gathered up an armful of split logs and put them on the stone hearth, returned to the double-stacked pile on the north side of the porch and brought in another armful. Once inside, he got a fire going, took the coffee pot which had sat on the cold hearth all night and hung it over the fire to get it boiling again and when it was hot, he'd pour himself a cup to warm up.

He went out to the chicken coop and pushed the snow to one side of the fence or the other so that the chickens would have a place to walk around in; he retrieved the grain bucket from underneath the building and threw handfuls of the cracked corn on top of the snow, then he opened the sliding door at the top of the ramp to let them out. He went in the door at the back of the coop and gathered 13 brown eggs placing them in an empty bucket so that he could take it back into the cabin.

Meanwhile, the dog was trying to catch two squirrels that were racing around the trunk of a large oak just out of his reach until he got tired of "their" game and plodded back to the porch where Ned had shaken out his blanket and refolded it in his favorite spot. He laid down to rest and kept watch on those mischievous squirrels.

Ned went inside and cut three thick slices of bacon and put them in the iron skillet before adding three eggs and as they were cooking, he poured himself another cup of coffee. Once they were the way he liked them, he set the skillet on the table next to his cup and utensils and pulled up a chair and ate his breakfast; it would have to satisfy him until later this afternoon. He'd put the venison in a roasting pan, covered it with another one and went out the cabin door and set it on top of the wood pile. Later this afternoon, along with a couple of potatoes and some carrots, he'd put them in with the venison to cook for his dinner. He had no idea where Todd was, let alone the Langstrom's or Pete. After breakfast, he cleaned the skillet, cup, and utensils before going out the door to get water for the horse trough in each stall. While he was in there, he'd get the snowshoes he found in the tack room, grab the shotgun with extra shells and go back over to Gus's barn to find out who was in there.

Todd had no idea that the snow would get deeper the farther he went up the trail toward the ranch. As the light of day was fading, he came upon a cabin and after a shout out, got no response. He dismounted and knocked on the door, still no response. He pushed on the door, which opened to reveal that it was the cabin that Moon had once lived in; he knew he was only about eight miles from the ranch. He decided to stay in the cabin for the night and continue on in the morning. He unsaddled the borrowed horse and brought the saddle with him setting it on the hearth, supplies the same using the light reflected off of the snow to find his way. He found some wood still stacked on the hearth as if Moon knew he'd need it. He took some fuzz from inside his coat pocket, and using the flint and rock that he always carried with him; he got sparks to ignite the fuzz. He piled on some pine straw and small sticks that he had shaved from one of the logs until he had a sufficient amount to keep the fire going, slowly adding the wood from the hearth. He pushed a small table and two chairs to one side of the fireplace and the crude bed frame to the same side against the wall opposite the table. He needed space to bring in both horses. Once he got them situated, he got out the small coffee pot that he always had with him and using a small kettle he had found on the hearth, managed to melt enough snow into water for each horse to drink. Warmth crept into the cabin slowly. He took a small branch out of the fire for light and found three candles on the far side of the cabin sitting on a window frame. By the light, he could see that there was more kindling and firewood stacked in the corner. He rummaged through one of his packs for the small sack of grain that he had for the horses and using his hat, put some in it for each horse. He took out the new blankets, one for each of the horses, throwing it over them, enough to help keep the chill out of their bones. Now it was time to take care of Mike and after that, himself. He went out and using both the coffee pot and the small kettle, he got more snow to melt down, first for Mike to drink and, again, some to make coffee. He took the biscuits that he had purchased nearly four days ago and set them on the hearth near enough to the fire to warm them plus two cans of beans that he had opened using the tip of his bowie knife around the top edge. He bent back the lids, setting them both next to the fire. Pulling one of the chairs close enough to the fireplace and with Mike by his side, they waited for their dinner to cook. His thoughts were about Priscilla and how she must be worrying about him. Once he got Ned squared away, and got done what he needed to do and he would try to get back in time for Thanksgiving, but more than likely it would be Christmas. The worst case was by March, next year.

* * *

While Todd was thinking about his new family back in Lander, Pete was thinking how long it would take to get back to

Gus' homestead given the fact that the snowdrifts were much deeper than he had anticipated. He knew he was going in the right direction but at times he had to lead rather than ride the horse and the mule through some of the deepest snow. He managed to find a draw where he could make camp for the night. At least, he had thought to bring a bundle of hay with him for the horse and mule to eat, he'd melt down snow for water for them, and he had some grain, too. But for himself, he hadn't taken enough food with him and after the first night he went to half rations. If necessary, he would stop every few hours to make a small fire for warmth to make some coffee to keep him warm. Going back to the mine, he hoped at least that the trail that he was blazing wouldn't be completely covered over; he'd have to get help from Todd to bring enough supplies up to Gus and Turk for them to survive through the winter.

* * *

Tom Murphy and Beth finally made it back to Lander on Thursday, much later than either anticipated. It had taken the stagecoach nearly four and a half days to cover the same ground, which under normal conditions would only take two days between Casper and Lander. Bridges were washed out, rockslides blocked the road in two places and even roads that had been used over and over for years, were indistinguishable along most of the route. They were both glad to be back 'home'. He walked Beth back to The Parker House, gave her a kiss on her cheek and said he'd see her tomorrow once he got things straightened out at the office and with Sheriff Hughes.

She made her way up the front steps and let herself in. She heard singing in the kitchen and as she went down the hall said,

169

"What is that I smell coming from the kitchen Mrs. Morgan?" She didn't get the answer she was expecting. Megan spoke up and said "I'm making some tea and toast for mommy she isn't feeling well today." As Beth rounded the corner, Megan practically knocked her over as she ran into her giving her a big hug saying, "Mommy will be so glad you're back; I have missed you." Beth hugged her back and had Megan sit down, "I missed you too, why don't you make some tea for both you and me and I'll take this up to your mom."

"Okay, do you want some cookies too?"

"That would be fine."

Beth wondered why Megan wasn't in school and thought that perhaps she had stayed home to help her mother out. Going upstairs, Beth set the tray on the table just outside the bedroom door, opened the door and found Priscilla propped up in bed dozing. She knocked on the doorjamb so that Priscilla knew that someone was there. Waking, as a tear ran down her cheek and she tried to get out of bed to give her hug, but she was very weak. Between crying over Todd not being there and not being able to keep much food down, she just fell back into bed. Beth went and got a washcloth and rinsed it with cold water and washed her face and said, "I guess you missed me, huh?"

"Missed you isn't exactly what I would have said. From now on, you can't leave me for more than an hour at the very most. Megan and I have been sick with worry about what happened to you; did Marshal Murphy come back with you also?"

"Yes, he and I rode on the stagecoach together. I was so grateful he was with me. It took us forever to get back here, but now I'm 'home' and we can get you back on a daily routine once again. I suppose the poor boarders have been eating in town since I left."

"Quite the contrary, we've had supper every night with them helping Megan and me get it together, but they will be glad you're back so that they can have breakfast again. That's one meal I couldn't make." They laughed as she brightened considerably. She ate the toast and drank the ginger tea that Megan had made. She told Beth that Todd had left the day of the storm and she had no idea where he was or how he was doing, especially after the reports that they were getting the further north you went. "I'm feeling he's alright, it's just that I don't know where he might be and I'm hoping he at least made it to Ft. Washakie to ride out the blizzard they had up there." She told Beth about the supply wagons that had to turn back and from a lone rider riding on a harnessed horse who finally made it to town after having endured Mother Nature's wrath by having to take refuge in a draw for three days until the sun finally came out and he could make his way here. Beth said, "I'm sure when Tom has to ride north, he can inquire at the fort, maybe he'll get some news for us. I'm sure that Todd is okay; it's the best we can hope for given the circumstances. Why is Megan home?"

"The school was damaged because of the storm, but starting Monday all the children will be going to the church for classes until school house is repaired. They said it would take about three weeks."

"That explains why she was in the kitchen, singing a little song I've never heard before."

"You know, I think she just made it up; she sang it to the "baby" the other night during the storm, surprisingly enough, the "baby" let me have a decent nights sleep for a change."

"Maybe she could sing it to the "baby" every night and you'd

feel better every day."
    "We'll ask."

-32-

"What do you think? If we ride all day we should make it to the ranch by late this afternoon," Pete said to the horse and mule. He'd been on the trail for three and half days and all he wanted was to sleep in his own bed, eat some decent food and rest for at least two, maybe three days before he'd start back to the mine with the supplies.

* * *

Ned woke with sore shoulder muscles, but other than that, he didn't feel too bad; the cabin was warm and he still had some of the venison roast left over, as well as one and a half baked potatoes, the vegetables were all gone but the pot of coffee was still at least half full. He shaved off a couple of slices of venison and put them on one side of the frying pan and cracked two eggs and sliced up the half baked potato into the pan as well, the breakfast would have to last until later that afternoon. Once breakfast was over, he cut off a one inch slice from the roast and sliced it into chunks for the dog before saying to him, "When you're done, you can go out and do your business, chase the squirrels if they are out today or lay on your blanket while the sun is shining on this side of the cabin." The dog ate what was put in front of him and when finished yawned, drank some water and went to the door waiting to be let out.

Ned decided today he'd tackle the snowdrift on the north side of the barn and get a path shoveled over the bridge to the ranch entrance, not that he was expecting anyone, but out here you just never knew if someone would come riding up the lane. By the middle of the afternoon, he strapped on the snowshoes to walk over to Gus's following the path he'd made earlier.

* * *

Pete figured he had about an hour to go once he got to the top of the rise that looked down toward where the homesteads were. He also saw a beautiful 8-point buck just below him feeding on the branches of an aspen tree. He dismounted, removed his carbine from the scabbard, set the resting rod he had purchased into the snow bank, took aim and fired using a 56-grain cartridge. It hit the buck right behind its right ear, a perfect kill shot. Making his way through the snow to where it was, he quickly hoisted it up on top of the mule, tied it down and finished his journey to the ranch. He saw snowshoe tracks leading in through the entrance near Gus's place. It made it easier to ride in using those tracks and as he rounded a bend in the lane, saw Ned cradling the shotgun in his arms as he approached a slightly open barn door and also observed two of the windows were open. He took the carbine out of the scabbard, Ned turned and saw him coming towards him and said, "Boy, you're a sight for sore eyes. I was just going to check and see who was in the barn, so I'm glad you came along." Ned opened the barn door and saw an old plow horse in one of the stalls and a boy no more than 11 or 12 looking back at them who said, "We meant no harm, we just needed a place to stay is all." Pete entered and heard something to his left, turning he saw a little girl holding a rag doll and a woman laying on the piled hay in the corner with one of their blankets over her, shivering, she said, "We're sorry mister, we didn't take anything except this here blanket for warmth and some of the grain so that we'd have something to eat."

Pete looked at Ned and vice versa. Neither knew quite what to say, but Pete finally broke the silence and said, "I certainly didn't expect this when I got back here. Now what are we gonna' do with these folks Ned, they can't stay here."

The boy said, "We were trying to get over the mountains, but the pass was blocked so we had to turn around. We've got no place to go, our wagon broke down north or west of here, pointing, my father took the other horse and set out toward the south in the hope of finding someone to help us, but we haven't seen him since."

His mother said, "I sure hope he got to somewhere before this terrible snowstorm trapped us here and he's okay." Before she could continue, Pete said, "No disrespect but trespassing is against the law."

"Ned remarked, "Generosity is a virtue Pete. You heard what she said and if she was your mother, you'd be happy to let them stay in the barn until they could be reunited with her husband."

"Good point, boy, but this is no place for her to stay in. You'll just have to let them stay at Stony Creek, where they'll be safe and warm."

The lady continued with her story. "My son, daughter and I were riding on ole' Blackie and he just kinda' brought us here. We managed to get the door open and once inside we put him in a stall, took off his harness and gave him some feed and hay. We all went upstairs and saw your three beds and just slept in them the first night we got here, but since then we've been down here." Ned thought to himself *if I'd only gone those few extra steps before the storm and peeked in the window, I would have seen them and they could have come with me over to the cabin.* He felt really bad that he didn't follow through; he couldn't just come out with it. In his later years, it would become one of his demons, until he got up the courage to say something about it, but by then it would have been long forgotten.

* * *

Todd got back on the trail around mid-morning and found that the snow drifted here and there making it difficult to ride along the old trail, though sometimes it was only a few inches of snow and he could make good time. Finally, smelling the cedar aroma from the smoke in a fireplace, he positioned himself to head for the front rather than the rear of his homestead he found that a path just wide enough for a horse was shoveled leading from the entrance over the bridge and into the barnyard. Not seeing or hearing anyone, he guessed that Ned might be out in the woods; he was surprised to see the roof over the entire porch and the double-stacked woodpile on the north side, as well. The extra hay stored on the side of the barn was covered; the wagon, though not covered was next to the south side of the cabin; there were paths leading to the gate by the corral, the chicken coop, the outhouse, and the barn door on the north side. In the barn, he found it clean with fresh hay, feed and water in the troughs in each stall, and the windows and the Dutch door open to air out the barn. The horses were in the corral frolicking in the remains of the snow or pawing for grass shoots underneath. He was duly impressed with all the work that Ned had done since he left. *I'll have to give the boy a raise, if he's going to do such a good job., I might as well find a way to get back to Priscilla and Megan and let him continue to run the ranch for me. He certainly doesn't need my help up here.*

-33-

"I didn't catch your name, ma'am?" Pete asked.

"It's Thompson, Emma Thompson. This is my son George and my daughter Mary; my husband's name is Richard when he comes back to find us."

"Well Mrs. Thompson as I was saying, you can't stay here. My partners and I built the barn to stay in when we come back from our mine up in the Tetons. It's rather primitive since we don't have a wood stove or even a fireplace and you apparently found where we sleep. I hope the accommodations were comfortable enough," he said rather sarcastically. "This is my neighbor," motioning towards Ned "and had he known you were here, he would have had you go to his cabin where you would have been warm and be able to at least eat some real food other than moldy grain. I think, for the time being, that if you can gather up what you have and we'll get your horse over to his barn and you settled in at his place. You'll be much safer and warmer there. You can take the blanket with you, I can always get it back when I go over there later."

"Thank you for not turning us out. We would probably have frozen to death if we had not found this barn." Before they left the barn for Stony Creek, they closed all the windows and doors. Upon their arrival, Ned saw Todd coming out of the barn and said to him, "Welcome back stranger. I had no idea if you were dead or alive, but I'm glad your back. We have guests so we'll have to figure this all out after we get Mrs. Thompson and her children settled in the cabin, get them warmed up and fed."

Pete arrived shortly thereafter and when he saw Todd said, "You're a sight for sore eyes, I am glad you are here. I've got good news and not so good news, but I'll wait until later to talk with you about that."

Ned got Mrs. Thompson and the children situated in the cabin and said, "Let me add some logs to the fire so's you can get warmed up and I'll fix you something to eat."

Todd had gone back in the barn to take care of his horses. He unsaddled the one and got the supplies off of Misty. Pete brought in his horse and the mule and got them in stalls, while Ned got Mrs. Thompson's horse in the end stall. The three of them walked over by the stairs leading up to the hayloft. Todd said, "We have a full house, not only in here, but in the cabin with only one fireplace and one bed. I know that all of us would like to be inside, but under the circumstances, I think that we'll let Mrs. Thompson and her children stay right there. The three of us can bunk in here with the animals and between their body heat and ours, we'll be comfortable enough. We can be thankful that a north wind isn't whipping through here and the sun is out nearly everyday warming the barn and cabin, despite the windows being open in the barn. Ned you can have the tack room back; Pete and I will either go upstairs to the hayloft or make our beds down here next to the stairs. We'll all have to eat inside the cabin since using the outside fire pit is out of the question for the time being. It might be a bit tight but we'll make it work."

Ned replied, "If you gents will excuse me, I'll start preparing what we are going to have for supper."

After Ned left, Pete remarked, "I'm guessing that you've been in the saddle about as long as I have. We need to just rest for a few days. I shot a deer just before I got here, so I've got to get it skinned, gutted and hung in a tree until I can cut it into steaks and roasts, wrap the meat and get it up into your cache.

"If you want, I can help and it will take half as long."

"That's a good idea and I'll be able to bring you up to date regarding the mine."

They brought the deer over to where the old temporary shelter was for the horses and laid it on a couple of boards across the side poles and cut the meat into steaks and roasts, setting them aside so they could wrap them in muslin before they put most of them up in the cache. Pete said, "I wanted to let you know that Marshal Murphy made it back here and told Gus and Turk that they needed to bring a wagon full of supplies up to the mine. After they got there, we built a wooden shaft down to the floor of the cave and a ladder to get up and down. Turk found that the seam ran horizontal along the floor instead of vertical. It runs pretty deep into the hillside and it's relatively flat so that makes it easier for us. We've been busy shoring up the inside as we go along; the only bad part is we can't use dynamite to get the rock out; otherwise the whole hill would cave in. We all came to same conclusion that it will have to be hand chiseled out of the floor and we'll go as deep as we can, but we have our limitations as to what we can and cannot get done for any length of time. It's backbreaking work. The three of us wondered if you'd be interested in a partnership?"

"What kind of partnership are we talking about?" Todd asked as a thousand ideas ran through his brain.

"We would do the actual digging, retrieve the gold ore and guard it until you could get it assayed in Lander. We were thinking along the lines of a 70/30 split."

"Actually, that's the best news I've heard since I got married two weeks ago."

"You finally did it. I personally thought I'd never hear you say that gal of yours would want to marry an "old" fart like you. She must see something in you that we don't," Pete said with a laugh.

"She's the best thing that ever happened to me including finding the gold. The worst part is being away from her and her little girl. I hope to change all that in the coming year."

"Well, what do you say, is it a deal?"

"Tell you what, let me get my head around all that's happened, take a walk and do some calculations and I'll give you an answer after I sleep on it. Is that fair enough?"

"Sure." They divide up the meat equally. "I need to go back to our barn for a little while and I'll be back for supper. Can I borrow your snow shoes to get back over there?"

"Here, take them and we'll see you back here around 6 pm."

* * *

After the meeting at the US Marshal's Office in Casper, Tom Murphy decided that he'd stay right where he was. He was given an expanded territory to cover including all of Fremont and Hot Springs counties. He turned down a promotion because he enjoyed the people he worked with in Lander; he enjoyed the time he spent with Beth and hoped to make it more permanent in the New Year. He knew he'd be gone for weeks at a time when performing his duties in this section of the Wyoming Territory, but he wouldn't have it any other way. He was given the reward for Todd capturing the gang of murderers and a letter from the territorial governor too. He had planned on giving it to him personally, but under the circumstances he decided to give it to Priscilla along with the letter. He had no idea if Todd was even alive. Since he was going to the Parker House for supper he'd take Priscilla aside and hand her the money and the letter.

-34-

"It looks like a lot has happened around here since we left," Todd said to Mike, who looked at him quizzically. "Let's go for a walk down to the pond." Mike ran ahead; he grabbed the rifle before he walked down to the pond saying to himself *I just need some time to think and there's no better place to do it than right here.* Finding his favorite tree, he sat on the side overlooking the frozen pond covered in white thinking wistfully about Priscilla and the fun they had swimming here. Looking down, he saw tracks of rabbit, wolf, and deer mostly over a week old, but one was fresh, a couple of hours old, cougar. He said to Mike, "If I didn't know better, I'd say hunting for game is going to get a lot trickier with one of those critters close by. All of us will have to keep our guard up until it either moves on or we take care of it." Mike settled in next to him as Todd scratched the dog's head and stared straight ahead, thinking.

* * *

Back at Gus's, Pete was busy hiding some of the gold that he had already found up at Todd's mine. He managed to chisel some of it out of the ground and he wished he had a way of

183

getting to Lander to find out whether it was high or low grade. But for now, he'd have to wait until spring. He also wanted to make sure that the squatter's didn't find their gold stash under the tack room floorboards. Apparently they hadn't and that was a good thing. He was sure that Todd would just say, "Yes" to the partnership without any conditions. Ever since Todd had worked it out that Gus and Pete could take over a section each under the Homestead Act and he wouldn't have to be responsible for it, made Pete angry. He didn't want to be tied down to any one property. But before he could sell it, he'd have to improve the property over the next five years; he'd do as little as possible. His goal was to get to California, not stay in this God forsaken frozen wasteland.

* * *

Todd thought a 60/40 partnership would be better and he'd even share some of it with Ned. The next time he planned to go trapping, he'd take Ned with him so that he knew what it took to help pay for the operation of the ranch. He would do some of the mining himself and he'd train Ned in trapping at the same time and make him responsible for maintaining the trap lines.

He saw anger in Pete's eyes, but he wasn't quite sure what or whom his anger was directed at. As long as it wasn't him, he wasn't going to waste any time thinking about it. He had enough to worry about.

* * *

After supper, Tom took Priscilla aside and into the parlor

while Megan helped Beth in the kitchen. He said, "I have a letter from the Territorial Governor for Todd and the reward for catching those murderers.. Under the circumstances, I thought it best to give it to you, rather than wait until Todd returned." Priscilla just looked at Tom not knowing what really to say other than "Thank you. I have a favor to ask."

"Yes."

"If you have to go up-country anytime soon, would you please inquire if he spent time at the fort during the storm and if he was all right the last time they saw him?"

"You know I'd do that anyway and I know you probably have been worried sick since he left, especially with no word one way or another. I'll be going the end of next week, so you've got a week to write a letter and put together another package for delivery." A smile came over her face and she gave him a kiss on his cheek and a hug as Beth walked in the room, and said, "just a friendly kiss?"

They both looked at each other, then her and Tom said "Well her husband isn't around and until you caught us…" She almost took them serious until she saw them starting to laugh and said, "You had me there, for a minute."

"I think I hear your daughter calling you Mrs. Morgan. Don't you think you should go see what she wants? I have to speak to Mr. Murphy for a few moments," she said with a twinkle in her eye.

With an unpredictable predator about he'd keep a wary eye and ear open as he walked back to the cabin. As he was walking down the lane, Mike ran ahead of him. Todd saw Pete coming over the bridge, and waved, but apparently Pete didn't see him. He noticed that the horses weren't in the corral anymore; he went into the barn to find Ned putting the last one in between the last stall and the wall, he put a halter on it and put one rope through one side and another through the opposite side and tied both to posts. He also had put a bucket of water, a bucket of grain and some extra hay where it could feed like the other horses and the mule. Looking up, he said, "with one extra horse, I needed to put it somewhere and the tack room was out of the question, besides with the three of us and the two dogs in here it's going to be close as it is. Do you have any idea what were going to do with Mrs. Thompson and her children?"

"That's one thing, I hadn't thought about, but by tomorrow I'll have figured something out, among other things."

Megan asked her mother "When is daddy coming home, I really miss him and Molly misses him, too?"

"I'm hoping he'll be home for Christmas; I don't think he'll be home for Thanksgiving, which is this Thursday."

"I heard you talking to Mr. Murphy and he said he was going to the fort. Do you think daddy's there?"

"Right now, I don't know where he is but we have to be strong and hope that he is all right; I am sure he misses us too."

"After I get ready for bed, can I sing to the baby tonight, he probably misses him too?"

"Yes, you can sing to the baby; now get yourself ready for bed. I'll be sitting in the rocker waiting for you."

* * *

Tom and Beth were sitting in the parlor and she said, "I'm worried for Priscilla; she doesn't know one way or another where Todd is or if he is even alive. I hope when you get to the fort, they have some news about him. I know it would be asking a lot, but do you think you could ride to his ranch on the hopes that he is there."

"Tell you what I'll do. If he isn't or wasn't at the fort, I'll go see his friend Joe; he lives about 4 miles from there to see if he saw him. As much as I want to find out about him, I have a lot of territory to cover before I get back here. There are so many new villages springing up and no law to speak of. Part of my new assignment is making sure they know that I am covering that part of the territory. I should be back in Lander by the 8th or 9th of December. "

"Now, where were we when I had that idea?"

"Let me turn down the gas lamp and I'll show you."

-35-

After dinner, everyone had gotten situated in the cabin or the barn. As they drifted off to a deep sleep or tossing and turning in fitful sleep, Mike woke immediately to the sound of a baby crying. A sound, that sent shivers up and down the spine of the strongest person or dog. He wanted in the worst way to go investigate, but Todd heard it too, and wouldn't let him go. Mike had already been in one scrape with the dog/wolf and a grizzly had seriously hurt one of his other dogs. He didn't want it to happen again. He quietly said to Mike, "You'll have your turn soon enough." He pulled the quilt and blanket up around his chin and had Mike curl up next to him while both of them heard the eerie sounds for another twenty minutes or so before it abruptly stopped.

The following morning, he let the dogs out, but said to both, "Stay"; "Guard." They both reluctantly did as they were told as much as Mike just wanted to find the elusive predator.

Todd had done some serious thinking about the mine, both before and after sleeping. He had an answer for Pete; he also thought about the Thompsons' predicament, but first, he wanted to talk with Ned. Todd lay back down on the bed of straw and waited for Ned to wake up. Ned came out of the tack room looking like he was ready to work when Todd said, "after you go to the outhouse, I'll meet you at the fire pit by the stream. We need to do some talking."

Ned thinking the worst replied, "Just give me a few minutes."

"Take your time, these old bones take a mite longer to get going than yours do." Todd pulled on his boots before standing up, put on a heavy denim work shirt, his coat, scarf, and carried his hat, gloves and a shovel with him. Walking down one of the snow paths toward the bridge, he called Mike and the other dog as he went to shovel out the fire pit. After clearing everything off, he went back to the barn; Pete was still sleeping fitfully; he had no intention of waking him, he only wanted to get the coffee pot and some coffee grounds. You could smell the coffee aroma by the time Ned got there. "Take a seat; we need to talk before breakfast. First, I wanted to tell you, that I am very impressed with everything you've done while I have been away, actually I didn't think you'd get to a tenth of what was on the list done and secondly, I'd like to know who helped you?"

"No one helped me, honest. I, I just... well to be honest with you both Gus and Turk gave me a lecture the day after you left and ever since then I have learned to pace myself and not try to get everything done in one day."

"I really didn't think that you had any help, it's not like you're in a town where you could ask for help at the drop of a hat or ask Curt to help you. Now what is still on the list that you think we could get done in two weeks?"

"You're not leaving again are you?"

"Not without you this time and you don't have to give me an answer to my question right now. I want you to think about it and by noon I want your answer." Todd poured each of them a cup of coffee and said, "You asked me what we were going to do with Mrs. Thompson and her children. It wouldn't be easy for us to take her to the fort because of all the snow; Lander is definitely out of the question. I was thinking that we'd just let them stay here until a thaw, then we could get them to the fort."

"But we're so crowded as it is and I know you'd like to get back into your cabin and be warmer."

"Sure, I would, but under the circumstances, I can't do that. If it was your Ma and your siblings, what would you do?"

"I would make sure they were taken care of first, then I'd worry about me."

"Exactly and this morning after breakfast, I'm going to talk with her; She'll have to rearrange the cabin to accommodate them more comfortably. We on the other hand, are going to make some additions on the inside of the barn, to better accommodate you and me. When you were looking through the piles of things in the barn did you by any chance find two bolts of muslin cloth?"

"I just put them in the tack room, I didn't know what they were for."

"I bought those months ago; they are going to help us make the cabin warmer plus the tack room and a room upstairs that we are going to build. Can I assume you brought the fry pan into the cabin when you were getting prepared for the storm?"

"Yes."

"Let me go back to the barn and get my pack, while you go raid the chicken coop for some eggs. I need to have breakfast now, rather than wait for the Thompson's to wake up."

They were almost through breakfast, when Pete walked out of the barn looking like what the cat may have dragged in.

Seeing them sitting at the table, he gave a weak wave and walked over to the outhouse. Todd said to Ned, "I have to talk to Pete, but first do both of us a favor and get me a couple more eggs; I'll make him breakfast. Then I want you to go back to the barn and let all the horses and mule out into the corral after you take my carbine and walk around the corral looking for tracks."

"Tracks, what kind of tracks should I be looking for?"

"Cougar." He just looked at Todd and shivered.

"It gives me the willies too. We're all going to have to make sure that the Thompson's do not go anywhere without telling one of us first or making sure one of us is nearby. It's bad enough that one of them critters' is out there," he said with a wave of his hand.

* * *

Priscilla had another night of restful sleep and she was down in the kitchen by the time Beth got they're saying, "Megan sang to the baby last night, rubbing her stomach, and I got a good nights sleep. I thought that I since I hadn't made breakfast for John, Edith and Mabel in such a long time that I should this morning. I think they are spoiled by all the attention you give them."

"Spoiled is it? And here I thought I was doing what you normally did all this time. Boy was I mistaken," she replied with a little laugh.

"What shall "we" make for them today? I already put apple-bran muffins in the oven and I was about to scramble some eggs and get the bacon going on the grill plate; why don't you finish with that and I'll go and wake Megan so she can get ready for school. We can all eat together." After breakfast, Priscilla said to everyone, "Tomorrow is Thanksgiving and I hope you will all be joining Megan, Beth, Marshal Murphy, Parson and Mrs. Samuels and myself for dinner unless of course you've made other plans."

"John and Edith said they would, Mable said she had been invited by the Henderson's to join them."

"I'll be making a light breakfast for tomorrow since we have to concentrate on getting everything done for the dinner." John, Edith and Mabel all left for work; Megan gathered up her books as she waited by the front door for the neighbor to drive her and the other children to school. Priscilla said to Beth, "I think I need to go sit down for awhile, can you handle all this."

"I have a system so don't worry. I'll have everything cleaned off and put away by the time you wake from your nap with the "baby".

"You read me like a book, don't you?"

"Yes!"

-36-

After Pete came out of the outhouse, he walked over to where Todd was sitting and said, "Mornin', thought I smelled coffee brewing. I could sure use a cup."

"And a good morning it is. I had Ned get you some eggs, how do you want them cooked?"

"I like them sunny side up."

While Todd was preparing his breakfast he said, "You asked me about considering a partnership with you and the Langstrom's. I am thinking along the lines of a 60/40 partnership with me doing some of the work. That would seem fair for all concerned."

"Gee, I don't know and without the others here to agree or not agree to that percentage, I'll just have to wait until I see them the end of this week."

"You're going back so soon? I thought for sure you'd be here at least another week or so. What's your big hurry to get back up there?"

"We started to run low on basic supplies and since I knew how to get here and back there, they sent me."

"Now that we have a family to take care of, we'll have to ration what all of us will need for the rest of the winter. Unless of course there is a thaw and we would be able to replenish

193

any of those supplies at the fort. What supplies are you going to contribute Pete?"

"I planned on bringing more work clothes, most of the vegetables that we have stored in our barn, blankets, more feed and grain for the horses and mules."

"I'll have to do some planning on what I can spare given the current situation; Ned and I are leaving in two weeks, we'll bring most of it up with us."

"You're going up to the mine?" Pete replied, surprised by Todd's response.

"Yes, it is one of the few areas where I can train Ned about trapping; I'm going to do some more exploring and working in the mine for at least two or three weeks before I head back down here. It would be a good time for the Langstrom's to take a break from all the work they have been doing. When they get back here, they could go to Ft. Washakie for more supplies, weather permitting of course."

Ned returned and said, "I didn't see any tracks; it's eerie quiet down in the woods, but I guess that's from our 'guest' being around and all."

Pete asked, "What are you talking about?"

"Apparently, we have a cougar in our midst. It made it's presence known with tracks that I saw yesterday down by the pond and with it's "talking" during the night while everyone else was sleeping; However Mike and I knew he was around",

"Great, something else to stir the pot, so to speak. It gives me the willies."

"Well join the two of us and by the way, I haven't had the chance to tell the Thompsons. I'd appreciate it if neither of you did either. I need to talk with her this morning. I don't want them any more scared than they already are."

Both Ned and Pete replied, "No problem!"

"Ned, I want you to show George and Mary the barn and keep them occupied while I talk with their mother."

Todd knocked on the doorjamb and Mrs. Thompson let him in. "I need to talk with you Mrs. Thompson, but first I have arranged for Ned to show your children around."

"George, Mary, I want you to go out to the barn and see Ned while I talk with Mr. Morgan."

"Okay, mom." The children took their leave and Emma said, "Can I get you a cup of coffee?"

"Yes, ma'am, one sugar and some condensed milk will be just fine."

After she handed him the cup of coffee, she took a seat, Todd sat on the hearth and said, "It's nearly impossible to get y'all to the fort because of the snow. I know you're missing your husband, but I miss my wife who is with child and our daughter. For the time being, I have a solution that I think will be of benefit to both of us. I would like you and the children to stay here at the ranch throughout the winter months. I frequently go trapping and tending to other property that I have up in the mountains. Just knowing that someone would be here at the ranch and be able to do the chores would solve some of my problems. I need to train Ned how to trap and tend to my other properties; I can't do that from around here. The four homesteads have all agreed that we won't hunt or trap any animals on our homesteads, unless they become a nuisance. Do you think that you'd be interested in my proposition?"

"I guess it depends on what chores you'd want us to do."

"I'd need you to collect the eggs from the chicken coop two or three times a week, feed the chickens; you'll need to put the horses that we don't take with us out into the corral daily, bring them in before nightfall and get them settled in their stalls. They all need to be grained, given water and hay daily. I need the snow paths that we currently have to the barn, outhouse, chicken coop, and over the bridge to the front of the property shoveled out if another snow storm comes through here and lastly, the stalls that the horses use, need to be cleaned out every day. The manure and straw mixture need to be shoveled out the back door of the barn onto the manure pile."

"I've been a housewife and other than taking care of the children, growing a garden, feeding and caring for the chickens and chopping wood, my husband did all the heavy labor."

"You could learn to do the other things, couldn't you?"

"I guess we could. What about provisions?"

"Right now we are pretty well stocked. We have meat in the cache, vegetables in the barn, staples over in the corner and I have some out in the barn, as well. We have enough feed, hay and straw for the animals from now till the end of spring."

"What about water?"

"We don't use a pump because we have a stream that, so far, has never frozen over and with all this snow around, you can melt it down."

"The only clothes we have are what we brought with us on the horse and that isn't much. How would we have enough to last us four months?"

"Ned and I have purchased new clothes recently, and if you're a seamstress, you could make them fit you and the children. We can share what we don't actually need of the store-bought clothes and from the deer skins, we can make other clothes."

"You can make clothes out of deer skins?"

"Yes, I was taught by the Indians last summer how to do just that."

"What about Indians?"

"We haven't had any trouble for quite awhile and the Indians that we know are friendly and helpful."

"What about wild animals?"

"Right now there is a predator in the area and before we leave in two weeks, we plan on killing it. Speaking of that, when either you or the children go outside to take a walk, make sure one of us is within shouting distance just in case you need us in a hurry."

"I'd like to talk with the children before I give you my answer."

"That's fine, we aren't going anywhere except to hunt for a turkey or two. Tomorrow is Thanksgiving and we plan on celebrating it. By the way, does your son know how to shoot a rifle or shotgun?"

"Richard was just beginning to show him, Why?"

"I thought if you'd let him, I would take him with me when I go hunting this afternoon for those turkeys."

"I think he'd like that."

"By the way, do you know how to use a hammer and nails?"

"Yes."

"I have a bolt of muslin and if you're willing, you can cover the walls in the cabin, cut out for the door, two windows and around the fireplace."

"I've never heard of that before."

"Where I worked before, we did that and it made the bunkhouse nice and warm from fall to spring. It keeps out the drafts between the logs. I'll bring it over when I come to get George; you can rearrange the inside of the cabin to suit your needs so that it is more comfortable than the way I had it. Excuse me while I get something from under the bed," he retrieved the bottle of whiskey. "Good for drinking, but mostly it's good for injuries and cuts, kills the germs."

-37-

"Great shot George! Now all we have to do is get one more and we'll be all set for tomorrow," Todd said, delighted that George did so well.

"My pa never let me use the shotgun, but he did show me how to use a rifle. He never told my Ma though. I guess he thought she'd worry about me knowing how to use it at a young age. Where we lived in Indiana, we had a lot of deer on the farm we were living on, but the best I'd done back there was a yearling buck."

"Heck, that's pretty good, when I was a youngster like yourself, I missed the first time I went out with my pa and my brothers. It took me several more times after that before I shot my first deer. You say you lived on a farm in Indiana, why did your Pa want to move?"

"Well, my ma told us that pa was in the war and while he was away, the sheriff came and said that he hadn't paid his property taxes. She had thirty days to make good or he'd come back and kick her off of the property and sell it. My ma pleaded with him to not kick her off the property and told him when my pa got back, he'd pay the back taxes and make everything right. He didn't get back right away cause he fought for, well you know, the other side of the conflict. When

199

other folks in the area found out about that, they forced us out of the county and called him a traitor. He wasn't a traitor Mr. Morgan, he just did what he thought was right at the time; he's always been a hard worker. Rather than explain to everyone why he fought for the south, rather than the north. He heard that out west you could get a piece of land, work it for five years or so, and it would be yours free and clear. We set out and almost got over the mountains, but had to turn back because the snow already blocked the pass. My folks hoped that they could get back to the fort at least and we'd ride out the winter there and try again in the spring. The wagon hit a rut in the trail and we busted a wheel, but without some help, my dad didn't have the strength to fix it. He decided that he'd go for help while we stayed with the wagon. It started to snow and ma was afraid that we'd get snowbound and without much food, we'd be dead by the time he got back. She made the decision for all of us to take the other horse and go find someone who'd be able to help us in our predicament. The rest of the story you already know."

"Good to know. I see yet another gobbler over by that windfall. If you are quiet, I do believe that you'll be able to get that one also." George edged, ever so carefully, quietly and when he knew he was in range, he fired.

Excitedly, Todd remarked, "Good shootin', now the fun part begins, plucking the feathers and cleaning them. Tomorrow, we'll roast them for our dinner."

* * *

"Well Pete, I think you've got everything that you need for the mine and I'm letting Ned go with you with the other

200

packhorse. He needs to get away from here for a while and get the lay of the land, so to speak, even though it's covered in snow, the exposure will do him some good. I'll be along in another week or so and we'll talk about the partnership when I get up there."

"I hope you get that critter if he's still in the area. That pelt will bring a good price come spring at the trading post. You will remember to bring what food you don't think you'll need for the Thompson's, right?"

"I will, don't worry so much. I wouldn't let my favorite miners' starve."

Pete led the way with a packhorse between him and Ned and the other packhorse behind as they made their way up into the foothills of the Teton Range.

* * *

Emma made the inside of the cabin very homey, more than Todd could expect given the size of it. She cut the muslin in such a way that at night she made sure it covered the drafty windows and door to keep in more of the heat given off by the fireplace; during the day you could roll them up and out of the way to let in the sunlight or fresh air in and have access in and out of the door. She put the bed opposite the fireplace on the north wall and with Ned's help, they built a single bed for George, made a third seat for the small table for them to eat on and a triangular cutting table to prepare meals on for the other side of the fireplace. They moved the bookshelf to the left of the fireplace and it still gave them plenty of room to move around in; they also had a chamber pot so that no one would have to go outside at night. Todd had rigged up

201

the smaller of the two tarps to cover the entire north wall from the northeast corner to the end of the porch to help cut down on the wind blowing against the stacked fire logs and the cabin. Todd and George shoveled snow up against it to keep it in place and in doing so, it added a bit of warmth to the bottom of the cabin. Ned had added a third row of split firewood before he left with Pete. Other than the chores that Todd had given them, they were in great shape while he'd be gone for a few days. Todd made it a point that tomorrow, he and Mike would be tracking the predator. Today, however, he wanted to finish the room up in the hayloft and get the muslin affixed to those walls and finish redoing the tack room to accommodate not just Ned, but the supplies that the room was intended for in the first place. While Mary was out front of the cabin playing in the snow with the dogs and her mother sweeping out the cabin, George decided to go up in the hayloft to see if he could help. "Mr. Morgan, it's me, George. Can I help you in any way?"

"If you want son, over on the far wall you'll see where we have stacked bundles of hay, it's become disorganized to say the least. Grab a pair of gloves over by the hook stuck in a bale and move them around so that we can transfer some of the hay in the pile next to the barn up here to the hayloft." The boy had certainly helped his father in the same manner many a time back in Indiana and he knew exactly what to do. Todd had only wanted to make the room in the hayloft big enough to hold his furs, but now since he was going to be sleeping up here he needed to make it bigger and have storage for his furs also.

* * *

Meanwhile in Lander, Marshal Murphy was trying to explain to Richard Thompson about trying to locate where his wife might be. "As I said, Mr. Thompson, I don't know what to tell you and until I ride up to Ft. Washakie and find out if your wife and children are there. There really isn't much you or I can do. You're unfamiliar with the territory and if you go off by yourself and get lost, there isn't anyone in a hundred square miles that can help you. I hate to be so brutally honest with you, but that's the reality of the situation."

"Well, if I am going to stay here for the winter, do you know of anyone who needs a hired hand and can offer me room and board; it's not that I don't appreciate the help that I have received here in town, but I prefer to pay my own way."

"Let me talk to a friend of mine, she may be able to use your help."

-38-

"I'll ask your mother, George, about you going with me tomorrow to track the cougar; but if she say's 'no' that's the way it has to be. I really don't want your mother and sister left alone while I'm gone. You're the man of the house until we can find your pa wherever and whenever that will be, understand?"

"Okay, don't ask her. I'm sure that before you go up-country we'll have a chance to go hunting again."

"If I show you how to frame a smoke house, do you think you could build one while I am up at the mine?"

"Yes, sir. I watched my pa build ours and I'm sure I can do it."

"Tonight, I'll make a rough drawing and show you where the lumber is."

The following morning, Todd said, "Mrs. Thompson, I should be back by nightfall, but if I'm not, please don't worry, I have Mike with me. I have enough food to last me for two days, my bedroll, kindling for a fire and my pistol and my rifle. I've left the shotgun; if you get in some sort of trouble, fire three shots in the air regardless of the time of day and I'll be back as soon as I can. I have instructed George in everything he needs to know while I am gone."

204

Using snowshoes, he started at the pond and followed a faint trail deep into the woods going southwest; Mike went ahead of him sniffing the snow for a trail. He was hoping that Mike wouldn't get too far ahead of him. Cutting a new trail, every hundred yards or so and making an arc back toward the southeast, yielded nothing. After several hours of doing the same thing, he brushed off the snow on a weathered stump and said to Mike, "We haven't found his trail yet. Maybe we got lucky and it's moved out of the area. He drank from his canteen, ate two strips of jerky and relieved himself before he headed northeast toward the Wind River when dusk overtook them. He made camp for the evening between two pines that crisscrossed each other with plenty of cover from the wind and drifting snow; he took the time to dig out under the logs finding rotted wood that would make a nice fire to keep them somewhat warm, and enough to heat a can of beans and a couple of biscuits. He pushed himself back into the crotch of the tree when he thought he heard a faint cry, like a baby crying, sending a shiver down his spine; Mike made a throaty growl. Todd said to the dog, "It's too dark for us to find it and neither of us want to get hurt or killed. We'll wait until morning to find his track. I need some sleep, you must "guard" for at least part of the night. After his meager supper, he set his blanket down, got on it and covered his legs with the other half of the blanket and got as comfortable as he could. Mike lay in front of him looking out into the blackness of the night.

* * *

Marshal Murphy said to Priscilla the next day as they were standing on the front porch, "I'd like you to meet Richard

205

Thompson, he's the man I told you about. Mister Thompson, this is Priscilla Morgan, she and her husband own The Parker House Inn and Stony Creek Ranch up near Bull Lake."

"Glad to meet you, Misses Morgan," shaking her hand. "Marshal Murphy has told me that you have some work for me to do around the Inn and some of the property that surrounds it."

"Yes, while my husband is up-country, I need someone who can make minor repairs to the house and barn; I also need trees cut down on two of our pastures and taken to the sawmill. If you think you can do that, I'll pay you $45.00 per month, plus room and board and you can put your horse with the rest of ours in the barn and out to pasture."

"I could, but where I come from work like that pays $60.00 a month plus room and board."

"Then I guess you should go back to where you came from. I don't know you or your work habits; the Marshal said you needed work and that's what I'm offering, take it or leave it."

"Thanks for your time, I'll pass and get work elsewhere, good day." He walked off the porch to where his horse was tied up and rode back toward town.

Tom remarked, "Well, I never expected him to turn down the work, especially from someone who doesn't have two nickels to rub together. You certainly offered him a fair wage plus room and board."

"Whatever happened to that young man that was in jail for disorderly conduct? I thought Todd had the idea that after he spent some time in jail and had time to think he'd make a good ranch hand."

"Funny thing, after I had him locked up for the four days in jail, which gave him a lot of time to think and when I told him he'd have to work off his fine, he said how much? So I told him $35, he took off his boot and emptied out a pouch with 20 double-eagles and gave me two of them and asked for the $5.00 in change. I saw him walk over to the livery, saddle up his horse and ride south. I haven't heard hide nor hair about him since."

"Well, I guess Todd figured him all wrong."

"I guess so. Is Beth here?"

"She's in the kitchen, do you want me to get her?"

"No, I'd like to surprise her. Tomorrow night she won't be available to help you with dinner, I am taking her out to dinner at the Wind River Inn. I have something to ask her."

"Is it what I think it is?"

"Could be, you'll just have to wait until she gets home tomorrow night and see." He left with a smile on his face; Priscilla was smiling too.

* * *

"Well Ned, you can see how big this country is when it's covered in white, now just picture it in green, then brown and white again, that's the three seasons up here."

"I always thought that there were four seasons?"

"Maybe where you grew up there was, but up here, there are only three colors, white, green, brown, so there are only three seasons."

"If you say so."

"I do. Do you like working for Todd?"

"Well, he is pretty straight forward about what he wants done, but there are times that I can't read him. He's distant and mysterious at the same time; there are other times when he is the most genuine person I think I have ever met I just don't know how you can be two people in one."

"I know what you mean, he suckered the three of us into getting homesteads, two of which he already had paper on. He had some shyster lawyer from Lander transfer the papers from him to Gus and me. Now they are our responsibility to develop, but if they were still his and he couldn't develop them, he'd lose everything. It takes some balls to get out of something like that and still keep a straight face and pretend he's your friend."

"Is that how you look at him, as a cheat?"

"You summed him up nicely not only a cheat, but a traitor to the cause."

"He'd give you the shirt off of his back; matter of fact, he has taken good care of you. Take last week for instance, he could have said to you, stay at your own place and feed yourself. But he didn't, he just shared our food, friendship and took care of everything."

"You don't understand kid."

"Oh, I think I do." They continued their ride toward the mine in silence.

-39-

"Well, Mike, I think that he is far off; maybe too far for us to track him in a single day. Might take close to a week to finally break his trail. If I hadn't made a promise to take the rest of the supplies up to the mine, I would be packing supplies for you and me to track him down, regardless of how long it took. We've been walking straight north for the last five hours and still no sign only sounds every now and then. It's like he's baiting us to come get him. He just lures us further and further north. I don't give up easily and we've been gone a good two days already. We need to go back to the homestead and get ready for our trip up to the mine."

* * *

"Mrs. Thompson, I am confident that while I am gone you will be able to take care of yourselves. Ned and I should be back in a couple of weeks or so."

"We'll be right here when you get back Mr. Morgan. You be careful." Emma replied.

"Remember, Mike is not to follow me; I want him here with you. He'll protect all of you to the death, if necessary, but I

209

prefer that he be alive when I come back. I'm taking the new dog with me. He needs the training that I gave Mike. I don't think that cougar will be coming back this way, but on the off chance it does and if Mike gets his scent, make sure you restrain him. George, remember what I said about the guns. For distance, use the rifle with the long grain bullets; use the shotgun for short distances; shot for turkeys and small game, slugs for varmints you want to kill in a hurry. Do not take any unnecessary chances. I want to see all your smiling faces when we return."

With that said, Todd reined to the left and rode over the bridge with the young dog in front of him on the saddle as they went toward the Tetons with the mule in tow.

After Todd left, George said to his mother, "I've got to get started on that smoke house so I'll be in the barn putting the frames together. If you need me, just holler."

"I'll be showing Mary how to get in the chicken coop and gather the eggs, feed them and to make sure she latches the gate when she leaves."

"I see that Mike is still lookin' for Mr. Morgan; I guess we should just leave him be, he'll come back to the cabin when he's good and ready." Mike was looking deep into the forest, and watched what sends shivers down a man's spine. It was walking slowly through the forest toward the Tetons, as well.

* * *

"Mom, I want daddy back in time to celebrate Christmas with us."

"I know you do Megan, I want him home too and I am sure he wants to be here with us, as well. Marshal Murphy did say that he hadn't stayed at the fort during the storm, but he was at his friend Joe's cabin for a few days until he could get back to Stony Creek. So at least we know that he was alright about a month ago."

"Is Beth going to marry Marshal Murphy?"

"He did ask her when they went out to dinner a few days ago, and she said 'yes', but she hasn't told me when. I would guess it'd be either the spring or early summer before they get married."

"Will I still be able to call her Beth or will she have a new name?"

"You can always call her Beth and you can call Marshal Murphy, Tom, but only after they get married."

* * *

After a few miles, Todd had put the dog on the ground and said, "Come" to it. After he had ridden at least ten miles, much like he would during the fall or the spring; the young dog had grown tired from all the walking so he picked her up once again and put her in front of the pommel and over the shoulder blades of the horse like he'd carry a newborn calf as he had done when they left the ranch. The dog would get used to walking great distances; it just took time to toughen up the pads on its feet. The snow was starting to get deeper the further they went. A trail had been cut through the snowdrifts and even though it was slow going, it was easier than forging a new one. He made camp off the trail in a grove of aspens with a rock wall behind him and a wide-open space in front. He found enough dried timber to make a fire for warmth and cooking. He had a feeling that something was watching

211

him, but couldn't see anything around the site and hadn't seen anything on his back trail, either. It was just one of those feelings that you got from time to time. He made ready the camp, got enough snow packed into the coffee pot for melting down into a few cups of coffee, heat the biscuits and jerky for supper. Then he'd do a first watch, a quick nap, a second watch and another quick nap. The horse and mule were tense, but not agitated enough where he had to stay awake throughout the night. They were a team, or at least they had been in the past. It was good to get back on the trail with all of them together again.

He made it through the night, no sounds, no problems with the horse or mule, but he was still tired, riding all day and keeping watch most of the night. And when the new dog guarded, he still slept lightly, enough to come awake should the dog start a throaty growl, but she didn't. He felt if he got in at least ten miles today that would be good. During the night a light wind had come up, with more clouds. He said to the dog, "New storm a comin', I can feel it in my bones. We best make it to the mine before it does though or it'll take us an extra day or two."

* * *

Pete said to the Langstrom's upon his arrival, "Ned came up with me, so we'll need to put him somewhere where he can sleep and he can eat with us. He is supposed to get the lay of the land."

"Ned," Turk said, "Welcome to the frozen north. We are going to put you under the wagon where you'll be sleeping and when Todd get's here he'll be joining you. We'll be having supper soon, so put your horse in our makeshift corral, get yourself situated under the wagon and then come over to the fire pit."

After he left to do what Turk suggested, Pete said to his partners, "Greenhorn, he has no idea how tough it is up here, he'll find out in a hurry. Ned was getting on my nerves on our ride up here."

"Oh, give him a break, he hasn't been in the wilderness for as long as we have and he's curious is all." Gus remarked.

"You were a greenhorn once yourself Pete. Don't be so judgmental about people." Turk added.

"To each his own. Todd should be here by the end of the week. After he get's settled in, we'll show him what you've accomplished in the mine, we can talk about our partnership again. Maybe by then, he'll agree to the original 70/30 split that I offered him. Sometimes he's a stubborn cuss, but business is business, and that's what we're discussing. It's nothing personal."

"He is stubborn, I'll grant you that, but he is a reasonable man and if I could convince him to just sell the mine to us, he wouldn't have to worry about it ever again. I'll work up some figures and we'll ask. It certainly won't hurt to try." Turk replied.

-40-

"We should send Ned out and see if he can bag us another deer or an elk before we run low again." Pete replied.

"That's a good idea 'cause I'm getting a feeling that we're in for another storm tomorrow or the next day for sure. I never thought I'd say this but I'm getting tired of winter. We have at least three more months to go before we can see green again." Gus remarked, agitated.

Ned had taken to walking nearly every day to get the lay of the land and looking for tracks. Today was no different, but in the distance, he thought he saw an animal stalking something. *To far to get a good clean shot.* He continued trudging through the snow and eventually came to the trail that he and Pete had used to get up to the mine, making it easier to walk. As he came around the bend he saw a horse, mule, and a person walking next to it along with a black and white dog trailing not far behind. He also noticed behind them another animal, stalking them. He took aim and pulled the trigger; Todd heard the whistle of the bullet as it passed him and thought to himself, *is that hunter blind?* The bullet just grazed the animal, causing it to flinch. Ned knelt and chambered another shell, a .58-grain cartridge this time and fired again. The bullet whizzed past

214

Todd, only this time, it hit the mark that Ned was aiming at just behind the eye into the brain and shoulder. The cougar tumbled head over heels, dead. Ned got up and continued down the trail and said, "Good to see you, boss."

"You crazy fool, can't you tell the difference between a horse and an elk, you nearly killed me."

"Oh, I wasn't shooting at you, I was shooting at the critter who was stalking you, just down the trail there," pointing. Todd turned around and saw a tawny colored animal and said, "It couldn't be, and not all this way to just get me or the dog."

"Couldn't be who?"

"Remember back a couple of weeks when I told you there was a cougar somewhere near the ranch."

"Yeah, but you don't think that's the same one do you?"

"I'm not sure. It could be another one. Mike and I went to try and break his trail just a few days before I left to come up here. He taunted both of us, but we never did break its trail. It just kept luring us further and further north. I'm guessing it could be him. Seems unlikely that a cougar like that would track a man all that way, though."

"Well, he'll make a nice pelt for trading, won't he?"

"Yes, he will. Tell you what, you take the mule and "your" dog and go up to the mine. I'll go and put a rope around it and drag it close to camp. We can skin it out later and use the insides for bait for some of our traps, starting tomorrow."

"Sounds good to me, but the Langstrom's and Pete are going to be disappointed that I didn't get an elk."

"Don't worry about them, we'll get an elk soon enough despite the fact that it's going to snow either tonight or tomorrow."

After he arrived in camp, he's greeted and Gus said, "Well, I hope you brought enough grub and extra supplies to last us awhile?"

"I did and a few comfort foods for your dining pleasure, like canned peaches, beets, stewed tomato's and green beans from my root cellar."

"I suppose you'd like to see what we've done down in the mine," Gus remarked.

"I would, but could we wait until after I get some sleep. I got very little of it on my way up here. If you'll just point me to where I'm sleeping, I'll be out of your way." They showed him the underside of the wagon that had been cleared out and fresh hay had been put down. They took the time to wrap a tarp around the bottom and banked snow against it so that it didn't blow open in the wind, making it a comfortable place to be.

"Now what?" was the first question out of Pete's mouth?

"Now what, what?" Turk responded.

"I suppose we'll have to wait until he wakes up in God knows how many hours before we get answers to either a partnership or a buyout."

"What's your hurry, it's not like he's going anywhere."

"I just like things settled is all."

"You know, ever since you got out of the hospital, your personality has changed; you're not the friendly, happy-go-lucky person we used to know. In the past, you'd wait until the grass would grow an inch before you'd ever speak. Now, you just want to get it done yesterday and you're a might testy, too." Turk responded.

"Tough shit! If you don't like the way I am, then you can buy me out too. I'll go to where I wanted to be in the first place, rather than being stuck up here in this God-forsaken place, shivering my ass off every minute of every day."

"Pete, slow down, no one blames you for a change of heart and we'd all like to be someplace else, but this gold strike is big and it will make all of us rich, richer than even our mine. So just settle down and let things come about naturally."

After a few tense seconds, he replied, "Ok, Ok, I'm settled."

* * *

Thompson as he has become known around Lander, found a job cleaning up in a saloon on the outskirts of town making almost half of what he was offered to work at the Parker House, but that was his choice. There were times when he got so drunk and no one wanted to be around him. The owner, who was a southern sympathizer, knew that he had fought at the Battle at Hartsville[5] in Tennessee and said to him one day,

---

5   The 39th Brigade, XIV Army Corps, was guarding the Cumberland River
    crossing at Hartsville to prevent Confederate cavalry from raiding. Under
    the cover of darkness, Brigadier General John H. Morgan crossed the
    river in the early morning of December 7, 1862. Colonel Absalom B.
    Moore, commander of the 39th Brigade, stated in his after action report,
    that Morgan's advance had worn Union blue uniforms which got them
    through the enemy lines.
       Morgan approached the Union camp; the pickets sounded the alarm,
    and held the Rebels until the brigade were on the battle line. The fighting
    commenced at 6:45 am and continued until about 8:30 am. One of Moore's
    units ran, which caused confusion and helped to force the Federals to
    fall back. By 8:30 am, the Confederates had surrounded the Federals,
    convincing them to surrender.
       This action at Hartsville, located north of Murfreesboro, was a
    preliminary to the Confederate cavalry raids by Forrest in West Tennessee,
    December 1862–January 1863, and Morgan in Kentucky, December
    1862–January 1863. Result(s): Confederate victory.

"You know you're okay when your sober, but when you get drunk you're of no use to me or yourself. I hired you because you fought for the gray. I was a southern sympathizer, too. I've started a new life after I moved out here and no one knows of my past associations. I know it's hard not having your woman around, but remember you left them to fend for themselves in a hostile environment; if they were lucky enough to find shelter, you'll find out one way or another come spring if they are alive. You're going to have to live with your decision and get yourself together. I'm going over to Henderson's and have them give you credit so that you can get yourself some decent clothes. When you're sober enough doing the job I hired you for, come back, otherwise your fired. You've got to find a way to control your drinking?"

"Go fuck yourself and the horse you rode in on. I drink to forget what I've done and it's none of your damn business."

"It is if you want your job back."

* * *

During sleep, Todd thought about Priscilla, Megan, and the new baby and about the promises he made. *'I won't overdo it anymore; I'll take care of myself so that I won't get so exhausted. I'll delegate more.' Right now though, I'd give anything to be back in Lander with them. Here I am up on this mountain worrying about gold, trapping, and cold temperatures, eating out of a can and pissing into the wind. I could be back in Lander eating off of china plates in a warm house with people I love and they love me back, working on building up the property there and not exhausting myself. What was I thinking?'* He woke up in a cold sweat and found the dog was lying at his feet; Ned was fast asleep at the

218

other end of their makeshift sleeping quarters. Peeking out from under the tarp to see if it was day or night, he couldn't see a thing. The storm was raging and there was nothing he could do. He propped himself up against his saddle, pulled the wool blanket up higher on his chest and thought about what he should do regarding the mine. *If they are thinking of a partnership, I'd do a 70/30 split just so I won't have to come up here and work it; or maybe one or all of them will just want to buy me out. I'm sensing that this mine is actually worth quite a bit because of all the work they're putting into it; I'd take a $100,000 and not a penny less. I know its worth that much based on what the metallurgist said, and the samples proved that.*

Ned woke and said, "Have any idea what time it is?"

"I haven't got a clue, its pure white outside and you can barely see your hand in front of your face. I'm guessin' the storm started sometime after I went to sleep."

"Yeah, it started just after dinner two nights ago. I made sure the horses and mule had a blanket over them and I got them as far up the draw as I could. I was so glad to see you. Pete is wearin' on my nerves. There are times when he's a real pain in the ass. I hate to say this since I don't know him all that much, but he has such a negative attitude."

"His attitude changed after he got injured. I think he blames me for his injuries, but it would have happened regardless if I were around or not. He was at the wrong place at the wrong time."

"Do you think we'll get any trapping done while we are up here?"

"It depends; you've been up here about a week. Have you been able to walk away from camp?"

"Yes, nearly every day. I don't know a damn thing about

mining and I didn't want to be in the way, so I took to walkin' and lookin' around."

"In your walks, what tracks did you see in the snow?"

"Some wolf maybe three miles north of here; closer to camp I found rabbit, I think weasel or something like that, bobcat, fox, and of course, elk. There are plenty of elk just over the ridge to the northwest about a mile or so. I found hundreds of horses in a valley about five, six miles northeast of here. I also found a few beaver lodges in two ponds to the east about two or so miles."

"You did good. Do you know how to set a snare trap?"

"Yes, My pa showed me how when I was a youngster. If we didn't shoot a deer for food, rabbits and squirrel's were all over the place. If you cook them right, they are mighty tasty."

"Well, later today or tomorrow, once the snow stops, you're going to make fifty snares for rabbits and martens. Then I'm going to show you how to set the steel traps that I brought with me for fox, wolves, maybe even a bobcat or two. The day after we set all those traps, we're going to see how good you are. Whatever we trap, we'll split 50/50 come spring when we sell them at the trading post; the cougar pelt is all yours.

-41-

"Megan, you were crying in your sleep, what's wrong?"

"I want daddy back here with us. It's just not fair. All the other children at school have their daddy, but I'm the only one who doesn't."

"I know how you feel, sweetheart; I want him to be with us too and I'm sure he'd rather be here with us, than up-country. I can't wish him here and we'll just have to pray that he is alright and will get back to us as soon as he can, safely."

"Okay, but I still miss him."

"Come here and we'll snuggle and later after you and I wake up again, we'll go downstairs for breakfast. I have to do some shopping in town later and we'll make a day of it. We'll go to lunch and afterward we'll go over to Henderson's for some new fabric. I want to make some more baby clothes, a new dress for you and a new dress for Molly and then we'll get an ice cream."

"That will be fun, but ice cream, it's so cold outside, how about a hot chocolate instead?"

"Whatever, you want."

* * *

"Ma, I'll go out and get some eggs while you and Mary get dressed, then we can have breakfast. I'll check on the horses while I am out there and see how Mike is doing. Can I bring him inside when I come back?"

"That's fine with me son. I'm sure Mr. Morgan has him sleep inside when he's here, but I feel better knowing he's in the barn with the horses, at night. That howling last night must be wolves. I sure hope they leave us alone."

***

Meanwhile, up-country, the cooking area was under the tarp, so that they could at least have coffee anytime of the day when they wanted it. Now that the snow had stopped, Todd and Ned could dig out and make their way from under the wagon over to where the campfire was. Todd said to the Langstrom brothers and to Pete, "I feel so much better after that sleep. A nice hot cup of coffee and a biscuit or two would do me wonders right now."

"Get it yourself; none of us are going to wait on you." Pete snapped..

"I guess Ned was right, you are a pain in the ass. What's gotten into you lately?"

"Sorry, all this snow all the time gets me agitated; would you like to see the mine?"

"Right after I have my coffee and biscuits. Ned, why don't you skin that cat and hang the insides up a tree for use in our steel traps later today; after that, make up about 25 snares and go northwest about a mile or two and set them; come back and make 25 more and go southeast and do the same thing. I have some business to conduct and when I've finished talking we'll get together and set the steel traps; Pete, I'm ready when you are, let's go see the mine."

They walked over to where a covered entrance had been built over the shaft that lead down to the mine floor. They climbed down the ladder and Pete said, "Once you get used to the light it isn't as dark as it seems. We've put lamps up every few feet so that you can see where you're going." Todd was impressed with all the work they had done in shoring up the sides and roof for about 300 feet or so. Pete continued, "We take turns, chipping away at the 'floor' where the gold seam is, then we take a break and someone else comes down to work. We've been at this for at least three weeks, working 16 hours a day. We have quite a pile of gold and granite rocks over there on the other side of the ladder, pointing. What we have done in the past at our mine is to bring it to the surface and chip out the gold from the rocks and put it in burlap sacks. We throw the remainder of the rock chips in a pile. We are undecided whether to do the same thing here or simply take them back to Gus' and do that work there. Course now, that's impossible because of all the snow, but come spring, that's what we'll do."

"I can honestly say I had no idea about all the work you had to do to get at the gold. Me, I'd just as soon sit by a creek, and sift sand and get some dust or flakes here and there. I'm guessing that it's time to do some serious talkin' about the mine and when the three of you want to take a break up top by the fire, let's talk business."

"Fine by me; Gus is up top already probably taking a short nap because it's his turn next to relieve Turk. I'll get Turk; he's probably ready for a break anyway. Let's say twenty minutes."

"Twenty minutes it is."

"Well, gentlemen, let's get down to business," Todd said to

the three of them as they sat around the campfire.

"We want to find out what your thoughts are about the mine?" Turk asked.

"When Pete came back to Stony Creek, he said the three of you were interested in a partnership. I said it was the best news that I had heard since getting married. He offered me a seventy-thirty split and I said I had to think about that. I've given it quite a bit of thought and countered his offer with a sixty-forty split because at the time, I had thought about contributing a share of the labor. After I got up here, I tossed that idea out the window, so to speak, and thought that seventy-thirty wasn't a bad deal after all, but I have another proposition.

Before he could say another word, Pete responded angrily, "Always a but! Why can't you just settle for what we're offering and let that be the end of it?"

"Well, Pete, if you'll give me a chance to finish what I wanted to say, maybe you wouldn't have been so quick to shoot your mouth off. So sit down, shut your mouth, and listen! If you want to buy me out, I'm open to that idea also."

"Well, you are thorough," Turk replied. Gus and I always thought you were that. I told the others just the other day that I'd work up some figures for a buyout. We all agreed, after some discussion, that we'd like to offer you $170,000.00 for the claim and the gold in the mine; you'd have trapping privileges any time you wanted to come up here, also."

"Can I take a few minutes to digest that?"

"Sure, take all the time you need. We knew you'd have to think about that proposal." Todd got up and walked around to the other side of the wagon, so that none of them could see him, *I wonder if I can get them a bit higher, course it's more than*

I was willing to take in the first place. I don't want to be greedy, but I know the value and quality of the gold seam and they don't; I really shouldn't take advantage of them like that, but what the heck it's worth a shot. I think I'll ask for a nice round figure like $500,000.00 and see what they say. After he relieved himself, again, he washed his hands in the snow and dried them on his buckskin pants, and walked back to the fire pit and sat down. "I'm interested in a buyout for $500,000.00."

Sputtering, Pete responded, "You're out of your fucking mind if you think we'd pay that kind of money. There is no way in hell; why you don't even know how much gold is in that seam."

Turk said, "Now we'll have to think about your counter offer. Give us some time to discuss it and we'll give you an answer by supper."

"I thought you would have to think about it." Todd figured they would come back with a smaller counter offer. *I'll ponder it for a few seconds before I agree and tell them it's a deal. I don't want them angry with me and after all, they've done a hell a lot of work to lay in timber, reinforcing the sides and roof, and put lantern hooks every fifty feet., They saw something in there and they know it's valuable.* "While you're palavering, I'm going to go set some traps and I'll be back in a few hours."

Pete replied sarcastically, "You do that, make sure one of those traps doesn't accidently spring back on you. Do be careful!" The other two looked at Pete and said to him, "Shut up and stop being a pain in the ass."

Todd doesn't know what's come over Pete, but he definitely doesn't like his attitude. He took the mule and the two sacks of traps, figuring that he'll be out of their way for at least two or more hours; he yelled for Ned to join him.

After Todd and Ned were gone, the three men turn toward each other and Turk says, "Look, he thinks he's getting a good deal and we all know that we have dug the shaft through the hill to about 300 to 400 feet; the seam didn't quit. We also know that there's the beginning of a second seam and I'm willing to bet the further we go there's even more gold. We won't know that of course until we keep tunneling, which is starting to get easier the farther we go. I'm bettin' that we've hit the mother lode and if so, we'll be rich beyond our wildest dreams. $500,000.00 seems like a lot, but compared to what were going to get, that's chump change. Are we all in agreement that it's a deal?" Pete is about to object, when Gus says, "Look Pete, if we don't agree to what he's asking, he might just tell us to get the hell off his property and then we won't have anything."

Throwing his hands up in the air, Pete replied, "Fine, write the damn purchase and sale agreement and all of us can sign it. He can put his signature or an X and when he finally gets to Lander he can have it recorded. We'll give him a letter to take to McDavitt & McIntosh that will state the transfer of the claim and mine to us and to transfer the $500,000 from our account over to his."

Three hours later he and Ned made their way back to camp. Gus and Turk motioned for him to come join them at the campfire. Todd said to Ned, "You can start skinning the martens we caught and I'll come join you just as soon as I am through talking with Gus and Turk."

After looking at his two partners one more time, Turk said, "We'll pay you the 500,000 dollars for the mine and ten acres that surround it. You'll have trapping privileges, as well. All three of us have signed a Bill of Sale. All we need is your signature, witnessed by Ned. Once you get to Lander, you'll have to take the documents to August McDavitt for the transfer of the claim over to us. Once it's recorded you can go to McDavitt & McIntosh and have them transfer the money from our account to yours."

"I accept your generous offer. Let me get Ned to witness my signature." Once signed, they shake on it and Todd said, "I think a shot of whiskey in our coffee is as good a toast as we can have out here in the snow, don't you think?" He produced the bottle from his shoulder sack and poured a bit in each cup on top of the coffee. They clink their cups in a toast and drink, all have a smile, except Pete.

-42-

"**M**erry Christmas!" Todd said a week later as they were sitting around the campfire eating breakfast.

"How do you know if it's Christmas?" Pete asked.

"When I left Lander a couple of months back, I started to keep track of the days, counting off every seventh day so that I knew when Thanksgiving was. I had intended to go back to Lander to be with my family for a few days, but the storm came along and disrupted my plans. You were there, Pete, we, celebrated Thanksgiving at Stony Creek and I knew that Christmas was about four weeks after that. I was checking my calendar yesterday and it's been 30 days since Thanksgiving, so we are as close to the actual day as it can be."

"That makes sense to me," Gus replied; "me too," Turk replied.

"Does that mean we get to share gifts and have a day off from working the mine?" Pete questioned.

"I guess whichever one of you is the boss can make that call. Ned and I are taking the day off and getting some much needed sleep. After we've rested, we are feasting on grilled elk, green beans and roasted potatoes and for dessert we are having canned peaches. I already gave Ned his present and

228

mine is waiting for me in Lander."

"What no presents for us?" Pete asked, being sarcastic as usual.

"I gave you, your gift already."

"What gift?"

"The gold mine."

"That wasn't a gift, that was a business transaction."

"And a mighty fine business gift it was too. Why I even wrapped it in "white" paper. Now if you'll excuse me, we'll see you gents in a few hours after our Christmas nap. Oh, and by the way, y'all are invited to Christmas dinner."

Todd crawled under the wagon, the dog wagged her tail, and he scratched behind her ears as she sat down between the two of them. "Really, a day off?" Ned asked. "By the way, what is my gift?"

"Your gift is, well your gift is…"

"Cat got your tongue?"

"No, the cat is dead remember," Todd, replied with a little laugh. "I was just trying to figure how to say it so that you didn't try to jump up and down while we were under the wagon."

"Well?"

"I am making you my foreman at Stony Creek and it comes with a raise to $60.00 a month."

"I don't believe it; have you gone loco?"

"No, I've watched you work through some tough situations, take on responsibility and learn how to deal with people. Up here under the harshest of conditions, you've shown me that you're ready to take on a more important role at the ranch. I was more than pleased with how you set those snares and the results were good despite the deep snow. I counted eighteen rabbits and twenty martens, it won't always be that way. Then I showed you how to use the steel traps and you got six red foxes and of course you already had the cougar pelt. You've shot four elk, not just for the food that we can use, but the hides will bring us a good price, too. Now remember, I said we'd split the trapping except for the cougar."

He continued, "At dinner tonight, I'm going to suggest that Gus and Turk go back to their homesteads, they need a break and you're going with them."

"But, I was hoping we would do some more trapping."

"I'm staying here to do some tracking and trapping. I'll be along two weeks after the two of them come back up here."

"What kind of tracking?"

"You said when I got here that you found a large herd of wild horses about five or six miles from here. I want to find out if they are the same herd I saw when I first came up here. If they are, I want to make plans to do some horse hunting come next summer. I'm inviting my friends from the Sweetwater Ranch and Timber Creek Ranch to come help me. I want to build up my horse holdings and that's the only way I know how to do it without it costing me any money, except paying for food for the help in capturing some of those horses. I don't mind sharing the herd with them for free help."

"Now, I understand why you're the boss." They laughed and each said to the other, "Have a nice nap. Whoever gets up first will wake the other."

After a fine dinner, stories and laughter, a playful snowball fight ensued before they all retired to their respective sleeping quarters. Todd said to Ned, "I think tomorrow morning, you and I will see if we caught anything else. I'm not going to do any beaver trapping this year. Last year the pelts brought in such a small amount of money that it's not worth all the effort to catch and skin them. We'll see when we turn in the other furs if the value for them has gone up. If they have, we can trap them during the fall." Ned yawned and could barely keep his eyes open before saying, "I am too sleepy to stay awake; goodnight."

Todd decided that now was a good time to write a letter to Priscilla.

Dear Priscilla and Megan,

This letter is long overdue, but under the circumstances, getting it to you was going to be a problem no matter when or where I wrote it. I want you both to know, that I have a burning desire to be home with you. Ned, Pete, Gus, Turk and I just celebrated Christmas up here in the Teton foothills. The weather is cold and beautiful, just not as beautiful as it would be if you were both here with me. You are my sunshine; there isn't a day that goes by that I don't think about you and wonder what you are both doing, Oops, I mean the three of you. If things go the way I hope, I'll be back by the middle of February, right around Valentine's Day. Priscilla, I have a Valentines Day gift that you won't believe.

Please say hi to Beth, the boarders, and Tom Murphy. By the time this letter get's to you, hopefully, I will be back from a trip up near Bull Lake to do some trapping for a week or so. Do be careful, especially with the cold weather. I am assuming you are getting the snow that we are getting up here; we watch the clouds head south toward where you are. I need to get some sleep; we have a long day ahead of us tomorrow.

Megan, I hope you are doing well in school and are drawing more pictures. Please give Molly and Jasper a big hug for me.

All my Love, Todd xoxo

PS - Tell Tom that we have a family at the ranch by the name of Thompson; if a Richard Thompson comes through Lander, let him know that they are being well taken care of. We will get them to the fort just as soon as there's a thaw or when spring gets to the high country.

* * *

He folded the letter and put it in an envelope that he had brought with him. He addressed it to Mrs. Priscilla Morgan, Miss Megan Parker-Morgan, Parker House, Lander, Wyoming. He kept the other envelope that Turk had given him; he must keep it in a safe place until he can get to Lander.

The following morning he said to Ned, "Before you leave tomorrow, I am going to give you two envelopes. You'll need to guard them with your life. The first one is a letter to my wife. If someone goes to the fort for supplies, take the letter to the Quartermaster with instructions that the first reliable that is person going to Lander take it with them and deliver it. Secondly, the other envelope is very important for my family and me. Do not keep it on your person once you get back to the ranch. Get one of the empty mason jars from the root cellar, make sure it is dry on the inside and put the envelope in it; seal it and put it somewhere that only you know where it is. If anything happens to me, make sure that only my wife gets it."

-43-

Turk, Gus and Ned headed out with a wave; Ned took up the rear with the mare loaded down with the furs and some of the meat from the last elk kill. The Langstrom's couldn't wait to get back to their homesteads; they both promised they'd be back in two weeks and be well rested.

"Pete, I'm going to set some wolf traps today, do you want to come along?" Todd asked.

"Naw, you go ahead and do that trapping thing, I'll just hang around here and straighten up the campsite, get the rest of the elk meat up in those pine trees next to the wagon and gather some more deadfall."

"You be careful while I'm gone. I'm leaving the dog with you for some added protection. I may not be back until late afternoon." He gathered up his steel traps, put them in a burlap sack with some meat for bait, his Sharp's, a canteen of water, a couple of biscuits and some jerky; he strapped on his snowshoes and set out for the area that Ned had told him about. He came to a stream about four miles from camp and decided to rest for a few minutes. He took out his compass to get a bearing.

While he was studying the terrain, he saw the palomino

233

stallion he had seen last summer making his way through the deep snow heading towards an opening between two huge boulders. He held back enough so as not to spook the horse and went into the cave. Since the ground was hard he had no way of knowing which way the horse went. Standing there he noticed several drawings on the cave walls depicting men with bows and arrows, horses, cattle and little children running away from a bear. *I wonder how old these drawings are?* He thought and continued to walk toward the sound of rushing water deep within the cave and saw another opening just beyond it. He made his way there and looked out upon a valley with steep canyon walls covered in pine, a long winding river that seemed to stretch forever, but no stallion and certainly, no herd of mustangs. *Well he came this way I'm sure of it. If I had more time I would follow the narrow trail to the bottom of this gorge and find which way he went and see if the herd is with him.* He made a mental note on how to get back here in the summer, guessing that if this is where the horse herd is they will have a rough time rounding them up. While he was looking out over the valley, the palomino actually had gone down another one of the paths inside the cave, drank from a spring-fed pool and waited for the man to get to the end of the path he was on. Using the gushing water to mask any sound, he walked back out of the cave and galloped away. Todd turned around thinking he heard something but dismissed it and went back out the way he came in. As he was walking along, he noticed several wolf prints and a bobcat print in the powdery snow. He went about setting his steel traps well off into the forest, masked his scent and covered his tracks. He'd check for results tomorrow afternoon and walked back toward the mining camp.

* * *

Ned arrived at Stony Creek, tied his horse and mule off before walking over to the cabin. He knocked on the cabin door. Emma Thompson wondered who could be out here in the middle of nowhere. "Who's there?"

"It's Ned ma'am, I just got back from up-country and I wanted to let you know that I was here."

"Please come in, is Mr. Morgan with you?"

"No, he's still up at the mine, he'll be back in about two weeks. I came back with the Langstrom's."

"You didn't by any chance see any other rider's out there did you."

"No ma'am, just lots of snow. I know you're worried about your husband, but you'll just have to have a little faith that he found shelter just like y'all did."

"It's just so hard not knowing whether he is alive or dead." A tear formed in her left eye and said, "The children miss him, too."

"Well in a few days I will be going to the fort to get supplies. I will make it a point of checking in with the quartermaster and see if by any chance your husband came to the fort and if he did, where he went too if he isn't there. I also need you to make a list of clothes, sizes would help, food or anything else that you might need."

"Thanks for being so kind to me and the children."

"We, Mr. Morgan and myself, appreciate all the help that y'all have been doing since we've been away; I hope Mike wasn't a bother."

"No, but he must have stared into the forest for at least two days after Mr. Morgan left. He didn't eat or drink, before he finally came back to the cabin and lay down on his blanket. Mary coaxed him to eat something and drink some water. We were worried about him."

"You just can't predict what an animal will do, but he's like that anyway; he's terribly loyal to Mr. Morgan."

* * *

"Megan you can be mad at daddy all you want too. I wish he had come home for Christmas too. We got snow on Christmas Eve and on Christmas day, which means they got it before we did. Just look out the back door by the barn and see how the wind has whipped up the fluffy, white snow against the sides of the buildings that you like to play in so much. It's nearly five or six feet deep in places. Now picture yourself up where he is and I am willing to guess that the snow drifts in places are at least that high and probably higher."

Crying she says, "I'm sorry mommy; I just want him home safe with you and me."

"I know how you feel. Why don't you write him a letter and I'll have Beth give it to Marshal Murphy. The next time he goes up to Ft. Washakie he can leave it for him."

"Okay, I'll write it now." Priscilla sighs and wonders about where he is and what he's doing. She prays every night that he'll be safe and get back to them, soon. Megan's letter is short and sweet.

Dear Daddy,

Molly, Jasper and I miss you. We had a nice Christmas, but it would have been better if you were here with us to open all the presents. I especially like the new dress, blue jeans, and the boots. I don't know what I'm going to do with them, though. Mommy and the "baby" misses you a whole lot too. I am going outside to play in the snow; do you get a chance to play in all the snow up where you are?

Love You, Megan

* * *

As Todd sat next to the fire drinking his coffee, his thoughts quickly changed. *If my calculations are correct, it's been nearly three weeks since the Langstrom brothers left for their homesteads. I can see why if you stayed up here for any length of time you'd go stir crazy. I've done what I came up here to do and I need to get back down to the ranch. I'm hoping that if there is a lull in all these storms, I can make my way back to Lander and my family. I have so much to do to get ready for, the horses that I'm getting from Jonathan; getting the pastures cleared for the summer roundup; I need to show Ned what he needs to get done at Stony Creek, as well. Wishing that they were back isn't going to make it happen, any sooner. I guess I'll do a little prospecting on my own at one of those streams I found yesterday near the beaver ponds."*

Later that afternoon as he was getting his supper, he noticed that Pete seemed more agitated than usual and finally, he said to Todd, "You know if you hadn't come along we would have all gone on to California like we planned to do."

"Where's this coming from?"

"I'm just sayin' that we had plans and now everything has changed. I wanted to leave just as soon as we had enough money in the bank; I want to live where it's warm; where I can feel the sand on my feet and go swimming in the ocean, not where I have to chop wood, dig in the dirt, freeze my ass off and most of all, not be with the likes of you. I don't need traitors and cheaters in my life."

"Who are you calling a traitor and a cheater?"

"You!"

"Are you blaming me for what happened to you?"

"Damn right I am!"

"I think what happened to you is terrible. I brought those bastards to justice not only for you, but also for all those other people who were killed, maimed, threatened and for all the property and animals that were destroyed during their wrath. You would have been hurt even if I didn't get to know you. They weren't after me. I didn't know a single one of them. Most of them were carpetbaggers looking for a free ride and when they couldn't get it, they turned mean and took it out on innocent folks, like you. When they came to my homestead, I stood up against those bastards and told them to get the hell off of my property and not to come back and if they did I'd be waiting for them.

"Now as to the War of Northern Aggression, I guess it depends on what side you were on. I lived in the south and defended what I thought was right. You lived in the north and you thought your side was right; so guess what Pete, no one actually won. Good, poor, rich, black, white, men, boys, women, babies were either killed or injured; farms and fields destroyed; towns burned to the ground all in the name of justice. While slavery was outlawed and that was a good thing, all the other parts of the war left a big hole in the Union. It will take decades for all of us to work together to make us a stronger Union. Now, you also say that I'm a cheat. I didn't cheat anyone. I had fully intended to use every single acre, all 640 acres of it as a ranch, but it was more than I could handle realistically by myself. When Turk found out that you could get 160 acres through the Homestead Act and after five years of working to develop it either as a ranch or farm, it was yours. He went and found that the section next to mine was still part of the program, so he signed up for that one. I told him that I wish I hadn't asked for four sections, he said that maybe you and his brother would want to get in on the Homestead Act. He asked the lawyer that I used if there was a way of having my name taken off of those two sections and have them signed over to you and his brother. Mr. McDavitt contacted the territorial governor's office to find out how that could be done and when we met with him at Ft. Washakie, he had his answer and the property was transferred from my name to yours and Gus'. Since, you're so pissed off at just about everything; I can see why you'd like to change your life and start over again. More power to you!"

"I don't know what to say."

"Don't say another word and by the way I'm leaving tomorrow for my ranch. I expected that the Langstrom's' would've been back here by now. If I see them along the trail, I'll tell them to hurry back here, so that you can get on with the rest of your life.

Goodnight!"

-44-

"Where in the hell is that boy anyway. I make him my foreman and now he thinks he can go and do anything he damn well pleases," Todd said as he looked down at Mike, who just sat there looking back up at him.

Ned on the other hand had been tending to a stump fire in the back pasture. When he saw George dragging in a deer, he offered to help him get it back to the barnyard. As they were walking down the lane with the dead deer between them, he saw Todd and waved with his free hand. As they got closer Todd said, angrily, "Been wondering where the hell you were. I've been looking and hollering everywhere for you. I need to show you what needs to be done around here before I leave for Lander. George knows what he's doing when he goes hunting for food to feed everyone back here. You don't have to go with him."

"I was tending to those fires that you and I started yesterday on the left over stumps and brush. I saw him coming in from one of the hay fields dragging the deer behind him. I thought it would be easier if I helped him get it here."

"I forgot about setting that fire yesterday. We need to be looking at the area I want cleared for the new pasture. I need to mark the trees that we want to leave and those that need to be cut down."

"George," All of a sudden Todd changed the subject, "I didn't get a chance to thank you for the job you did on the smoke house. Once you get that deer skinned and the meat cut up, you can put it in there and fire it up. We'll see how well it's built after we take them out in a couple of days and before we put the meat up in the cache. Make sure the deer skin is scraped as clean as you can get it before you role it skin side out and placed up in the loft."

"Thanks Mr. Morgan; I enjoyed building it; I'll get the deer meat cut up and put it in the smoke house in short order."

"Ned, come with me!" Todd said once again, sounding angry. "Sorry, I got upset with you a few minutes ago, I forget sometimes that I say things and don't remember that I did. Once we get the trees marked, I'll start cutting them and you'll have three months to finish everything, including the fencing and a pond full of water. Once I leave here, you'll be in charge. After the ground dries out enough, I want you to take Mrs. Thompson, George and Mary to Ft. Washakie in the buckboard so that she can find out what happened to her husband. While you are there, you can stock up on whatever supplies you need at the same time. I should be back by the end of April and we'll prepare the skins for trading. I plan on taking them to the trading post at the fort, but don't be surprised if Hanson tries to low-ball you. He does it with every tenderfoot trapper, but you're going to have to grow a set of balls bigger than his and not back down from a price you think is fair."

Ned replied, "I'm getting a headache with all the things that I've got to get done between now and then. Do you think I could ask Mrs. Thompson if it's all right for George to help me do some of the work? I'd gladly give him part of my pay."

"Tell you what, I'll ask her and if she says yes, I'll hire him to work part time, until he has to leave with his mother when you take her to the fort."

The three of them worked from sun-up to sun-down for the next week, felling trees, moving them to a spot where George could trim the branches, stacking the useable ones for posts, the rest for either firewood or to be burned on top of the vegetable gardens; then came the stump pulling. The ground was hard because winter wasn't ready to give up just yet. The horses strained against the harness to move the stubborn stumps and those that wouldn't budge no matter what they did were left until spring got there. Next, they laid out where the posts would go in once the ground thawed, piling ten to twelve per pile. They decided to make them longer than the other posts, just in case they wanted to add a third strand of barbed wire. Tomorrow, Todd was leaving for Lander and he said to Ned, "Remember when I gave you the two envelopes?"

"Yes and I did what you asked me to do."

"I need that mason jar that you put away."

"Let me get it for you." He went over to the outhouse, and lifted up the wooden seat where they sat and in a corner, wrapped in muslin, sitting on a shelf, away from any moisture, was the jar that he had hidden for Todd.

"I'm not sure I should ask why you put it there."

"Who would think to look in there?"

"You do have a head on your shoulders, don't you?"

"I always thought I did."

Todd's last words were, "See you the end of April, be careful; work hard." He ambled down the lane toward the back gate,

Mike running ahead of him. He, Misty, Mike, and Moon's horse made their way south along the ice-encrusted sides of the bold creek toward Ft. Washakie. Joe's place came into view and he thought, *"I'll stop in, share a meal before I have to move on."* He rode up to Joe's cabin; Joe's wife came out and said, "Joe not feeling well, he sleep, eats in cave. He tells me to stay away. You may camp down by stream if you want."

Todd decided that it would be best if he just went to the fort and said to her, "Tell Joe I stopped in; I hope he feels better soon."

At the fort, he made it a point to stop in at the Commander's Office. Upon entering, the young private who usually had a bad attitude, was wearing corporal stripes and said, "Mr. Morgan, it's good to see you after all these months. You helped me to look at life differently and I am grateful. You were right, once I got my act together and stopped acting like a fool, someone would take notice. I just got my second stripe a week ago."

"Good for you. Is the Colonel in by any chance?"

"You missed him by a day. He went to Lander and from there he was taking the stagecoach to Casper. Should I tell him you called?"

"Yes, just tell him I'll see him the end of April." He walked over to the trading post to see Hanson.

"Hanson, where are you?"

"Mr. Hanson is no longer here," came a woman's voice from the storeroom in the back of the building. She walked out front and said, "My name's Maud Bricker and this is my store now."

"Please to meet you Mrs. Bricker, my name is Todd Morgan."

"I'm not a misses, just call me Maud, everyone else does."

"Okay Maud, last spring when I traded my furs, I had a $900 credit with Hanson and I have used about $250 of that since then, leaving me with a balance of $650. Are you going to honor that amount?"

"That's why Hanson is no longer the owner of the trading post. He was overcharging prices and skimming the difference in what was on the books, except you. He didn't charge you more than what the actual product cost was and the balance on your credit is +/- $650. I never did find out why he didn't overcharge you like he did the others."

"Because he knew if I caught him at it again, I'd disembowel him on the spot."

"You're serious aren't you?"

"You bet! I never trusted him and I made such a stink

the first time I traded with him, I guess he figured I meant business."

"Well now that I know, what do you want to charge?"

"I only need a few things this trip; my ranch foreman may be in here from time to time. His name is Ned Hogan and I'd like you to extend him the same courtesy that you've extended to me. Will you be taking fur trades in the springtime like Hanson did?"

"Not this year. I don't know how to properly grade them. I haven't got a clue as to what the going price is per pelt, skin or fur. The closest fur trading establishment is in Lander, that's to the south of us."

"We'll take our pelts, fur and skins to Lander. I need to buy some things for my wife and daughter. I'll take ten yards of that calico cloth, a cowgirl hat for a 10 year old and 6 steel traps and that should do me for this trip. I also need a receipt with the total amount and what my new balance will be."

"She took about 20 minutes to do the calculations, and then told him that the total amount of his purchases was $24.50. That leaves your balance at $625.

"Good, that should last us through the remainder of this year. See you next trip."

"Bye Mr. Morgan."

With a wave of his hand, he was off for Lander. Arriving well past midnight, he decided to just go to the jail and see if they had an empty cell where he could sleep until morning. It wasn't customary for him to do that, nor was it for the sheriff's office to let anyone just come in for a nights sleep and leave in the morning. It had been slow most of the week and the deputy on duty knew him and said, "Sure you can sleep here, but in the morning you'll owe me for coffee."

"I'll be out of here by sunup anyway. I'm going to put my horses in the barn the sheriff uses. I'll be right back." He slept peacefully through the night and was gone even before sunup. Not wanting to wake Charlie who was sleeping in another empty cell, put two dollars and ten cents on the desk with a note, "When you get done with your shift, go to the café and have yourself a decent breakfast on me."

He stopped by Tom Murphy's office before he went home, but Tom wasn't in yet and thought to himself, *"Tom must be keeping banker's hours these days."* He saw the school wagon full of boisterous children pull away from the Parker House and as he neared the house he said to Mike, "Won't she be surprised when she get's home from school today; Let's go surprise Priscilla." He rode into the yard, took the horses into the barn, unsaddled Misty and removed the supplies and pack frame from the mare and told Mike, "Stay!" He put the new traps next to the saddle and took the packages he had bought for Priscilla and Megan with him. He scraped his boots on the side of the stairs and knocked on the frame surrounding the screen door. "Who is it?" Came a reply from a voice he wasn't familiar with.

"I just wanted to see the owner of this here property."

Beth came to the door and almost dropped the bowl of flour she was holding and said, "I don't believe it."

"Well believe it; where is she?"

"She's up in bed; do you want me to go wake her?"

"No, I want to surprise her." With that said, he sat on one of the steps on the back staircase and removed his boots before going upstairs. He opened her door and stared at her while she slept in her white cotton nightgown. Her head was resting on her down-feather pillows, with her feet propped up on another. He slipped out of his buckskin shirt and got in bed next to her as quietly as he had when he left months ago. He just starred at her face, so angelic it looked, her hair as smooth as a newborn's and it smelled like wild flowers. A strand of hair was laying on the bridge of her nose, so he blew it gently so that it would bother her, she started to swish it away with her hand and suddenly woke, turned her head to the right. She rubbed her eyes to make sure she wasn't dreaming, turned and put her hands on his scruffy face and gave him a long, long kiss; he kissed her back. "You have no idea how long I have yearned for you to be next to me in our bed. I just want to hold you and never let go."

"I thought about you every night and as I wrote in my letter, I would be here just as soon as there was a break in the storms. It's just two weeks later than I anticipated."

"What letter?"

"The last one I had Ned take to the fort about two months ago with instructions for the quartermaster to give it to the first reliable person coming to Lander. I guess there was no one to get it here."

"Did you get Megan's note?"

"No, I didn't."

"Well Tom was going to the fort and Megan was so mad at you that I told her to write you a note. I guess no one thought to give you that one either."

"Why was she mad at me?"

"Because you didn't come back for Thanksgiving, you missed Christmas and she wanted her "daddy" home no matter what."

"She'll be surprised when she gets home from school today, I guess. I will set a glass of milk on the table with a note that says, "Cookies are in the parlor, come get them." I'll be there with a plate of cookies for her. What do you think about that?"

"I think she'll drop the glass of milk." They laughed together for the longest time.

"I need to take a bath and get into some clean clothes, it's been awhile."

You mean I'm actually going to see your birthday suit again?"

"Which one, the before or the after?"

"Both, I missed both of you, but most of all I've missed my best friend."

"Well I don't know. I was going to give you a Valentine's Day gift, but I guess I'll just have to wait until after my bath. On second thought, I better ask the baby if its alright for the gift I want to give you first and we'll make that a Christmas present; the other gift that I have will be for Valentine's day."

"Take your bath first before you give me the Christmas gift, ok?"

"Your wish is my command." He slipped out of his long johns and socks while she watched. After he bathed and dried off, he quickly got under the covers. She was warm and wet as his touch was soft and caressing; they came quickly, lost in the throes of passion, trying to make up for the love and companionship of too many months separated. They held each other as he gently rubbed her tummy, and soon fell asleep in her arms. She gently got out of bed so as not to wake him much like he did before he left so many months before. As usual though, he looked exhausted. All the hard crease lines on his face, were a telltale sign of all that he'd been through. She put on her underclothes, her nightgown and went into the bathroom and washed her face, combed her hair, then slipped on a bathrobe and slippers. She quietly went out of the room and down the back stairs to the kitchen; she needed a strong cup of ginger tea and toast. He woke to find her gone and just laid there a few minutes before he got up and went to his dresser. Everything was as clean and orderly as it was the day he left 5 months before. After he got dressed, he looked in the mirror, borrowed one of her combs to comb his hair, "I've got to get a haircut and a shave before Megan comes home, if she see's me this way, she'll think a bear has moved into the house." He went downstairs and found Beth and Priscilla in the kitchen just finishing up their breakfast saying, "Is there anything left for an old man like me?"

Priscilla replied, "Old you're not! You just proved that a few hours ago." He blushed, she laughed. Beth hid her expression behind her hand.

"What do you want for breakfast?" Priscilla asked.

"What I'd like is a stack of pancakes a mile high and the largest glass of buttermilk you can pour me. You only get so many choices up-country. Eggs, sometimes bacon or shaved venison steak, potatoes left over from supper, hard sourdough biscuits or muffins if someone can get them to me more than once in 5 months."

"So what is my Valentine's day gift?"

"Why don't I say it's more of an 'our' gift."

He retrieved his saddlebags and took out the muslin wrapped mason jar; she looked at Beth and both of them looked at the jar. He released the seal and took out the envelope, removed the legal paperwork and then took out the letter for release of funds and gave it to her. She unfolded the letter and her eyes nearly popped out of her head and said, "Is this for real?"

"It's as real as it gets and after I go to town this morning, I'll get the legal paperwork taken care of with August and then you and I can walk down the street to McDavitt & McIntosh and get the financial part taken care of. Then you can go to every store in town if you want to and buy whatever you want. How's that for a Valentine's Day gift?"

"I'll have to send you away more often if this is what you're going to bring back for us." Beth was curious; Priscilla said to him, "Do you mind if I show her, otherwise she'll pester me until I do."

"Go ahead, but first put some pillows on the floor behind her just in case she faints." She gave the letter to Beth who sat down at the table, read it, looked up and said, "I don't know what to say, its, its overwhelming."

"While I'm eating my breakfast Priscilla, why don't you go take your bath, then we can go into town and take care of all this."

Beth asked, "Are you going to stop in and see Tom?"

"We can; I stopped by his office earlier but he wasn't there yet."

"He's been dealing with a man by the name of Thompson ever since the beginning of November; he probably was trying to get him sobered up. He can explain everything to you when he sees you."

-46-

Megan said goodbye to her friends as she got out of the school wagon and ran around to the back of the house. She thought she saw a dog's nose sticking out of the barn door. Rather than investigate, she went up the stairs and into the house. She set her book bag on the chair before taking off her hat, coat, and gloves. Saw the glass of milk and a single cookie, and didn't think much of it. She noticed a note in the middle of the table with her name on it, she opened it and read "Sorry, I didn't get a chance to make more cookies, come see me in the parlor." She finished drinking her milk and ate the rest of the cookie as she skipped down the hallway. Turning the corner she saw her "daddy" lying on the couch in the corner of the parlor, while her mommy was playing the piano. She couldn't believe her eyes and ran to where Todd was nearly tipping the couch over as she collided with him. "Daddy, daddy, you're home," smothering him with kisses. "Please don't ever leave me again." He held her in his arms for the longest time. Her mother said to them, "Is there room between the two of you for the two of us?"

Megan responded, "Not right now mommy," and went back to hugging Todd tightly, afraid he'd leave again. He gently put her over next to him on the couch and said, "Don't you think its time to let mommy and the baby come sit with us?"

"I guess so, but I'm sure that mommy had you part of the day while I was in school. She can have you again after I've gone to bed too." Todd looked at Priscilla and she back at him as they both stifled a laugh. The three (four) of them hugged each other.

At supper, John, Mabel and Edith were all glad Todd was back and during supper they asked how the winter was going in the up-country, what he had done, and other small talk.

John said, "I suppose now that your back, you'll be taking care of the horses at night?"

"Actually John, I probably won't have time. I thought if you're willing, you could still do it."

"I've enjoyed it, it makes working during the day more pleasant and I can't wait to come back here at night knowing that I'm doing something useful."

"It's settled then, keep up the good work. Mabel, Edith how have you been doing since I last saw you?" Taking turns they said what they were doing and where they worked. Edith said, "Are you going to be doing business with the new bank in town? I'm the Head Teller their now"

"What new bank?"

"Remember last fall after the banking scandal and you got the governor to lend $100 to everyone so that we could all survive until new arrangements could be made?"

"Yes."

"Well, McDavitt & McIntosh took over the failed bank and created The Wyoming Co-Operative Bank in place of it for everyone. Each customer gets one share ownership and can attend the quarterly and annual meetings if they so choose."

"I think that's wonderful. Priscilla and I will be in tomorrow to open up a new account with you."

"We will look forward to seeing you." With dinner finished, Mabel and Edith retreated to the parlor, where Mabel sat down at the piano and began to play; Edith picked up a book she had been reading and chose a seat by the fireplace. John excused himself and went up to his room where he changed his clothes before he went out to take care of the horses. Todd and Megan helped Beth clear the dishes; Megan helped Beth dry them as she had been doing for the last few months; Todd and Priscilla returned to the dining room, sat back down and he had another cup of coffee; she had ginger tea. He said, "I might just beat Megan to bed tonight after all the work I did today."

"Work, what work," she said with a twinkle in her eye. "I thought you rather enjoyed the 'work' you did today."

"Oh, I did indeed and I could get used to that kind of work. But after months of sleeping on the cold hard ground up at the Tetons or on a pile of hay in the barn after working 12-14 hours a day, I just wanted to make sure that where I lay my head down tonight is not all a dream. I just want to get to bed under your quilt and nestle my head on a down-feather pillow next to you and fall asleep."

"Sorry mister, but "daddy duties" come first?"

"What duties?"

"Making sure that Megan has brushed her teeth, gotten into her night clothes, said her prayers and have her daddy read her a book before she falls asleep with 'Molly'. Once you are finished there, you can get in our bed where her mommy and her little brother will be waiting for you."

"Ah, ha, there is no rest for the weary."

"Not in this house."

After he was sure that everything in the house was secure, he went up the back stairs and went to their bedroom, got out of his clothes and slipped into bed next to his wife, gave her a kiss on her forehead, said good night, turned over and fell into a deep, peaceful sleep. She snuggled close and kissed the back of his neck.

<h1 style="text-align: center;">-47-</h1>

After he'd been back for a few days, Priscilla became concerned about him sleeping all the time. Even when he was so exhausted and worn out from working too much, he had never slept this long. She had an appointment with the doctor and she'd ask him if there was anything to worry about. At her doctor's appointment she explained about Todd sleeping so much. The doctor replied, "Don't worry about Todd sleeping so much. In a young man such as your husband, it isn't uncommon for him to sleep for long periods of time especially if he didn't get enough when he was working. However, if he starts sleeping twelve to fourteen hours every day, let me know."

Todd wanted to start writing down what needed to be done at the "ranch" as he came to call it and then go over it with her; talk about finances before Megan got home. He had promised that he'd play with her, Jasper and Mike in the snow, something she had been looking forward too..

During lunch Todd said to her, "Depending on when I get a reply from Crusty, I'll need to make a trip to Sweetwater Ranch to pick up my horses. I wanted Megan to come with me. I also plan on asking John if he could take some days off, as well."

"How long do you think you'll be gone?"

"Not more than a week."

"She'll have to miss school."

"Actually, I planned it so that when she is out on spring break and she won't miss any school."

"Why do you want Megan to come along? She's never been away from here for more than a couple of days. I'm not sure it's going to be any fun for her?"

"Because I have a gift for her at the Sweetwater and I thought she'd like to see it there, rather than wait until I got back here."

"Why can't I go?"

"Don't you think that would be tempting fate? You'd be bouncing in the saddle and we don't want the baby to come any sooner than he has to, now do we?"

"You do have a point there. Can you give me a hint as to what that gift might be? A mommy should have some idea don't you think?"

"Not this time, I want Megan to show it to you when she gets back."

"Okay, she can go, but you've got to promise me you'll keep her safe and she won't be in the way."

"I promise and with John along, the two of us will make doubly sure she is safe and has fun too." After they got home, he changed into his work clothes; she needed to take a nap for a couple of hours. He went out to the barn and found Mike acting silly, and said to the dog, "What's gotten into you? Did you find my bottle of whiskey or something?" Mike just looked at him as if to say, "You keep me in this barn for two days and you wonder why I'm so giddy. I could go crazy chasing the same field mouse from one end of the barn to the other and back again."

"I think you need to run, let's go find Jasper and I'll take the two of you down by the river before Megan get's home." Standing in the road in front of the property next to Priscilla's, he looks through the trees that are stripped of their leaves and makes a mental note of where things are throughout the property, saying to himself, *I'll have to make a sketch of this later. I'll need to clear at least 80 acres, put at least half in open pasture and the rest in hay with a mix of buckwheat, alfalfa, and timothy on 20 acres and 10 acres in rye for variety. I'll order one of those new two-horse sulky plows, so we can plow two rows at a time, probably be able to get seven to eight acres done each day.* He was brought back to reality when he heard the dogs barking at something down by the river. He ran to where they were and saw the body of a man half in and half out of the water on the riverbank. He went down to check and see if the man had a pulse, he didn't. He said to Mike, "Guard!" He took Jasper back with him to the barn and tied him up. He put a halter on Misty and rode into town to find the sheriff or Tom, whichever one was available.

The sheriff came back with him and they hoisted the body up in the wagon the sheriff had brought and said, "I'll get doc to do an autopsy. I'll send a telegram with a general description of the man to the Wind River Township and another to the fort to see if anyone had been reported missing."

* * *

"Beth, have you seen my daddy?" Megan asked after she got home from school.

"I think he went for a walk with the dogs, I'm sure he'll be back soon."

"Okay, if he comes in the house, tell him I have to get my homework done first and then I'll be out to play with him and the dogs."

"I will; do you want your milk and cookies?"

"No, I want to get everything done so that I have plenty of time to play in the snow." First, she went upstairs to her room, changed into her play clothes and then came down the front stairs, sat at the dining room table and did her schoolwork. Todd came in the back door and said to Beth, "Has Megan gotten home yet? I was supposed to play with her today."

"She's in the dining room doing her homework. She said she had to get that done first, then she'll be out."

"OK, I'll be in the barn, she can find me in there." While he was In the barn, he looked around estimating what he could do to accommodate some of the horses and new foals he'd be getting; he went up in the hayloft to see how the bales were stacked, finding it in disarray, *"I need to get George down here to straighten this all out, but that won't be for another month. I guess tomorrow, I'll have to do it."* After he returned to the downstairs, he opened the doors at the back of the barn and went out into a small paddock, just big enough for foals to run around but nothing else. He went outside just as Megan was coming down the back steps; she ran to him, all excited, and he said, "You go find Jasper and Mike and hide. I need to look at the north side of the barn first and I'll count to 100 before I come find all of you." She ran to find the dogs; he walked toward the pasture first, around the back of the barn and over to the other side which in the spring and summer had bushes and brambles growing all over the place. He gets to thinking; *this is the perfect location for adding an addition to the existing barn.* He yells out, "96, 97, 98, 100 ready or not here I come." He found Jasper in the bushes on the side of the house right where she put him and told him to "stay"; Mike was more elusive; he kept changing where he was hiding as he watched Todd come look for him. Matter of fact, he got clear around the house and came up behind him quietly and barked, scaring the be-jeebers out of Todd who turned to scold him, but realized he'd been made and shooed him away. Now to find Megan, who was lying flat on her stomach on the porch, under the swing watching him find Jasper and then watching Mike scare him and continued to watch him as he walked around the yard checking behind trees, bushes and scratching his head saying out loud, "I give up Megan, where are you?"

"I'm up here daddy, can't you see me?"

"If I could see you, I wouldn't have given up so easy," he said laughing. She threw a snowball at him, it missed and he said, "So it's a snowball fight you want huh?" He lobbed several large snowballs in her direction as they splattered on the porch railing or the floor, splashing her with snow. She was laughing so much she wasn't watching where she was standing and fell off of the porch. He caught her just in time and they rolled around the snow, laughing all the time. "Megan, why don't you and I make snow angels for mommy and the baby?"

"Oh, that would be great daddy." He did one first; she followed. He picked her up so that there weren't any footprints and carried her to the backyard where he put her down, dusted the snow off of her and put the dogs in the barn. The two of them went up the stairs onto the back porch where Beth said, "before you come in this house, take off those boots and get the rest of the snow off your clothes, I don't want wet floors in here."

"Yes ma'am," they both replied.

"Yes ma'am," they both replied.

-48-

Priscilla had just come downstairs after her nap and saw the two of them standing in the hallway. Megan said, "We made snow angels mommy, come see!"

Todd put a shawl around her shoulders and they all went out on the porch; she stood in front of Todd. He had one hand around her waist and one on her shoulder, holding her close. Megan pointed over the railing to where they were.

Priscilla said, "They look lovely and no footprints either."

Megan looked up at her mother and said, "They were made by angels who just floated down for you and the baby. Why would there be any footprints?" Todd smiled, bemused, as she turned to see his face and said, "You're right, what was I thinking." Megan winked at Todd and they all went back in the house and got ready for supper.

Shortly thereafter, Mabel, John and Edith, came in the front door, shed their wraps or coats and hung them in the hallway. As they headed for the dining room, they all said in unison, "We wondered who made the snow angels in the front yard, one big and one small?"

Megan's innocent reply was, "by angels, who else?"

All of them couldn't help but smile. After dinner, they retired to their rooms while Todd, Megan and Priscilla helped

Beth clear the dishes.

Later Priscilla said to him, "I thought I heard horses and a wagon going down the road while I was falling asleep."

"You did. While I was out with the dogs this afternoon, they were down by the river barking. I went to see what all the commotion was about and I found a dead man on the riverbank. So I went into town and got the sheriff. He brought the wagon that you heard."

"How dreadful, was it anyone we know?"

"I've never seen him before. The sheriff said he'd send telegrams upriver to see if anyone was missing."

"It's so sad when someone dies that way."

"Please don't let it worry you. I'm sure the sheriff will get to the bottom of it sooner or later."

"Let's hope so."

"Now that you're wide awake, tomorrow morning I'm going into town to put up my help-wanted posters. I have got to get started on the new pasture and hay fields. I also want to get started on enlarging the barn; I'm making a sketch of what I want so that you'll know what's going on too. I was also thinking that we should redo the upstairs to make our living quarters separate from the boarders; they need their space and we need ours. What do you think?"

"I think your going in too many directions. Why don't you concentrate on getting the pasture and hay fields done first, then the barn and finally the upstairs? We have plenty of room to accommodate the baby. Beth and I decided to move the linens from our closet to the hall closet and make our closet into a nursery. It will hold a large cradle, rocker and changing table/dresser. Megan's room is right next-door on one side and the bathroom on the other side. Our bedroom is plenty big enough for what we like to do."

"I thought you told me more than once, that our love making was what got you into the condition you're in now."

"Oh, I did, but I didn't say that I never wanted to stop making love, now did I?"

"Come to think of it, you didn't, shall we?"

"No, I'm too tired tonight."

"You can't possibly be tired, you just got up from a two and half hour nap."

"Tell that to your energetic child growing inside of me and see what he says to you."

"Fine, I have to finish with my help-wanted posters and finish drawing my re-design of the barn anyway. I'll come to bed after I've finished and I won't wake the two of you either." After kissing her, he left and she went into the bathroom to get ready for bed; he went downstairs to the kitchen, got a glass of buttermilk and sat at the table making his posters, his barn sketch and the estimated costs.

* * *

Up-country, Ned was having a heck of time, even with George's help, in getting out a huge oak stump that sat in the way of the new pond.

"I can't just leave it here and have us dig around it. But then again, it would make a nice diving platform if we ever wanted to go swimming in the pond."

"We best get to chopping all the roots so the horses will have an easier time pulling it out, 'cause the way it stands right now they can't," George replied. After two days of struggle, the huge stump finally moved enough to where they could pull

263

it out of the way. As Ned looked down in the hole, he was surprised to see large rocks with gold flakes on them! He thought *if I didn't want this stump out so badly, we'd never have found this gold; I can't wait to tell Todd.*

"George, I think that for the time being, we'll just move a bit further south for the new pond. It was good that we got that huge stump out of the way though and I think we've done enough work for today."

After supper Ned said to the Thompson's, "If you'll excuse me, I need to go to bed, it's been a long day." He went back to the barn, made sure all the horses were settled in, the doors and windows were closed. He took a lantern back to the tack room, set it on a workbench, stretched, scratched his back as far as he could reach, turned the lantern off and crawled into his cot, exhausted. Ned's mind didn't "sleep" though. It was very active as he dreamt of all the things he could buy with all the money he was going to get from the gold.

* * *

Priscilla woke early to find that Todd was not there, *not again, he wouldn't dare,* she thought. A few minutes later he came in the bedroom from the bathroom with a washcloth held up to his nose, "I can't figure this out, I'm sleeping and thinking that I'm drinking something, but I don't like the taste. I wake up to find that I have a bloody nose and it's dripping down the back of my throat. I guess I better go see the doc later this morning."

"I'll go ask Beth, maybe she knows what's causing it. Why don't you just lie back down, keep your head back with the washcloth on your nose. I'll get dressed and go find her."

Shortly afterward, Beth came in the bedroom and said, "A bloody nose is not uncommon if you got in a fight, but knowing you that didn't happen unless it was a pillow fight with Priscilla, I'm guessing it's from being in the cold weather. When the air gets cold, it dries out the inside of your nose, the skin cracks and the tiny blood vessels can't take it anymore. I'd suggest using warm salt water and sniff it up your nose two or three times a day until the air gets moister. If it continues, you should see a doctor."

"Whew, I thought it was something really bad. I guess when I work in the hayloft later today I should wear my bandana."

"Good idea," Beth replied.

Megan got up for school and on the way past the bedroom door, she said, "I had fun yesterday."

"So did I sweetie, have a great day at school." Todd decided to stay in bed until the nosebleed stopped. A half hour later, Priscilla came back in the room and said, "You really scared me; I thought you had left again without telling me."

"I promised you I wouldn't. I don't want to be away from you, Megan or the baby, any more than you want me to be away."

"Are you going into town later this morning? I know you want to get your posters up.. Can I go with you?"

"Of course you can. Is there anyplace special that you need to go to?"

"Yes, I need to place a catalog order for a cradle and a new rocker for the baby's room. I already have the dresser, which will also be the changing table."

"If I was handy like my pa was, I'd build you a cradle for our baby, but when it comes to fancy furniture like that, I'm all thumbs."

"Well I like you just the way you are, you're handsome, intelligent, strong, and a good lover,"

"Just good? I thought I was great."

"Well, after this one is born, you can show me. Maybe we can go away after the baby is about six months old. Does that sound good to you?"

"Yes, and I'll let you pick where you want to go. Until the baby is born, what should I not do? I don't want to hurt you or the baby?"

"In about 6 weeks, I'll start lactating so that the baby can be fed after it's born,"

"You mean like a mother cow does for her calf?"

"Exactly like that, only her nipples are much bigger." She laughed. "Then the baby is going to start moving around to get ready to make his entrance into our world. The doctor told me the baby should be coming around the end of June or the beginning of July. I know you'll want to move our horse herd upcountry, but I'll need you here with me, so you'll have to put that off until at least six months after the baby is born. Will you be okay with waiting?"

"I will."

"What other plans do you have that you haven't told me about yet?"

"I guess when I figure them all out, I'll let you know. Why?"

"I'll have to have some secrets too."

"You wouldn't keep secrets from your husband would you?"

"I would."

-49-

He decided to take the surrey; it was just too cold for Priscilla to walk all that way to town and back. He would put one of the posters on the wall outside of the Cattlemen's Association office and another in the window at Henderson's. When they got there, he said to Joshua, "I have your horse blanket and pack frame out in the surrey. How much do I owe you for keeping it so long?"

"Not a thing. I knew you'd be back sooner or later; it's not like you were never coming back."

"With all the deep snow and one storm after another, I was beginning to have my doubts."

"By the way, the sheriff was looking for you."

'Thanks" as he walked out of the store. Priscilla was down at the telegraph office, placing her order for the items she wanted. It was as good a time as any to go see what the sheriff wanted.

Sheriff Hughes said to Todd when he walked in his office, "Remember that fellow we fished out of the river a few days ago?"

"Did you find out anything about him yet?"

"Not yet, but after we got him back to the undertaker's, we found this in his back pocket, handing Todd an envelope

267

I thought maybe you'd want it back." Todd looked at the envelope. It was the letter he had sent Priscilla over nine weeks ago that she never got.

"I might be able to help you find out who he is."

"From that envelope you can tell me that?"

"In a matter of speaking, I can. I sent this letter along with my foreman over two months ago. We were out trapping and I told him when he went to the fort for supplies to give it to the quartermaster. In turn, it was to be given to the first reliable person going to Lander. Now I know why my wife never got the letter. I would contact the quartermaster's office. They can probably tell you who it was given too and any other information about him."

"Thanks, I'll let you know what I find out."

After Priscilla finished placing her order, she came out and found Todd sitting in the surrey just outside the office. He said, "Let's take a ride out to Hiram Bender's and after that, I'll take you to lunch at the Wind River Inn. How does that sound?"

"I'm getting hungry already. You know we are getting to be regulars there. I guess the food agrees with all three of us," she said as she patted her stomach.

"I should see Tom afterwards. Remember when I said that I sent you a letter a while back and you said you didn't receive it?"

"Yes, I remember." He pulled the water soaked letter from his pocket and told her where the sheriff found it.

"In this letter is information about a family that has been staying at the ranch until a spring thaw happens and we can get them to the fort. I also asked that you let Tom Murphy know who they are and if he sees or hears about a Richard

Thompson to tell him his family is alright."

"Tom came to me about four weeks ago and asked if I could hire him as he got separated from his family and needed work. I explained to him what I needed done and how much I could pay. He turned the job down, because he wanted more than what I was paying. I heard later he was cleaning the spittoons and the outhouse at the 'Dusty Boots Saloon' on the south end of town, took less than I offered and has turned into a drunkard."

"That's too bad. Maybe I should go see this man and let him know about his family."

"Tom has been trying to keep him out of trouble by having him do extra jobs around the jail and between him and Sheriff Hughes, it seems to be working; they also let him sleep it off when he gets really drunk so that he doesn't hurt himself or other people. They were hoping that come spring, they would hear some news about his family."

"Well, I've got the news they are seeking; maybe Tom should go with me to tell him. I'll drop you off at home after lunch. I'll saddle Misty and go back and see Tom. I told Megan I'd play with her again this afternoon outside, but I'll be a little late in getting back."

"I'll just have her work on her piano skills."

Arriving at the Bender farm, he asked Hiram if the ski runners were finished.

"Yes, but it's a might late to be using them now."

"I know, but I'll have them for next year. How much do I owe you?"

"$37.50." He paid for them and with Hiram's help got them loaded in the last seat of the surrey and tied them down tight. They waved as they went down his lane to the main road, turned left and went toward the Wind River Inn.

Todd said to Priscilla after they were seated at the inn, "I hope to be able to hire two men at least. If it's alright with you, I'll pay them out of the Co-op account."

"That's all right with me. Is that the account that were going to use for paying our bills?"

"Yes, I thought it would be easier than taking money out of the private bank account. I'm hoping that we can put whatever income you get from the Inn, my trapping, which I am sharing with Ned, and any other money that we get throughout the year into the Co-op; we'll leave the other one for our investments. Do you like the idea of me paying off Parker House with the money that I get from selling the furs later this spring?"

"Right now, I could see where that would be a benefit, but let's wait until you sell them and see how much you get this year from them before we make that decision."

"I was doing some figuring the other night and between the two properties, we need about $4700 a year to cover all of our expenses and wages and another $1000 for incidentals. Right now we have $2600 in the Co-op from the old account that I had at the Lander Bank & Trust; you had about $1700 in there also. I hope we'll get about $3900 from the trapping which I have to split with Ned and that should give us a total of $6300 give or take a few dollars. I also wanted to tell you that I did some panning up at a stream near the mine and got one small bag of dust and flakes and I had a satchel full of the rocks from the mine before I decided to sell it to them. I haven't had it assayed yet, but I'm hopping it brings in about $8000 or $9000 on top of everything else. I was going to put $7000 of that in the private account, also."

"Well that would certainly set us for quite awhile and I wouldn't always have to worry about whether I'm going to have enough boarders to cover my expenses. I think that Edith is going to rent something closer to work. She has been dropping hints for several weeks now. "

"She has the room in the front of the house over the parlor, right?"

"Yes, what are you thinking?"

"Well if she does decide to move out, let's not fill that right away. I want to take some measurements and see if we join our bedroom with the room she's in, we would have a separate parlor for ourselves. We could rearrange the current rooms, make a bigger bathroom, all on the second floor with little to no inconvenience to the two remaining boarders."

"I thought we agreed that we wouldn't do anything on the house until the pastures are done and enlarge the barn, first."

"A fellow can dream, can't he?"

"For some reason, dreams turn into realities and with everything that's going to be happening over the next four or five months, we have enough to worry about."

"Okay, I won't turn that dream into a reality until you say so."

-50-

"Mrs. Thompson, why don't George and I take Mary for a walk, so that you can have some alone time for awhile?"

"That would be just great. How long do you think you'll be gone?"

"Well, I was planning on going over to the Langstrom's and Byrd properties like I'm suppose to do every couple of weeks and then we'll walk back through the forest. It should only take about an hour or so."

"You'll make sure Mary will be safe, won't you?"

"We won't let anything happen to her." The three of them walked past the fencing and down the lane with the dog running ahead of them, toward Turk's. Turk hadn't cut an opening out to the country road that was slowly taking shape as more and more homesteaders were settling on their parcels. He put up a gate when he was doing the fence line, but he never finished putting in the lane to the house that he was building. Ned said to Mary and George, "I usually just go through the gate he put up where he is running his fence line, but it's more fun to go just a bit further and cut in through the forest between his property and the next property. Then you climb over the corner fencing and go through the woods to where his foundation is that he put in during the fall."

Just as he was about to climb over the corner fence, a bullet misses his head by inches and he said to himself, *now I know how Todd felt when I shot that cougar that was stalking him. I wonder who's shooting at us; all we're doing is climbing over the corner fence.* A man on a swayback mule came out of the brush and said to them, "You're trespassing on my land."

"Well sir, this property belongs to Turk Langstrom, but if you think we were on your property, we're sorry. I'm Ned Hogan and these are my friends. I check on the property that we are on now every couple of weeks and I occasionally just climb over the corner fence so that I can look over this part of the property for the owner."

"Where'd you say you came from? I thought I was the only homesteader up here in these parts?"

"No sir; Todd Morgan actually settled on the first homestead a couple of miles down the road; Mr. Langstrom has this one, his brother is in-between the two of them and a friend of theirs is on the back side of both of the Langstrom brothers."

"A Todd Morgan, you say?"

"Yes, sir.

"Does he also have some property in Lander?"

"I don't know anything about property in Lander. Why?"

"Oh, I was just wonderin' is all? I don't take kindly to strangers, but if you say your just checking on the property and I'm guessing it's to keep squatters off, am I right?"

"You're right. In the past we've encountered carpetbaggers, squatters and skunks of all shapes and sizes and we're just tryin' to keep it peaceful for everyone that lives up here is all."

"I'd suggest the next time you find a better way to get on Mr. Langstrom's property, you hear me?"

"I hear you loud and clear, I won't be coming close to your property again. Could I tell my boss your name?"

"Tell him my name is Parker."

"Is that your first name?"

"Last."

"Thank you, and again, we are sorry for disturbing you." Ned, Mary and George made their way through the forest and came out in an opening where Turk had put in his foundation. They walked past the foundation and through some hedgerows before find some deer resting in a grove of aspens. Upon hearing them approach, they quickly scattered.

"I'd like to know why when you're hunting them, they aren't in a group like that, just resting," said George.

"You got me; I've never come upon them in a forest where they are just resting," New replied. They continued to walk towards where Pete's homestead is, but see or hear nothing. But Pete hasn't put anything on the land yet so Ned doesn't expect anything to be amiss there. Despite all the snow they've had, they cross over a dry creek bed and walk up the divided fire line that was put in by Todd and Gus after the forest fire up past Bull Lake almost a year ago. George asked, "Why did they do this, it seems like a waste of time, to me?"

"Well, Mr. Morgan was caught in a forest fire that nearly consumed the area where he had been trapping. He made it out to watch it burn down through two draws right to the lake's edge and then it just smoldered for days. He decided that he'd take the time to cut a clearing all the way from the front of their two homesteads clear through Mr. Byrd's place to the back line of the homesteads. They pulled the stumps, plowed the soil under, and planted wildflowers and grass, so that if a forest fire ever came this way, there would only be green grass, not kindling for the fire."

"Still seems like a waste of time."

* * *

"Todd, what are you going to do today," Priscilla asked.

"I thought I'd finish restacking the hay bundles in the loft; then later this morning, I'm going to walk the acreage next to the barn to see how far it goes back and make notes on what I find. I also thought of taking the dogs with me so they would get some exercise. Why?"

"Beth and I are going into town and we won't be back until early afternoon and I thought maybe if you were going to be around, you would keep an eye on the place, for us."

"I can do that while I am up in the hayloft, I'll open the doors on both ends so that I can look out every now and then. Are you expecting someone?"

"Not really, I just have a feeling that someone is coming here today."

"Well when you leave, just make sure the front door is locked, so that if anyone comes they'll have to come into the barnyard and the dogs will let me know. While you're in town can you get me some Cherry-wood pipe tobacco? I'm almost out."

"Sure, just one pouch or do you want me to get two?"

"It's better to buy just one at a time so that it stays fresh".

Priscilla got ready to leave while Todd headed for the barn to do his chores. He led the horses and the mule out into the pasture as well as the dogs by way of the double-dutch door and closed the bottom half leaving the top open and proceeded to open all the windows. As Beth suggested, he tied his bandana around his nose and mouth so that the dust didn't cause his nose to dry out and bleed again before he headed up the stairs to the hayloft. Around 11 am he heard the dogs barking and went to the hayloft door that looked down on the barnyard. He saw a tall, thin-set man in a black topcoat, tan colored Stetson, and shinny black boots with silver spurs riding up on a magnificent black stallion. Todd yelled down to him, "Can I help you?"

"I was looking for the owner of the property."

"I'm one of the owner's, what can I do for you?"

Taking a notebook from the inside of his coat pocket, "I am supposed to talk with Priscilla Parker."

"Give me a couple of minutes and I'll be right down." He dusts off his clothes, undoes his bandana and walks down the stairs, and wondering what this is all about. He comes out into the barnyard; the man has gotten down off of the stallion and tied it to a post by the watering trough. Todd walks over to him and says, "I'm Todd Morgan, who might you be?"

"My name's Whitaker, John Whitaker. I represent the people who owned this place before it was sold a few years back to Mrs. Parker through the Lander Bank & Trust Company. How might I ask did you become an owner of the property?"

"Well, I married Mrs. Parker."

"Is she home?"

"Not right at the moment, but whatever you have to say to her, you can say to me."

"Not to be rude Mr. Morgan, but I came to here to talk with her and what I have to say, does not concern you."

"Whatever concerns her concerns me."

Whitaker realizes that it's pointless to continue the discussion, "I'll go back to town and come back here at 3 pm." He mounts and rides out of the barnyard.

* * *

The Langstrom's and Pete Byrd were having a time of it when Gus says, "Using a pick against this granite is like hammering nails into a brick wall. Pete, are you sure we can't use a small amount of dynamite to loosen the rocks and hard earth around where the seam runs along the floor bottom?"

"We'll, I'm not a hundred percent sure. We have never encountered a horizontal gold seam before. It's always been in the walls or along the ceiling. I guess if you're game, we can try a small amount back toward the entrance and see what happens. We probably should all be topside just in case the walls or roof of the mine cave in."

"Well nothing ventured, nothing gained. The worse that can happen is the whole hill will just collapse into what we've already dug and the best we can hope for is it'll crack open the seam and we'll be able to retrieve the gold easier," Gus said hopefully.

Turk responded, "When do you want to do this?"

"Let's do it in an hour. It'll take me about 40 minutes to set the charges for 50 feet and I'll need you to throw down 2 bundles of the hay, one of those wool blankets, a hammer and box of nails. Once I get everything in place, I will run a 100 foot wick up to the top and one of you can light it."

"That's fine with us," the brothers respond in unison.

* * *

Todd was in the kitchen having something to eat when Priscilla and Beth got home from shopping. He told her that John Whitaker, a representative for the people who owned the inn before her wanted to talk with you, alone. He wouldn't discuss anything with me. Does that name ring a bell with you?"

"I've never heard the name before."

"What do you want me to do, be here or not be here when he returns?"

"What I want you to do is take Megan for a walk when she gets home from school. I will be alright. Beth will be in the kitchen in case he gets annoyed with my answers and you've shown me how to use the derringer. I won't let him hurt the baby or me. I promise."

"That's just why I think I ought to be here, just in case. Beth can take Megan for a walk."

"Just do as I ask, please!" He retreated to the back porch to wait for Megan thinking *I don't really want to leave, but I'll accede to her wishes; I'll saddle Misty and Megan can ride sidesaddle and I'll lead her into town. I'll take her to the apothecary for an ice cream and down to the general store to buy a new book.*

* * *

Walking along, they noticed vultures circling overhead and Ned said to George, "I'll go ahead and see what it is while the two of you stay back here. Don't come up unless I whistle." He checked the shotgun, one slug, and 1 shot just to make sure. As he rounded a bend in the road, he saw a dead elk fawn lying in the snow being torn apart by three wolves. He was downwind from their direction and as quietly as he can, changes the one with shot to another slug; he gets within twenty feet before they notice him with bloodied jaws, snarling as he approaches. Firing from the hip, he kills one outright, the second one is wounded and limping away as he chambers two more slugs and fires as it makes it's retreat, killing it. The third is nowhere to be seen. He whistles for George and as he sees them, yells, "George, keep Mary away from here. I'll bring you the shotgun. I want you to take her home and come back with a horse and bring three steel traps from the tack room and don't forget to bring back the shotgun. Can you remember all that?"

"Yes, I'll be back as quickly as I can," as he takes his leave with his sister.

Ned makes quick work of gutting the wolves took the innards and sets them aside next to the dead fawn; then he scrapes the hides as much as he can with the bowie knife before rolling them into two bundles. When he gets home, he'll stretch them on a frame and hang them out by the hayfields high up enough to dry out after he finishes scraping away the remaining guts. He finds a stump with the open field to his back and facing the trail, and waits for George to bring the traps back.

<h1 style="text-align:center">-51-</h1>

Exactly at 3 pm, there was a knock on the front door of The Parker House. Priscilla having been briefed by Todd composed herself before she opened the door. As John Whitaker entered the hallway, "How can I help you, Mr. Whitaker?"

"May we sit somewhere in private?"

"Certainly, come into the parlor and I'll close the doors." She sat in the large round chair by the window, he in the straight-back chair next to the piano.

"My firm has been retained by Dr. and Mrs. Harold Johnston regarding this property. They were the previous owners and had listed it for sale with the Lander Bank & Trust Company. The original asking price was $5000 and you made a written offer of $4100 that was accepted with a $500 down payment, leaving a principal balance of $3600 to be paid over a 15-year period. Am I correct so far?"

"Yes, but what does that have to do with you and the Johnston's?"

"Well, Mrs. Parker..."

"It's Morgan now," she interrupted.

"The Johnston's were financing the purchase of said property and the bank agreed to be the collecting agent for them.

As I was saying, you were making monthly payments to the bank for the Johnston's in the amount of (looking at his notes) $45.00 per month, $10.00 going to the bank for administrative costs and the remainder of $35.00, partly being principal, partly interest. Up until a few months ago, the Johnston's were receiving timely payments before they abruptly stopped. They recently found out that the bank was in receivership and the owner of the assets was the Territory of Wyoming."

"Yes, that is correct until recently when the Wyoming Cooperative Bank took control of the assets."

"But we, I mean they, have not received any payments from them."

"We were all told that until the trial of the president, bank manager and the head teller took place, not to make any payments until everything was settled with the court action; we all agreed to keep what we owed and to make the payments owed on those notes once the new bank was formed. I made my payment this morning."

"Despite what you just told me, the Johnston's contacted their lawyer who had looked into the receivership of the old bank, and with the understanding that some bank would eventually take over the assets, he proceeded, with their permission, to start foreclosure proceedings. Our firm, Whitaker & Whitaker, Kansas City has the authority to seize this property, all its furnishings and animals, unless privately owned by another person, and proceed to auction, effective immediately. Your lawyer, Mr. August McDavitt, was made aware of several foreclosure notices and he should have contacted you before my arrival."

"As I said, this morning I paid the bank all the past months in arrears and they in-turn were going to apply all of it to interest and principal to the holder of the note, which I'm guessing is the Johnston's."

"I'll check with my office when I go back to town, but until I am notified, I will proceed with the auction on the courthouse steps at noon on Monday and your property along with others will be sold to the highest bidder. If the amount is less than what is owed to the Johnston's, you will be responsible for the difference, plus the attorney's fees and our fee's, of course."

"Like I just said, I have made restitution to the bank and I'm sure the Johnston's will be paid forthwith all the payments that were withheld by the territorial governors office."

"And as I said," raising his voice, "unless the whole balance is paid in full plus the expenses incurred before noon this coming Monday, I will take possession of this property. I expect that you and your illegitimate child from Nebraska and from what I can see, another child probably conceived the same way, are to be off the property by Monday noon. By the way, tell your husband if he interferes, I'll have him arrested for assault, which I believe in Wyoming, is a punishable offense with not less than two years confinement in the territorial prison in Cheyenne. Do I make myself clear on everything that I have said, Mrs. Parker, or is it really Morgan, as you say?"

"How dare you come into my home and make accusations that my daughter a bastard! And you have no right to characterize my unborn child in such a manner, either. I want you out of my house now. If my husband was here you'd be eating those words."

"I assure you madam your husband is no match for me." He got up, put on his black hat, and left.

Priscilla was thinking *what I'd like to do is push you down the front stairs.* Beth came down the hallway, seeing her crying and said, "I heard bits and pieces and I'm sure everything will be okay; I thought he was very rude and insulting."

She's beside herself and after wiping away her tears said, "I'm going up to my bedroom. I have to sort this out by myself. Please tell Todd and Megan that I will see them during supper." She went in the closet and took down a box that had her legal paperwork in it and set it on the bed. She began to sort the paperwork into three piles – Birth, Marriage, Inn. She starts reading the paperwork about the Inn first, making notes on a piece of paper; next she reads the paperwork regarding her previous marriage and her current marriage, jotting down a few notes there also. Finally she gets out Megan's birth certificate making sure that everything is in order. Since everything looks in order, she'll consult with August tomorrow, even though it's Saturday. *I need to know what options I have regarding all the issues and try to figure out who he may have represented in the past and what wrong information he has about my past marriage and the legal birth of my daughter.*

* * *

Pete tells Turk and Gus, "stand over by the wagon where the horses are while I light the fuse." Counting the seconds they hear a muffled explosion with a little smoke coming up the shaft and drifting away in the light breeze. They walk the horses back to the new corral they recently built spanning the creek that will have adequate forage and trees for shade during the spring and summer; they go over by the fire to warm their hands and have a cup of coffee. Pete wants to give the dust time to settle back down to the floor of the mine before he moves the bales of hay and takes down the blanket that he had nailed to the support timbers and anchored on the bottom with rocks. Once down the shaft, he does what he had been thinking and finds that the walls didn't cave in and the floor has been opened enough to where using picks to remove the gold will be much easier and noticing that there is more gold showing than what they had originally seen. He calls for Gus and Turk to come have a look-see.

-52-

"My ma got worried when she had heard the gunshots, but I told her the single shot was made by a grumpy old man on the homestead next to Mr. Langstrom's and the three shots were made by you killing two wolves." George said in a calming voice.

"Did you make sure that Mary was safe?"

"Yes, she didn't cry and did what she was told while I got her back to the ranch. The horse was skittish as we were coming over here, but he settled down as I was talking to him. Are you going to set some traps for the other wolf?"

"Yes, but I think there's more than one wolf, so I plan on trapping as many as I can, while I can. We don't need any of those critters around here scaring your ma or sister, or trying to get at our horses. We'll set the traps out on the fringe and one right where the fawn was. We'll come back later tomorrow or the day after and see what we caught."

* * *

"I don't want to talk about it, Todd, it's too upsetting." Priscilla said as they were sitting down to dinner.

"Look sweetheart, we promised that we'd be honest with

285

each other and I don't want you so upset that the baby gets affected or that you get sick over this. With that said, I would like you to tell me what transpired between you and Mr. Whitaker."

"After dinner we'll take a walk and I'll tell you what transpired during my meeting with Mr. Whitaker."

As they walk down the road, Megan takes Jasper and Mike with her onto the property next to the inn. Priscilla had been composing her self as they walked along and said, "First thing, I want you to know that I love you with all my heart and no matter what happens, we can be happy wherever we have to live, if it isn't here. Mr. Whitaker seemed to question my marriage to you; he had some information regarding my previous marriage, about the legitimacy of Megan's birth, but he wasn't forthcoming about where he got that information. The other part that he was very emphatic about was the Inn. Even though I just paid the late payments that I didn't make because of the directions from the governor's office not too pay them, he didn't seem to believe me. I have a receipt from the bank that I am now caught up to date. But, I was looking through the papers that the bank gave me when I closed on the property and it reads "that if my payments are in arrears for two months or more, regardless of the circumstances, the owner of the mortgage note can proceed with foreclosure; it also states that I may be liable for any legal expense incurred regarding the foreclosure itself." But it doesn't say that I'm liable for any collection fees in relation to the mortgage or any legal expenses. I may lose the inn and there isn't any thing I can do about it, legal or otherwise. What I don't understand is why August didn't come see me when he got notice of the pending action against me."

"I don't either, but I'll sure find out why."

"I don't want you to go off half-cocked about this. We have to set a good example for our children. We will approach this as a business, not a personal issue, together, alright?"

"Okay!" He said dejectedly.

"Now, as to our marriage, I remember that before I moved here, I spoke with an attorney in Omaha where I was living at the time. He assured me that because my husband abandoned Megan and me, and that I hadn't heard from him in over five years, and he gave us no support at all, that I could have him declared legally dead. I went to court, the lawyer presented the facts and my divorce decree was granted with him in abstention, and my marriage was dissolved. Holding up the paper to Todd, she said, I received this paper stating all that. I moved here, bought this house and made it our home and a business; You came along and we fell in love, made love and decided to make it permanent for Megan, our unborn child and ourselves, so I don't see what he possibly has that could take that all away from me, I mean, us."

"I don't either. I think for the remainder of the evening that you should put all this aside and go downstairs and get a cup of ginger tea and have some leftovers, you hardly touched your supper. I will get Megan ready for bed and then I'll join you in the parlor."

* * *

"I think we've hit the mother lode. Look at all that gold! Now if we can just get it all out, taken back to Lander to get it assayed and turned into cold, hard cash, we can retire in style in San Francisco." Pete said enthusiastically to the other two.

"Hold on their partner, I think your getting way ahead of yourself. You know as well as I do that what looks good on the surface, may not go down more than a couple inches or feet, if were lucky. The only thing we can do is work this 50 foot section where we did the test blast and see just how much there is; then we'll do the next 50 and so on." Gus replied with Turk concurring.

"Maybe so, but just look at it, you've got to admit it's surely more than we expected. We wanted to loosen the hard rock, but it sure looks like we hit pay dirt if you ask me."

"We got lucky and that's all I'm going to say on the subject. You know what the doc said, no strenuous work and be careful with your breathing. Since you were burned, your body can't take the pounding you were doing to yourself before the fire!." Turk said with his hands on his hips, practically yelling at Pete.

"To hell with the doc; I want to do my share of the work for all the rewards we'll get out of it."

"And we both appreciate your sincerity Pete, but you wouldn't do yourself any good if you worked yourself to death, now would it?"

"Okay, okay I'll do what I can for the mine and to keep the camp in good order, take care of the horses and keep us fed. I do think though that the next trip back, we'll have to get some cement, lumber and roofing materials to build us a permanent structure to live in and to make the mine shaft more safe. I don't want either of you to get hurt while you're down in that hole working."

"Agreed, now lets set up a system to get the rock out of the seam as we go deeper; could you also rig up that blanket at the end of this 50 or 60 feet to keep the dust from the other parts of the shaft from filtering its way back up this away?"

"I'll put the bales of hay on the bottom to make sure it stays in place, too."

-53-

"**N**ed, where are you?" came a small voice from down in the barn.

"I'm up here in the hayloft Mary, what do you want?"

"My mother would like you to have supper with us tonight. Please say yes. She is worried about you."

"Tell her that I'll come. I just have to finish what I am doing and then I should be done within the hour."

Thinking to himself he calculated *I've got 120 each of martens and rabbits, 10 elk hides, 16 wolf skins and 1 cougar. That should bring in a good amount and guessing that the prices will be the same or higher especially on the elk and cougar skins, it might come to close to $5000, split 50/50, except for the cougar pelt. Todd owes me all my back wages from October thru April, $420 total. I could get a haircut, bath, and some food other than the critters I hunt or trap, like maybe a steak or two and several new shirts, pants and still have money left over to hold me the rest of the year. I think I'll share some of the money with George; he helped me with the trapping. I could also get some gifts for Mrs. Thompson and Mary.*

* * *

"Todd, what are we going to do if Whitaker gets a bid on the Inn during the auction?"

"Then we'll live with it. As much as I'd rather live here in the comforts of this house, I have my property at Stony Creek. It would be tight, but I can always add a room or two to the cabin and make it right comfy for you, the baby and Megan. I can always bunk in the barn with the animals."

"You'll do no such thing, you'll be in our bed, right next to me."

"We could sleep in the barn and the children could have the cabin."

"With me breastfeeding the baby every three or four hours, I'd have to go back and forth between the cabin and the barn, then none of us would get any sleep."

"I'll figure out a solution."

"Seriously, what are we going to do?"

"I may have to do some lying, but the horses are all mine; some of the furniture in the Inn was loaned to you by your neighbors and friends; including the surrey and all your personal items. If Johnston wants the property back that much, we'll make sure there isn't anything left that isn't nailed down or came with the property when you rescued it after years of neglect."

"I wish August would listen to reason, but it appears that the law is on Whitaker's side in this fight and August's hands are tied. He told me this morning that we aren't the only ones in this predicament. There is the lumber mill, the haberdashery, the apothecary, several farmers and a ranch. Seems the doctor holds notes on all those properties, so it isn't just us. I feel bad for the farmers, they had a bad year last year and were hoping this year they would at least break even or make a little profit."

"Well there's one thing that the doc doesn't own."
"What's that?"
"Our ranch at Stony Creek."
"Amen."

* * *

"I was thinking about what Todd said before he left, that Hiram Bender near Lander, makes wagons. We could have him make two wagons to our specifications that can haul the heavy rocks with the gold in them between here and Lander." Turk said to his brother and Pete.

"That's going to cost us money."

"Pete, I don't know whether your just plain greedy, dumb or both. Once we have all this rock up top how are we going to get it down to Lander?"

"The current wagon should be good enough. You used to get all the supplies up here and that was a heavy load."

"You have a point, Pete, but sooner or later that wagon is going to break down. Then what are you going to do, carry the gold on the pack animals until they drop dead from exhaustion. We have got to be more practical about all this. We share equally on purchases and on the gold."

"I still don't want to spend that much money."

"I think what you need Pete is a trip to town so that you can get laid, have a good drunk, get laid again and have some food other than what you trapped or shot."

"I think we all need a trip to Lander." Gus offered his opinion.

"Well from the looks of the sky, it isn't going to be anytime soon. It looks to be a big snowmaker. So we better get the horses situated; tidy up the camp, get more deadfall stacked up and be prepared for what Mother Nature has in store for us come sundown or sunup at the latest."

-54-

Priscilla said to Todd, "Despite all of our efforts to the contrary, it appears that the auction is to take place on Monday. Everyone involved agreed that none of us would bid on each other's property. Also, Mr. Whitaker is going to have a hard time getting any buyer's from the surrounding area, especially at this time of the year. Maybe the circuit court judge or Tom will hear something from the court in Cheyenne for a stay in the proceedings and the auction will be put off; we can also hope that Dr. Johnston has a change of heart. If he had proceeded with due diligence, we could have been paying him all these months and none of this would have happened. After having talked with the other business owners who were in the same predicament and understanding the implications of the auction for her family and their future, she commented to Todd, "It's giving me a headache.".

"I am sure glad that I didn't start on cutting down all that timber or enlarging the barn. But the one thing that I miss the most is your smiling face and your outlook on life, our life. Ever since this mess started, your whole demeanor has changed." Todd said as they were standing on the front porch.

"I'm sorry, but when you put so much time and effort into

making a house a home for yourself and other folks and someone comes along and pulls the rug out from under you, it makes me sad and mad. It's just not fair."

Turning her around and placing his hands on her shoulders, looking into her deep hazel eyes he said, "You've got me, Megan, and the baby. What more do you need?"

"You're right, I don't need a thing but the three of you." She gave him a tender kiss. As he is holding her close, he begins to caress her. "Stop that, we'll have plenty of time for that later" giving him a playful punch. In between laughs, he says, "That's my girl."

There's a planned meeting after Sunday church services for everyone who is affected by the proceedings that are to take place Monday morning. August McDavitt stood in front of everybody and waited until it quieted down. "If I had the authority, I'd stop this auction today, but I don't. We've been neighbors and friends for years, but that doesn't excuse me from what I have to do. It pains me to have to be the lawyer on record for this auction. Despite what Mr. Whitaker may have told you about your property and what you can and can't take with you, he is wrong. They may do things differently in Kansas City, but here we follow the law as our territorial government has set forth. I want everyone to listen to what I am going to tell you. Any animals including your dogs, cats, chickens, horses, cattle, pigs and goats that weren't on the property when you bought it are yours to keep; the same thing applies to your furniture, pictures, pots, pans, dishes, silverware, etc. Basically, it comes down to what was or wasn't there at the time of sale to you. I'm asking that you don't destroy any buildings that you may have built or any improvements you've done. Whitaker is the type of person who'd have you arrested for destruction of property or worse. Sheriff Hughes or Marshal Murphy would hate to arrest you but they wouldn't have any choice on the matter."

A man in the back asks "What if I've got snakes or skunks on the property, can I leave them there?"

"Another person responded, "Why not, we've got a snake that is going to slither in and take it away from us." Everyone can't help but laugh and concur.

"Are there any other questions?" No one asked if there was. "I'll turn this meeting back to the parson," August said.

"Please bow your heads, *Dear Lord, we beseech thee, that you will make this right for your children in their hour of need; that you will watch over them and guide them for what might happen to their homes and businesses come tomorrow morning. Amen.*"

Everyone responded, "Amen" loud enough they hope that it wakes Whitaker from his sleep at the Mayfair Hotel. Everyone files out of the church, thanks the parson and August for their guidance and walk away slowly and quietly. Even the children are somber not knowing what will happen tomorrow. Todd said to Priscilla, "Why don't we go to the café for Sunday dinner and afterwards, Megan and I can take a walk with the dogs while you and the baby take a nap."

"You'll get no argument from me. I can use a good home cooked meal," she replies with a little laugh just before they walk into the café. It seems like most of the congregation had the same idea.

* * *

"Well, Emma, that storm last night was only rain, so I'm guessing that our winter storms are almost over. I am thinking that within a couple of weeks we can pack you up and I'll take you to the fort first and if your husband isn't there, I'll take y'all to Lander. Todd's wife has a boarding house and perhaps you can stay there until we find your husband, and you can get on with your lives."

"I don't quite know what to say. It's been an emotional journey over these last several months that we have endured. I mean, who else would have been so kind to take us in, given us a place to live, where my son could learn so much and where Mary could learn things that she never would have except on this ranch. If I had my druthers, I'd stay right here, but you have to have your cabin back and I have to find my husband and hope that he's been alright all these months." She gives him a little kiss on his cheek and then hugs him, but doesn't seem to want to let go. Ned turns beet red and said "Weren't nothin', I'd do the same for kinfolk and all of you have given me what I miss most, my family."

"Well, consider us as your family from now on. Perhaps, I can convince Richard to homestead near here and we could at least be neighbors. The land is fertile, the air clean and with all the water here about we wouldn't have to worry about irrigation for any crops we'd have to grow. The only drawback is the lack of a school and a church. Maybe if enough homesteaders move here, we could start a small town and in time, those needs would be met."

"You'll just have to wait and see, maybe he's already got something established where he ended up after all these months."

"What are you and George going to do today?"

"We'll be putting in the fence posts for the new corral and I hope by the time that I have to take y'all to Lander, that'll be done."

"I'll have supper ready for you when you come in for the night."

"That would be nice. After a long day of working, sometimes there isn't enough left in me to make even the simplest of meals."

* * *

"Todd, I don't want you to get angry but the other day when that Mr. Whitaker was here, he said some really disgusting things to me about Megan being a bastard child; he also implied that the baby was one too. He upset me so much, I cried. I asked him to leave and to keep his opinions to himself. I told him that you don't take kindly to folks who try and hurt us either verbally or physically. He said you were no match for him and I believe him. Please don't do anything that will jeopardize things like the Inn or our children."

"You mean like take him out behind the livery and teach him some manners."

"Exactly, that."

"How about I wait until after the auction and then I'll teach him some manners."

"No, that's exactly what he wants you to do so that he can destroy our family. Whatever he thinks he has on me, I'd rather let August or the Judge settle it once and for all, so that we won't have any skeletons' in our closets."

"Well he better not say a thing in front of me, I just might clean his clock in front of everyone."

"I want you to promise me you'll control your temper in his presence. I only told you because I didn't want you to hear it second hand."

"I'll control my temper." He replied through gritted teeth.

Monday started off as any other day in the southwestern part of Wyoming with a cloudless azure blue sky. Everyone had decided to meet at the church and walk together down to the courthouse.

The Judge began the proceedings and said to the crowd, "Ladies and Gentlemen, by the power vested in me by the Territory of Wyoming, 5th District Court, Sweetwater County, I hereby commence to adjudicate these Auction Proceedings on three businesses and The Johnson Ranch, The Parker House Inn and several farms in and around the City of Lander. The purpose of the auction is to satisfy foreclosure action taken by Dr. Harold Johnston who is represented today by John Whitaker, Esquire, Kansas City, Missouri. Sheriff Hughes and US Marshal Tom Murphy are here to keep the peace. If anyone tries to disrupt these proceedings, you will be charged with Disorderly Conduct, fined $50 and spend 30 days in jail. Do I make myself clear on this matter?"

Everyone, including Whitaker, said "Yes, your honor."

"Mr. Whitaker would like to say a few words before we begin the proceedings."

"I want you to know that this isn't personal. I do this sort of thing every couple of weeks all over the country. It's not something that I enjoy, but out of necessity, it must be done. Whenever an agreement can't be reached with the aggrieved party, it usually results in an auction and that's why we are here today. My office informed me that over the last few days, a few of you have made payments for notes held by Dr. Johnston, but that doesn't preclude the auction of those properties. The fact of the matter is you were all in arrears for four to six months and by law, the foreclosure process must go forth. Any monies that you paid on the debt owed will be credited, but the fact remains you are still in violation of the contract that you all originally signed. Neither this territory nor any other state will stand in our way of collecting what is justly due to the aggrieved party. Are there any questions?" Not one person said a thing.

"Okay, Judge, let's begin."

"The first property up for auction is The Parker House Inn, do I have a bid of $6100?" No one answers; will anyone give me $5000?" Again, no one answers. He doesn't get one single bid and sets a paper off to the side of the table. Whittaker said, "Okay, we'll deal with that property latter. The next property is the Apothecary Shop do I hear a bid of $3000? No one says a thing and on it goes throughout the afternoon, not one single bid for any of the properties. He says to the crowd afterward, "Well, I must say this is the toughest auction that I have ever presided over, but this solves nothing, I'll bring in out-of-town buyers if I have to."

A voice in the crowd said, "Go ahead, we're not surrendering our town to the likes of you or anyone like you." Another voice can be heard, "When you come back with your out-of-town buyers, you won't know the place."

"Just what does that mean?"

"If you leave today with your hat in your hand nothing will happen to you. But if you don't, you won't be able to sleep tonight and that fine horse you have over at the stable may go missing in the dark."

"Are you people insane, I am a representative of the law and threats against my person and my property, I take seriously."

"Who threatened you?" came a new voice within the crowd.

"None of us heard a thing. We was just bantering between one another is all? You must have been mistaken about what you think you heard. None of us law abiding citizens would do anything to hurt you."

"I suppose you harbor traitors and cowards amongst yourselves?"

Someone speaks up in the crowd, "To whom are you referring too?

"Todd Morgan."

That got Todd's attention, he had encountered this same bullshit before from a number of people. He tried to convince them that he had fought on both sides of the war and held no grudges against anyone, even though he spent two years in a northern prison camp under deplorable conditions during the incursion. Everyone started to look for him in the crowd, seeing him standing beside his wife and Marshal Murphy. Now it was getting personal and he aimed to finish it once and for all. "I'm right here Whitaker, what lies are you spreading about me now?"

"Lies, you're the liar Morgan and a traitor to your country; a coward."

"Well Whitaker, if these fine folks weren't here I'd teach you some manners. If you have a personal grudge against me, we should be able to settle those differences between the two of us and not involve anyone else, don't you think?"

"Do you deny that you fought for the South during the War of Northern Aggression?"

"No, I don't deny it and I don't deny the fact that I spent time in a prison in the North during the war; I don't deny that fact that I also fought for the North under Colonel John Wilder, 1st Cavalry of the West, either. I did a lot of brave things on both sides and I did some things that I'm not proud of either. Most of all, I came out here to Wyoming to get away from the likes of people like you who judge first and don't take the value of man for what he has done or what he can do. I guess there is no justice in this world when all free men have to put up with innuendo without someone getting the facts right the first time." As he started to walk away from Priscilla and Tom Murphy, Whitaker drew his pistol and fired a shot in the air. Todd thought about stopping, but kept on walking. He didn't have his gun with him but he was going to get it; another shot nicked the edge of his heel causing him to stumble and fall. As he got up, he turned and walked past everyone and went up to Whittaker, slapped him as hard as he could without drawing blood, and said, "Next time, if there is a next time, you'll have to face me." He turned and walked away and Priscilla caught up to him, "I love you for being my hero and we won't let him ruin our lives." Tom Murphy caught up to him and said, "Do you want to press charges against him."

"What good would it do, he'd just bring all that bullshit up in open court and I won't put my family through that humiliation again. I'll just leave it where it is. The court of public opinion is more powerful than any court in the land." Over the next several days, people in Lander had a different respect for Todd Morgan.

-55-

"Well, that was a surprise last night. No snow, just rain. Maybe we can get out of here quicker than we thought." Gus said.

"I'll believe that when I start to see some green through all the white and we can load up the wagon with the gold ore and take it back to your place Gus." Pete remarked.

"I think that we should go directly to Lander and bypass my place. We have enough of the gold that has already been chipped out of the rock itself. We might have to add a day or two to go directly to Lander. Since we'll be blazing a new route, but it will be worth it in the long run; we'll just have to repeat it several times over the remainder of the spring, summer and fall. I don't think we'll be doing any more winter encampments up here again. We should consider hiring some guards and maybe some miners to continue our efforts up here though."

"That does make more sense. I guess when we get done in Lander, we can all spend a few days getting drunk, laid and drunk again if we want too." Turk responded and said, "Now remember Pete, we have to place an order for those two wagons, and we'll need eight horses, either Belgians or Percherons. Todd should be able to tell us who sells those types of horses. We also need to get some mining supplies while we're in town. Since you are so fired up about being able to help, it'll be your responsibility to get the horses, wagons and supplies that we will need. Your partners, on the other hand, will make sure that you get laid and drunk."

"You know the two of you are real pains in the ass. I was just sayin' that I wanted to help since the two of you are doing all the physical work."

"You've done your share of physical work in the past, and we both know that if you hadn't gotten injured, you'd be in the thick of it again, but you can't. It'll kill you for sure and besides, who would we have to pick on then?"

"You're still a pain in my backside."

* * *

"I say we sell the inn to Beth and Tom, Priscilla." Todd said in an offhanded comment. "He's retiring before they get married in four weeks. He mentioned to me awhile back that he wished he could find a place like this and become a gentlemen farmer. We don't need to be burdened with all the legal maneuverings that Dr. Johnston is going through to recover his precious money. We could sell it for exactly what he's owed including those legal fees and he can deal with Whitaker. According to the judge, Whitaker has been instructed not to come back to Wyoming in the future. If he does, he'll be found in contempt and jailed on sight anywhere in the territory. I was at the Cattlemen's this morning and I saw a notice for a farm that was for sale in the Wind River Township. The town has a nice church, a small school, even a few stores and it would be twelve miles closer to Stony Creek. We could build your dream home from those humble beginnings," he said earnestly.

"I'll think about it once this son of yours stops waking me up every night; you'd think he's the only one involved in this birthing process. Never again am I going through this for you or anyone else. Do you hear me Todd Morgan?" Priscilla said emphatically.

"I hear you Mrs. Morgan, but I'm willing to bet that when you had Megan, you said the very same thing, am I right?"

"Oh, shut up!"

"Temper, temper. You're loving it and besides, who better to be a mommy, than you."

"You know if I weren't in such a tender state, you'd be eating those words right about now." As she looked down at her expanded stomach saying, "stop moving around inside of there, it's uncomfortable and you have at least six weeks to go before you can come out, do you hear me John-Michael?"

"I thought we agreed that we would call him John."

"That was before he started all this moving around, now he's back to being called after both of our fathers."

"Okay, I'll stop teasing you and I'll try to talk to our son about being nice to his mommy tonight so that she can get a decent nights sleep. I'd really like to take a look at that farm though. According to the poster, it has 125 acres, some farm equipment, a 16-stall barn, paddock, well, river frontage plus 80 acres cleared for planting or pasture, 35 acres in woods and 10 acres of partial clearing set on a little knoll, a perfect spot for a new house for the Morgan family. The asking price is $8,500.00. We could self-finance using our investments. We have all that cut lumber from the trees that we brought in last fall to the mill just waiting to be delivered. What do you say?"

"I know you'd buy it for investment anyway, but I'd like to see it first, just to satisfy my curiosity. Can we set up an appointment for Saturday and we can go over in the surrey?"

"I'll have Mark at the Cattlemen's make the appointment. Is there anything you need from town, while I'm there?"

"I need some more ginger tea and soda crackers. Megan needs new shoes and how about a treat or two for supper tonight."

"Megan and I will be back in a couple of hours. Are you ready to go to town, Megan so that your mother can have a couple of hours to herself?"

"I'm ready, daddy."

* * *

"Mrs. Thompson are you ready?" Ned asked as he was waiting to help her get up in the buckboard.

"I'm just making sure that I have everything and for one last look around. I am actually going to miss this place."

"You'll be back for a visit someday. I am letting George ride my horse and the three of us will be in the seat. I'll be taking all the furs to the fort first, stay the night and tomorrow, we'll be on our way to Lander if we don't find your husband there. I just want to make sure that the gates are locked down tight; the doors and windows in the barn are secure, then we'll be ready. George make sure you tie that knot tight on the horse that's following the wagon; come on dog, let's go." They make their way down the lane to the back gate. George rides ahead and swings the gate aside and, once they are through, he makes sure that it is secure and puts the double rope through it like Todd showed him.

306

* * *

"I swear Pete, if you get stuck one more time, you'll be fired as a team driver. We need to get another few miles under our belt before we stop for the night."

"I'm doin' the best that I can. It's not my fault that the dad-blasted gold is so heavy."

"Exactly my point about getting specially built wagons to haul the gold ore from now on out. This wagon is good for supplies like tools, food and hay. It wasn't built to do the type of haulin' we need done."

"Spend the damn money for a new wagon and stop yellin' at me. If you think you can do a better job, we'll trade places."

"Will the two of you stop bickering with each other and get a move on; otherwise it'll take us an extra week to get to Lander." Turk yelled at Gus and Pete.

* * *

"Okay Megan, let's try on one more pair of shoes and if they don't fit, we'll just have to wait until we get to Casper and look for a proper shoe store that can size your feet perfectly for one or two pairs of shoes." "I'm sorry daddy, but the shoes are pinching my feet and it hurt's."

"You're probably going through a growth spurt and your feet decided it's time for something new. A little wider and they'll fit. We'll just tell mom that we'll wait for our trip to see Beth and Marshal Murphy get married. Is that okay with you?"

"Yes and maybe Mom will find some shoes also."

Epilogue

The last chapter Hearts (Burning Desire) summed up nearly every character in this book. Each of them had a mission - be it getting to where they needed to be, finding the right outcome of their quest, ridding themselves of a painful memory or starting a life where everyone is content with the outcome.

Book 3 – Diamonds (The hand that was dealt…) continues with their quests and only time will fulfill the outcome of your reading pleasure of this new series.

There is one caveat however, you the reader will have to wait until late summer of 2021 to find out how the remainder of this series comes about. Ah, the advent of more suspense, intrigue and heartache.

About the Author

Born, raised, and educated in Rochester, New York. My intent was to study Agribusiness after high school. The Vietnam Conflict was just ramping up and the local draft board had other ideas for my future, which in turn changed my long-term outlook. I was given a five-day window of opportunity, either accept the draft board's decision and go in the Army or enlist in one of the other services. I chose the US Air Force and that turned out to be the best decision I ever made.

I served a total of 34+ years in the US Air Force, including Active duty, NH Air National Guard and US Air Force Reserve, which included Iraq I. I retired at the rank of E7 (Master Sergeant). Using the GI Bill, I got an Associate's and a Bachelor's Degree in Business Administration.

In my later years, I earned a Master's Degree in Educational Media. I have owned a variety of businesses over the last fifty years. When I wasn't working for myself, I worked for Department of Employment Security in Massachusetts; Virginia Community College System, retiring from John Tyler Community College, Chester, Virginia.

My writing career began a couple of years before I retired. I was enamored with the west and used my initial passion for wanting to be a farmer to help write my stories (though I never did follow that passion). These stories are to entertain you as well as educate you about US History.

I am a member of Western Writers of America and Citrus Writers.

I share my time between Florida and North Carolina.